The
GREAT
AND
DANGEROUS

CHRIS WESTWOOD

FRANCES LINCOLN
CHILDREN'S BOOKS

Text copyright © Chris Westwood 2012
The right of Chris Westwood to be identified as the author of this work
has been asserted by him in accordance with the Copyright,
Designs and Patents Act, 1988 (United Kingdom).

First published in Great Britain in 2012 by
Frances Lincoln Children's Books, 4 Torriano Mews,
Torriano Avenue, London NW5 2RZ
www.franceslincoln.com

A catalogue record for this book is available from the British Library.

ISBN 978-1-84780-249-1

Set in Palatino

Printed and bound by CPI Group (UK) Ltd, Croydon, CR0 4YY in January 2012

1 3 5 7 9 8 6 4 2

❧ 1 ❧
THE DRIVE-BY

Our last call on the after-school shift was a 32374 in Stoke Newington. Alice Edritch never knew what hit her.

The shots were fired on a cold and rainy November afternoon as she left a newsagent's in Shacklewell, stuffing packets of Quavers and Twiglets into her bag. When she stepped outside, Alice was twelve years old. Now she'd be twelve forever. Even before she hit the ground, her ghost was tearing across town, becoming more lost and confused with every silent step.

Four hours later, the street corner was ablaze with colour – sprays of crimson and bright yellow flowers stacked high against the dim brick walls. A white chrysanthemum cross lay on the newsagent's step and tacked to the wall above it was a photograph of Alice, a thin-faced girl with straw-coloured hair and an easy, buck-toothed smile.

The newsagent's door was locked and bolted and iron shutters covered its windows. The lights were on at a twenty-four-hour grocery store and the laundrette next door, but the rest of the street was deserted. The only sounds were those of the rickshaw's wheels trundling through puddles and potholes as our teammate Lu steered us along.

Watching from the passenger seat, Becky Sanborne gave a heartfelt sigh. 'That poor kid. She wasn't any older than us.'

As new recruits to the Ministry of Pandemonium's subdepartments of registration and salvage, we'd already faced many strange and terrible sights, and sometimes there were sights that made me want to turn away and weep. This was one of those times.

'So this is a 32374?' Becky said. 'Can't say I know all the numbers yet but I suppose that's what it means – gunshots.'

'Yes, a drive-by,' I said. It was the second I'd personally seen. 'Probably gang-related. The girl was an innocent bystander, hit by accident.'

'That's dreadful.'

'All the numbers are dreadful.'

Before our shift began, the 32374 had arrived on a list with five other names and numbers in the receipts office at Pandemonium House, our secret headquarters off Camden Passage. The lists may as well have been written in stone. The telegraph that churned them out had no opinions. It simply told us how it would be, and we were powerless to save those it named – the soon-departed – from what was coming. Our mission was to guide them afterwards, before anything worse could happen.

Because worse things *could* happen. We all knew that. The enemy wanted those lost souls too.

Lu hauled the rickshaw north, her heels sending up a misty trail from the wet road. A dedicated, stern-eyed girl in her late teens, she was responsible for transport on our team, but transport wasn't her only area of expertise. In combat she was fearless, and I'd once seen her decapitate a reptilian demon with a flick of her wrist. In the heat of battle you'd want Luna San Lao – we only ever called her Lu – on your side.

She turned off the high street onto a narrow courtyard, pulling up outside the main entrance to Abney Park Cemetery, where Alice had last been sighted by an off-duty Ministry field agent. Becky rolled off the seat and ran to the gates, peering into the dark.

'She's here,' she said through a shiver. 'I just know she is.'

Starting inside, we snapped on our Ministry-issue flashlights. Becky flinched when hers found a hooded figure crouching by the path, but it was only an arch-shaped headstone. Mine fell on a stone angel which stood on a towering plinth. The angel's face was peaceful, its lips on the edge of a smile. For some reason the smile made me nervous, so I flipped the beam away to where the path began to fork. The shadows of trees and monuments crawled along both overgrown routes.

'Which way, right or left?' I said.

'Right,' the girls both said at once, and we set off in search of Alice Edritch.

The afternoon rain had turned the fallen winter leaves to mush on the path. Sliding and squelching along, we whipped our flashlights around at every slight sound, a rustle of tree branches, a scuttling of bugs over mossy green headstones. As the path wound deeper inside the cemetery, the high street noise faded and I began to notice another sound almost hidden by the breeze, a whisper of voices chanting in a weird, reverse-sounding language, like a backwards-playing tape.

'What're they're saying?' I said.

Lu wasn't sure. 'It's enemy speak. I don't know the

lingo but I'd guess they're warning us to stay away.'

Becky seemed to have picked up something else. 'Hear that? Careful now. Alice is close, but she isn't alone.'

Another path took us past a black marble cenotaph and a man-sized stone eagle with outspread wings. The trees were less thickly tangled here and the path gradually curved towards a clearing where the whispers were closer. Closer still was another sound, the one Becky had been tracing from the start: a muted sobbing.

Past the trees the outline of an old chapel loomed in front of us, its spire piercing the sky like a blade. The place was in ruins, had been for years. All its entrances were barred and padlocked, and the building's gutted innards blossomed out of the dark when we turned all three flashlights on it.

On the floor just inside the bars a hooded dwarf statue stood with its back towards us. Further inside, another figure cowered in a pool of shadows among the rubble, its knees drawn to its chin. The figure was moving but it wasn't alive.

'Alice?' I said.

The girl turned her head to the light, lifting a hand to shield her eyes. Her pale face was as darkly smudged as her school uniform, a bloodstained blue blazer and grey pleated skirt.

'What did you call me?'

'Alice,' I repeated.

'And who're you?'

'I'm Ben, and these are my friends. We heard you were in trouble and came to help.'

'You're not the first,' Alice said. 'The ones before you said they'd take care of me. But I didn't like the look of them and I didn't trust them.'

'You did right,' Becky said. 'They're liars, and the last thing they want is to take care of you.'

Alice's ghost mulled this over, saying nothing.

'Do you remember what happened?' I said.

'Some of it, but it's fuzzy. It was on my way home from school, I think.'

'That's right. You went into a shop. . .'

'Yeah, and . . . and someone ducked inside past me as I came out. I didn't see his face, but he seemed scared and in a rush. I thought I heard a car backfiring, and then it was like I'd been punched, here and here.' Her fingers hovered near but didn't touch the dark wounds about her neck and chest. 'I went cold. I'm still cold. And the next thing I knew I was running, but how did I get from there to here?' She looked around. 'I don't know this place at all.'

The breeze stiffened, the whispers inside it becoming busier, louder. We had to act quickly. The enemy were never far away at these times.

'Listen, Alice,' I said, offering my hand. 'We can't take back what happened to you, we can't undo it. But we can take you somewhere safe. Will you step out and come with us?'

She sat there listening to the breeze, sucking her thumb, unsure what to do, but then her face cleared and she scrambled to her feet and came forward, lifting her fingers to mine.

'OK,' she said. 'Yes, I will.'

A kind of electric charge passed between us when we touched. Sparks of silvery light fizzed about our fingers and wrists, and Alice stared fascinated at the magic show, taking another step to the bars. As she did, a great wrenching and crashing sound came from the trees as if something huge had toppled or torn itself up from the earth, and the earth rumbled and shook underfoot.

'We're out of time,' Lu said. 'Quick, before it gets here!'

But whatever *it* was, it was already here.

It came into view above the chapel in the same

instant Alice slid outside, a raging, smoky, black cloud that seeped from the heights of the trees. It had no clear shape, or rather, its shape was changing all the time, whirling and unfolding in all directions. At its centre were two foggy red points of light that glowed like Chinese lanterns. By the time it reached the spire, blotting it out against the sky, we were running, retracing the path through the trees, Becky leading and Lu urging us along from behind.

'Faster,' Lu called. 'No, faster!'

As we ran I had to keep checking Alice was still there – her grip on my hand was so faint – and her eyes were tearful and wide with fear. The cloud was already at our backs, a cold wave careering through overhanging branches, showering us with dead wood and droplets of rain. An earthy, decaying scent filled the air.

Becky stumbled ahead, gesturing wildly at something she'd sighted. 'There. . .' she cried. 'There, and there!'

There was an explosion of soil and leaves close by. My flashlight swept past something like tendrils or long fingers shooting out of the earth. Further on, another larger shape was surfacing near an ivy-choked cross, head and shoulders scattering

8

mulch, dead eyes peering from a face that was mostly moss and mud. It was happening everywhere, little bursts and sprays of earth as others dragged themselves up from the depths.

'That cloud-thing,' Lu said, her usually calm voice cracking. 'It's bringing them out!'

Alice whimpered as I bundled her along and, in front of us, Becky let out a squeal of surprise and vanished from sight as the ground suddenly swallowed her up.

Something had ripped itself up from the path, opening a deep rectangular gash across it. Sprinting ahead, Becky had seen it too late. The flashlight fell from her grasp, struck the edge and went out before rolling down into space.

Becky tumbled in straight after it.

'Becky?' I put on the brakes, managing to stop just short of the drop, at the same time releasing Alice's hand. 'Here, Lu!'

Lu was at her side in a flash, guiding Alice around the grave-like opening, then pausing to peer down inside it.

'She's gone,' Lu said, then added less certainly, 'Is she gone?'

'I . . . I don't know.'

I turned a flashlight around the moist walls, which quivered with worm and bug activity. There was no reply, only another soggy eruption of soil behind us, and another, nearer to where we stood. Away to my left, a nimble dark shape flashed through the undergrowth. I was still staring after it when a slippery hand shot out of the earth to close on my ankle.

The shock nearly drove me out of my body. A scream stuck fast in my throat, and I only just heard the small voice in the darkness below me.

'Damn it, I knew there'd be nights like this.'

Forgetting Alice Edritch, forgetting everything else for the time being, I dropped to my knees and reached with both hands to bring Becky slithering clear of the hole and back to solid ground.

'You all right?' I said.

'Do I *look* all right?' Her face was a mud-slicked mask. Taking a moment to catch her breath, she was wiping a dollop of dirt from her chin when her eyes widened at something past my shoulder. 'Oh no. . . What the hell?'

They were swarming the path behind us, a risen army of walkers. Called into being by that cloud-thing in the trees, they were already too many to count and others were still rising to join them. The majority were almost human in shape, but were blighted with missing or decaying limbs and wagging misshapen heads, while some lacked heads altogether. All of them were coming our way, and they weren't exactly dawdling.

'*Do* something,' Becky moaned.

'Do what?' I said, too numb to think.

'Whatever it is you do. Picture it. Imagine it.' She spat out a mouthful of dirt. 'Just make it happen and soon, OK?'

She meant the gift, a gift I hadn't known I had until Mr October explained it a few short months ago. It was a sign, he'd said, of my developing skills. I still didn't really understand it, I couldn't switch it on or off at will, and I couldn't find it now.

'Run!' I said.

Becky looked daggers at me. 'Is that the best you can do?'

Alice stopped whimpering and started to bawl.

'Shut up and move,' Lu said, yanking her on.

We took off in pursuit, skirting around the gaping hole. There was a flurry of movement in the trees as we rejoined the path, and a spindly figure tore out of the dark, looping its arms around my chest and neck.

I strained and twisted and clawed to break loose, but its strength was tremendous, crushing air from my lungs.

Becky had meanwhile stopped and doubled back, flinging herself at the attacker, pounding her fists against the rotting mask that passed for its face, but the thing swung a heavy paw, toppling her off her feet.

I never saw her hit the ground. If she was hurt I couldn't tell how badly. A clammy hand had closed over my eyes, blanking out what little light there was, and a stream of grave breath washed into my face as the walker spoke.

'We've warned you, Harvester. We don't give ultimatums. You've crossed us once too often – and now you're coming with us.'

No chance, I thought. I'm staying where I am. But you – you're going back where you came from, you're going empty-handed, and you're going there right now.

Perhaps that was all it took, the simple, crystal-clear thought Becky had asked for, because the thing suddenly yowled in pain and shuddered as if it had been shot, loosening its hold and shrinking away, and then Becky was on her feet again grabbing my wrist.

'Come on,' she hissed. 'No dawdling!'

The ground heaved. There was a hollow roar followed by the stunning white blast of an explosion, which sprayed fragments of stone and dirt from the chasm. A fountain of light poured upwards, flooding the path, covering everything. Trapped in its brightness, the walkers wailed in ear-splitting voices and flapped at the air like vampires in the sunlight. And there was something else inside the light, a swirling and gathering of specks of darker light that seemed to take physical form, reaching like hands to draw the enemy into itself and down inside the gash. The one that had attacked me went first.

I looked on, awestruck, unable to budge. At least ten had fallen screaming below before Becky dragged me away. A chilling howl followed us on the night air as we ran, the mournful cry of the enemy counting its losses. They must've thought they'd had this 32374 in the bag, but we'd stolen it from under their noses.

We slithered on up the path, not daring to look back. Soon there was light and traffic noise ahead and then the welcome sight of the rickshaw at the gates with Lu settling Alice onto the seat under its red and gold canopy. Above and behind us, the angry cloud backed off into the trees, the red lights inside it fading out one by one.

Hearing us nearing the top of the path, Lu turned and faced us impatiently, hands on hips.

'Well, what are you waiting for?' she said. 'We don't have all night.'

⊷⊷ ≼◆≽ ⊶⊶

A train clattered overhead on the bridge as Lu stopped the rickshaw by London Fields station. Helping Alice off the seat, I took her hand again, and again she marvelled at the show of lights when our fingers met.

'They can't touch you now,' Becky said. 'It's nearly over.'

'What happens next?' the girl said. 'I won't see my folks or my mates again, will I? I'm supposed to go somewhere else.'

'Yes.'

'So what do I do?'

'Let Ben show you. It's easier than you think.'

Alice nodded. She seemed to understand. This was as far as we went, but she still had much further to go. Her point of departure under the arches wasn't much to see, but after the train had passed it was quiet and private.

The others hung back while I led Alice the first few steps of the way. Somewhere in the darkness ahead there would be an opening, a solid door handle and the place of access beyond it. Alice tensed her grip on my hand as I felt for the handle and turned it.

'Nearly there,' she said.

'Nearly. Just another few steps.'

'Should I be scared?'

'Not anymore. The worst is over.'

'All right,' she said after a pause. 'I'm as ready as I'll ever be.'

A radiant golden-orange light bathed her face when the door opened. Alice blinked into it, more curious than afraid, the doubt slowly leaving her eyes. My fingers tingled when she let go, and she moved through the flaming doorway without a backward glance.

That was the last we saw of her. The light drenched her from head to toe, and for a moment she looked made of light, all aglow, and then she was part of the light itself. Wherever newly-departeds went, Alice was there now and safe.

I closed the door. Darkness settled under the

arches again, and I plodded back to the rickshaw where Lu was going through a stack of cards to check the next call on her shift and Becky was wiping mud from her cheeks.

'How's it looking, Lu?' I said.

'Busy as ever. An 11629 in High Barnet. Then a 5821 on the Westway, a 62822 in Regent's Park. . . I'm all over town again tonight.'

'A 62822? That's no fun. We should come too. It's early and you can't do all that alone.'

Lu took hold of the rickshaw's handles, hoisting the vehicle around into take-off position. 'You know the drill. You've got school in the morning. I'll tag along with another team and you two will go home and sleep.'

Then she set off, her slight but strong figure towing the vehicle through shadows by the station and past the rows of blue-shuttered warehouses towards Lamb Lane.

Watching her go, Becky said, 'Did any of this really happen? I feel like I dreamt it.'

'Take a look in the mirror later. Then you'll know.'

She glanced up at the bridge. 'You were brilliant back there at the cemetery, Ben. Thanks for, well, doing what you did. Mr October would've been proud.'

The mention of Mr October's name put a lump in my throat. With Dad gone, he'd been the nearest thing I'd had to a father. He'd led us to our True Calling, watched over us and taught us all we knew. We were only here because of him, but he hadn't been seen or heard of since Halloween, when enemy fire had ripped him to pieces, and I couldn't face the thought of never seeing him again.

'I don't know about that,' I said. 'I didn't do much.'

'If you say so. But I swear you don't know what you're doing half the time. *They* know, though – they know all about you. You're a threat to them. They'll target you.'

'Like I wasn't a target before?'

'Well, I suppose we all are now, and we only made things worse for ourselves tonight. It won't stop there.'

I wanted to say she had nothing to worry about, but we both knew that wasn't true. This wasn't the kind of work you chose to do. The work chose you, it never got easier, and we both knew the risks.

We went our separate ways from there, Becky heading for Richmond Road while I cut under the bridge to London Fields, tugging up my collar against the mid November chill. Crossing the park, I had to dive off the path to avoid two cyclists racing side by side, headlights blinking like eyes in the gloom. They passed without slowing, taking a path to Broadway Market, and I set off again towards home.

✤ 2 ✤
THE UNNAMED

In the maisonette on Middleton Road, I took a microwave dinner through to the living room and put on the TV to drown the noise of a neighbour's stereo, as Mum often did when she was home.

Sometimes the TV lulled her to sleep at night, and twice before she'd flown to the Canaries with her friend Ellie I'd found her napping on the sofa when I came down in the morning. The place had felt empty while she'd been gone, but Mum was due back from her holiday soon.

There wasn't much on TV tonight, and I was still buzzing from the after-school shift, so I turned the TV off and went up to my room, lifting my sketch pad from the shelves where I kept my prize possessions, my collectible comics, annuals and action figures.

The most recent additions were a tin trinket box containing the four-leaf clover chain Mr October had given me in Victoria Park and a pocket-sized volume of Ministry dialect, *The Pandemonium Guide to Apocalypti Idioms & Phrases*, a book of enormous power which I wouldn't be ready to read until the words on its pages stopped moving about.

I carried the sketch pad to the bed and flicked through it. Sooner or later everything I saw, imagined, or felt ended up here. The last thing I'd done was a portrait of Dad, which I'd drawn while sitting on his bench in the park before winter took hold and the park became too chilly to sit in. It was a good enough likeness that when Mum first saw it she wept.

'You're his spitting image,' she said, and I realised that whenever she looked at me she was seeing him too.

On a fresh page I roughed out a head and shoulders of Alice, the 32374. I wanted to show her as I'd first seen her, smiling like her photo outside the newsagent's, not as the petrified child we'd found in the cemetery. I softened her outline with my thumb and roughed out the eyes and nose, but I must have fallen asleep before I started on the smile. When I woke to a startling crash of bricks and stone outside, I was still fully dressed with the sketch pad beside me and Alice Edritch had no mouth.

Not long after we moved to Middleton Road, council workers had set about restoring a building across the street. Their chipping and drilling began every morning at eight on the dot, so on school days I didn't need an alarm. They were back for the Friday shift.

In the first week of November the numbers of hard hats had doubled and the two-storey building had started climbing another level, cutting off our view over Lansdowne Drive. Now the work at the top looked set to rise to yet another floor.

Wherever you looked, London reached for the sky. Past the construction site, above the rooftops across the park, the horizon was broken by many more tall buildings, still rising, and an army of cranes stood above the city like dinosaur skeletons. How much taller would it all go, and how would the city know when to stop?

Downstairs, I sat with tea and toast at the kitchen breakfast bar, trying to ignore the building opposite. Its front wall had once been a playground for graffiti artists, covered top to bottom with stencilled cats and rats and police and thieves. For a time Mr October had left private messages for me there, messages no one else could see. But ever since the enemy started using it to make threats against Mum and me, I'd avoided looking that way at all.

A cold gust rattled the window behind me, as if

something were trying to feel its way indoors, and I stiffened, hearing the front door thump.

The post had come early, bringing three bills and a postcard from Mum in Lanzarote, her second card in a week. On the front was a sculpture by an artist called Manrique, a face constructed from blocks of stone with car hubcaps for eyes. On the back, Mum's scribble was even more legible than last week's. Either she'd mastered left-handed writing or the change of climate was doing her more good than the two months of clinics back home had. We couldn't pretend she wasn't still sick – the gradual loss of use of her right hand and arm had only been a symptom of something more serious – but the signs were good.

Darling, she'd written. *You don't know what you're missing! Wish I'd been able to persuade you to come. Time's going too fast here – and I'm loving it. Great views, sun shining, good food. Went for a camel ride yesterday! I'm so much better. They say sometimes you have to be in another place to really find yourself. And I think I have! Will explain all when I see you.*

Much love, Mum xxx

PS: Hope Ross is taking good care of you. Otherwise he's in trouble!

Ellie's husband Ross had been assigned to keep an eye on me while they were away. Mum had refused to go unless someone did, and we'd argued about it – I didn't need nursemaiding, but I couldn't go with them. The Ministry's work took up all my spare time. In the end I'd given in, and Ross either phoned every day or visited with food parcels. He was a Spiderman fan, so we always had something to talk about when he came over.

Anyway, Mum sounded great, happier than she'd been for ages, happier than I'd expected her to sound so soon after the trauma of seeing Dad for the last time, knowing she'd lost him forever. Leaving the postcard in the kitchen, I grabbed my school things and hurried out across the chilly balcony and down the stone stairwell to the street.

Winter was closing in, bringing darker mornings and biting air. House lights burned along Middleton Road and drivers travelled with their headlamps on. On Queensbridge Road, work traffic crept by at walking pace and a 236 bus blocked the crossing between the lights and the safety island. Towards the back of the bus, three faces with hollow, dark eyes stared out through the grubby windows.

It's just the gift, I thought. It's always there. You

try to forget about it but it never forgets about you.

I'd seen more and more of this lately. Those were the faces of the unnamed dead, lost souls who travelled the city night and day on journeys that had no end. They were everywhere among us, but the Ministry could only help those whose numbers and names were on their lists. Those anonymous ones, too many to count, were out of reach.

Edging around the stalled bus, I waited on the island while a taxi rolled past in the other direction towards Dalston. The taxi's fare light was on. Its driver had no passengers as far as he knew. He wasn't aware of the two bedraggled grey-faced females seated behind him.

They were probably in their mid to late forties and the state of their hair and shabby clothing suggested they'd been homeless when they died. They were looking straight at me, and one of them waved and mouthed something to get my attention.

Hey you. Yes, you. I know you see us. So what are you going to do?

After that I had to stop looking and move on. There was only so much I could take. It still amazed me that these two worlds existed side by side and I could see both, but I often wished the gift would be still, stop yelling and leave me alone.

But I couldn't ignore the unnamed. Most days I'd see them in traffic queues or sitting in greasy spoons. Some would wink and doff their hats, others would hang their heads, knowing there was nothing I could do. I saw one now on the outskirts of De Beauvoir Town, sitting at a tin table outside the Portuguese café where I sometimes came with Becky. They served the best hot chocolate in town here.

The man's blueish complexion and sopping wet clothing told me he must have drowned.

'I'm sorry,' I said. 'I can't. . .'

He didn't look up but stared forlornly into the gutter. Music drifted out from the café, a 1960s pop song which I knew from somewhere but couldn't quite place. Another figure stepped outside, a wiry man wearing a snappy dark suit and carrying a double espresso. His cropped black hair and steely eyes were instantly familiar. This was Joe Mort, one of our field team leaders.

'It's OK, he's with me, and he *does* have a number,' Joe said, seating himself at the man's table to take his first shot of morning espresso. 'Damn, that hits the spot! How's tricks, Ben?'

'Oh, not bad.'

I was never too sure what to say to Joe Mort. There was something hard and edgy about him that made me glad to know we were on the same side.

'Heard you did good last night,' Joe said. 'By the way, this isn't a 3618, in spite of appearances. His name's Freddie Bannister and he's a 78414, strangled and dumped in the canal.'

'God, that's awful.'

'Yeah, it wasn't great,' Freddie said.

'Any idea who did it?' I asked.

'Came at me from behind. Never saw his face. Took my wallet too,' Freddie said. 'Not that I had anything in it.'

Joe blew air from his cheeks. 'The perp's still at large.'

'Perp?' I said.

'Perpetrator. Out of our jurisdiction. Wish we could follow these things through, dish out a little poetic justice, if you catch my drift, but payback isn't part of our remit. So I'm going to have a little confab with Freddie here . . . figure out what I can do for him.'

'OK,' I said. 'Better leave you to it. Nice meeting you, Freddie.'

Freddie nodded but didn't reply.

'Maybe see you on the next shift,' Joe said as I started away. 'Hey, but watch your step till then. Word is, the enemy are coming back strong after the kicking we gave 'em at Halloween. Take care, Ben.'

'I will. You too.'

There were diversions like this every morning on the way to school, encounters with colleagues, looks and stares from strangers, always a feeling of being observed. The shorter days gave the enemy cover. They lived in the dark, and while you never knew when they'd come out, you could be sure that, at some point, they would.

Today I felt watched more than ever – from every shop doorway and every empty side street I passed. And from higher up, too, from the gaping windows of unfinished skyscrapers miles away across town, their black skeletons standing tall against the morning sky. Watchers everywhere.

Looking up, I suddenly remembered where I'd heard the song in the café. Dad used to have it on vinyl when I was little. He'd bought it in a second-hand record shop and played it on an old Dansette record player. 'The night has a thousand eyes,' the song went, and I thought, yeah, and so does the morning.

3
THE WHISPERER

Turning onto Mercy Road, I found Becky waiting by the steps above the crypt tea rooms, rubbing her hands together and stamping her feet in the cold. 'There's a stranger in town,' she said when she saw me. 'The second new kid on the block this week.'

'Beg your pardon?'

'You're slow today, I can tell. There's another new kid in our class. Name's Decker.'

'Then why not just say so?'

She sniffed and turned to watch a maroon and grey procession of pupils heading down from the bus stop across the street to the school gates. The old Victorian school building looked haunted even by day, with its turrets and cupolas and dark windows.

'Listen, Ben. . .' Becky said in a hushed voice. 'I've got much more important news than that. I saw Sukie on my way here just now, and she said the enemy are—'

'Hang on. We're not supposed to talk about this at school.'

'We're not in school yet,' she said.

She had a point, but classified Ministry business wasn't something we could discuss anywhere we'd be overheard. All the same, Sukie was one of our highly-skilled Ministry colleagues, and whatever she'd told Becky had to be worth hearing.

'So what did she say?' I asked. 'You'd better be quick.'

But the first bell was ringing across the school yard.

'After,' she said. 'It'll have to wait.'

'Yeah. After.'

It was clear from the start that something was wrong in Miss Neal's class. There was a mood, an atmosphere neither of us could explain. Becky sensed it even before we reached the classroom, pulling back sharply in the corridor.

'Feel that?' she said. 'It's cold in there. But not a wintery cold, no ordinary cold.'

'Then what?'

'Not sure. Just a feeling.'

'Harvester! Sanborne!' Miss Neal bellowed

behind the door. 'No loitering out there. You're late!'

If Becky's reaction had made me wary, Miss Neal's shout put me on full alert. She hardly ever raised her voice, if anything she tended to lower it in anger, and in any case the bell had only just rung off. We were seconds late at worst.

Seated behind her desk, Miss Neal looked flushed and irate, a large woman with eyes too small for her face, a storm cloud brewing around her. As we came in she took up a biro and tapped it against her wristwatch.

'What time do you call this?'

'Nine o'clock sharp, Miss,' I said. 'Time for registration?'

'The question was rhetorical, Harvester. Your insolence is noted.'

'Sorry, Miss.'

'Now sit down, the pair of you.'

'But I wasn't. . .' I began, then thought better of it. 'What's rhetorical, Miss?'

'Shush.'

Becky elbowed me. There was no point in answering back. I'd only dig a deeper ditch for myself if I did.

'Sit,' Miss Neal said. 'I won't tell you again.'

As we turned away, I noticed another odd thing. Instead of the usual fidgety, scuffling morning rabble, the class were sitting to attention, alert and perfectly quiet. The icy expressions of the twins Dan and Liam Ferguson seemed to have spread to everyone else.

Well, almost everyone else. The other newcomer this week, Fay De Gray, was a nervy, shrunken violet who went into hiding between lessons and looked alarmed if you so much as spoke to her. Perhaps she was homesick or lonely or had other problems we didn't know about, because twice this week she'd burst into tears for no obvious reason. Fay cowered over her desk, head in hands, whimpering, but no one took any notice of her. All eyes except Fay's were on us.

Becky's old gang – Matthew, Ryan, Curly, Devan and Kelly – occupied two pulled-together tables with a spare chair at the near end. They'd been mates since the infants and Becky still sat with them in most classes, but they'd been growing apart since she'd made friends with me. Her involvement with the Ministry meant they saw less of each other these days, and the gang of six were now more like five. As she went for the free chair, Ryan laid a hand on its backrest and spoke politely but firmly.

'Sorry, that's taken.'

Becky flinched. 'Excuse me?'

'It's taken,' said Kelly.

The others exchanged a knowing look and a nod. Becky stood there, stranded, unsure which way to turn. After a long moment she headed for my desk and sank down, flustered, while Miss Neal began calling the register.

'What was that about?' I said.

Someone – I believe it was snot-nosed Tommy Farley – shushed me.

Becky shrugged, opened her bag and slapped her books and pens loudly on the desk.

Someone else shushed her.

'Raymond . . . Michael . . . Fay. . . ' Miss Neal read in a lifeless monotone, not looking up from the register. 'Tommy . . . David . . . Liam. . .'

Becky muttered something under her breath which I didn't catch, and looked at me with worried green eyes.

'What?' I said.

'I'm not supposed to say, but what Sukie told me earlier – she wasn't kidding.'

'Not now. . .' I said.

'That's enough!' Miss Neal smacked her desk

with a flattened palm. 'You two – yes, you two. Since whatever you're discussing is clearly so important it cannot wait, you might like to explain it in detail. Not here and now but in a thousand-word essay you will write after school during detention. My detention.'

Becky sighed and shook her head.

'Aw, Miss. . .' I groaned, feeling every smug look and triumphant grin in the room bearing down on me. Since starting here in September I'd never been made all that welcome by 8C – I'd always been an outsider but never an outcast. Apparently we were both outcasts now.

'With your permission, I'll move on,' Miss Neal said. 'Now, everyone, are you paying attention?'

'Yes, Miss,' answered every voice in the class except ours and Fay's.

'Good. Then I'd like you to welcome a new face to 8C. This is Simon Decker's first day at Mercy Road, and I'm sure most of you know how it feels to be in a new place surrounded by strangers, so make your new classmate feel at home by saying hello.'

'Hello Simon,' the class chimed as one.

He was sitting alone at the back by the window, a small boy with straight-combed hair as black as ravens' wings, a pale narrow-chinned face and the coldest blue eyes. His thin lips quivered as if he were muttering to himself. First day nerves, I supposed. He answered the class's greeting with a shy nod of his head.

'And I hope, Simon, you've taken note of the kind of behaviour that is and isn't acceptable here.' Miss Neal's piggy eyes fixed on me. 'At Mercy Road we have rules like any other school, and if you abide by those rules you'll do well. Now I'm sure the rest of the class would like to welcome you properly during the break, but first let's proceed with our lesson.'

The lesson was Maths. Probabilities. For instance, the probability of a six-sided dice throwing an even or odd number, or a two-sided coin coming down heads or tails. Not my subject. It never had been. But I couldn't help thinking, and what's the probability of twenty-six students and one teacher switching personalities overnight? What are the odds of that?

For the next forty minutes all you could hear were the pages of exercise books being turned and scribbled on. At the back, Simon Decker mouthed silently, and every so often Miss Neal gave me dark looks. At one point Raymond Blight flicked a paper ball at my neck, but no one noticed or commented on that. Had the whole class been brainwashed or what?

It came as a relief when the bell went, breaking the spell. The lesson ended, books were bagged, and the scramble for the door began. When I looked to the front Miss Neal had gone from her desk, but on the board she'd left a reminder:

B. Sanborne & B. Harvester, 8C, 3.15 p.m. 1,000 words.

Half the class lingered behind, not pressing for the door but towards the desk where Simon Decker sat peering out the window at the yard. Two girls closed around him, Mel Kimble perching on his desk, Sarah Knox sliding onto a chair beside him.

'Wassup, Simon? I'm Mel. Pleased to meetcha.'

'I'm Sarah. Welcome aboard.'

Others, even Becky's old gang, flocked round like autograph hunters, and through the crush I saw something that both irritated and unnerved me. Decker turned from the window, and his lips stopped moving long enough to form the semblance of a smile as he looked straight at me.

That look reminded me of something else, a warning the enemy had sent me last month, posting it on the graffiti wall across from our place on Middleton Road. *We can get to you and yours anywhere any time*, the message had said. Perhaps I was

reading too much into it, but just then Simon Decker's
eyes seemed to say the same thing.

✦ 4 ✦
STRANGE AIR

Every lesson that day had the same strange air, the same orderly well-behaved class, and teachers who, for some reason, had all decided to clamp down on us. Even English with Mr Glover and PSHE with the usually pleasant but horsey Miss Whittaker went the same way. For the most part we were walking on glass.

'It's like a virus,' Becky said after school, following the corridor that smelt of stale varnish to Miss Neal's room. 'Something that's making everyone nuts, including the teachers.'

'Yeah,' I said, only half-listening, still shaking off Simon Decker's look. 'What do you think it is?'

'Not sure, but I don't like the way it's all aimed at us. Did you see how my old mates treated me?'

She tailed off, again stalling at Miss Neal's door as if she expected something to leap out from behind it. I pushed it open and led the way in, and Becky reluctantly followed. Miss Neal wasn't here yet and the room felt lighter, airy and safe.

'I've never had detention before,' Becky said, looking around the empty space.

'Me neither.'

'We'll be late for our shift.'

'I know.'

'Suppose that's their plan?' Becky said. 'Suppose that's what Sukie was getting at?'

Earlier, at the crypt tea rooms where we spent most breaks, Becky had finally had a chance to explain her morning exchange with Sukie. Walking to school on Richmond Road, she'd spotted Sukie with a 3624 who'd jumped in front of a midnight tube train at Old Street. The young woman's departed soul had wandered the streets all night and could have been lost forever if a field agent hadn't called Sukie to assist. Sukie, whose mind-scanning capabilities made her an expert tracker, was consoling the weeping woman on Holly Street when Becky turned up.

'Word of warning,' Sukie said. 'This 3624 swears blind she didn't mean to do it. She's never given a thought to suicide in her life. She just got *engaged*, for crying out loud. Someone on that platform popped the idea of jumping into her head before the train came in. Something's changing. Seems they're using different tactics now. Be careful, keep your ears to the ground.'

'Different tactics. . .' Becky mused as we settled at a desk near the front. 'Are they smart enough to mess with people's minds? Make them behave differently? Make them jump under trains?'

'I suppose they *must* be that smart. Otherwise they wouldn't be much of an enemy, would they, and the war would've been over ages ago.'

She looked at the detention notice on the board. 'Do you think Miss Neal's one of them? Or one of them did something to change her?'

'It wasn't just her. It was all the kids and staff, even the principal. When I saw him coming downstairs after lunch, the look he gave me made me want to dig a hole to hide in.'

She opened her bag and took out a pen and exercise book. 'What will we write? A thousand words about what we weren't talking about?'

'We can't do that.'

'We'll have to make something up.'

'What else can we do?'

'Shush.'

There were footsteps outside, but they quickly passed along the corridor. Another fifteen minutes went by before Miss Neal appeared, crossing to her desk without a word. I expected her to start yelling again, but her look was placid as she sat, folding her pudgy pink hands together in front of her.

'There seems to have been a misunderstanding,' Miss Neal said. 'I believe I owe you both an apology.'

'Excuse me, Miss?' Becky said through a cough.

'I wasn't quite myself this morning,' Miss Neal said. 'When I called you here for detention, I think I was overreacting to your little confab. Consider your thousand words written and your sentence already served.'

She forced a smile. I exchanged a quick glance with Becky.

'If you're sure, Miss,' I said.

'I am, and that's the end of it.' She pinched the bridge of her nose. 'Aren't the lights in here awful? They give me such headaches. I had an unusually bad one first thing today, a migraine.'

'I get those too sometimes,' I said, trying to be conversational.

'I think this old building brings it on. It's so dark in places, and the fluorescent lights are so harsh in others. And some parts of the school are colder than others, have you noticed?

Sometimes I think I'm seeing things.'

'Sometimes we see things too,' Becky said, blurting it out without thinking. A look from me sealed her lips.

'Really, what kind of things?' Miss Neal said.

'Just shadows,' I said quickly.

'Yeah, shadows,' Becky agreed.

Miss Neal looked out at the fading sky. 'Anyway, if you suffer from migraines as I do, Ben, you'll understand. They can make you snap at the slightest thing, as I snapped this morning. I'm sorry.'

'That's OK, Miss. Good you're feeling better now, anyway.'

'Thank you, much better.'

This was more like the Miss Neal we knew, but she still seemed distracted, or perhaps she was just embarrassed by a dramatic mood swing she couldn't explain. Rising from her chair, she wiped our names from the board and started for the door.

'You're free to go, by the way,' she said as she went.

＊＊＊

'Well, that was bizarre,' Becky said, returning up the

corridor a minute later. 'Really bizarre. She's right about the cold spots, though. Miss Whatever's room for one.'

She meant Miss Whittaker's, where I'd first seen the stranded fire children, and where, for the first time since his death – although I hadn't known it was him at the time – I'd seen Dad.

'Yeah, it *is* colder in there,' I said.

'And here.' Becky stopped where the two main corridors intersected close to the centre of school. 'See this?'

She exhaled a pale mist on the air. I put out a hand and felt the temperature plummet. The cold spot, about a metre across, had to be ten degrees cooler than where we'd just come from.

'Miss Neal's was even colder first thing,' Becky went on. 'But that was a different kind of cold. And I'll tell you something else for free. Whatever came over her this morning, it wasn't a migraine, no way.'

I nudged her along. We had to make up time. 'What else could it be?'

'The new kid. The whisperer. Decker turning everyone against us, even my mates.'

'Now you're sounding paranoid.'

'You saw what I saw. Anyway, I'm keeping my eye on him.'

Leaving the gloomy building for the deepening dusk outside, we crossed the yard, searching our pockets for gloves. A raven called in the darkness above us and crossed Mercy Road to land on a TV aerial. We were at the school gates when another, more violent sound made us both stop – a shriek of car tyres to our right – and a sudden blast of headlights whited everything out.

The vehicle, travelling at high speed, swung to the curb, bumped up and over it onto the pavement and did an emergency stop in front of us, sliding to a halt under a streetlight.

It took me a long moment to recover from the shock, and then I had my first clear view of the car. It was just about the most gorgeous vehicle I'd ever seen, an early 1960s Ford Mustang convertible with its black top down, a long sleek cream body and red leather interiors. Lu sat behind the wheel, her hair unravelled by the wind from its normal tight bob and plastered about her face.

'Don't just stand there,' she said. 'You're late. They sent me to get you.'

While Becky squeezed into the back, I took the

passenger seat. 'What happened to the rickshaw, Lu?'

'Annual service. This is the best they could come up with to keep us going.'

'Not a bad loaner.'

She frowned, crashing gears, working the accelerator until the engine boomed like a jet's. 'It's not bad. I'm still getting used to it. Put on your belts, though. It doesn't corner too well and I don't have a driver's licence.'

'Ah.'

This snippet of information was still sinking in when she whipped the Mustang off the curb and went serpentining up the street with the speedometer nudging sixty. I found my belt and hurriedly clipped it on.

Two blocks along we went into a kangaroo hop, and Lu had to fight the steering wheel to avoid ploughing through the red phone box on the junction. Nearer the top of Mercy Road she again mounted the pavement, the Mustang's near-side demolishing a grocer's fruit and vegetable stand, scattering red apples and green bananas. The top end of Mercy Road was quiet, there wasn't much more damage Lu could do there, but I worried about what might happen when we hit the busier

Islington streets closer to headquarters.

'Have you driven a car before?' Becky called from the back. 'Just wondering.'

'I've driven lots of things,' Lu said. 'But no, nothing like this. I'll get the hang of it soon enough, just you watch.'

'You couldn't slow down, could you?' I called above the engine.

'Slow . . . down?' The thought had never occurred to her. 'Too busy. No time, and you have an important meeting before we start the rounds.'

'Me? A meeting with who? What about?'

'Something about the incursion last month. They didn't explain. They just said to bring you double-quick.'

'That's all you know?'

'That's all.'

It didn't sound good. The incursion, the night the enemy stormed headquarters, had been all my fault, and if the meeting had anything to do with that I'd rather not go at all. Maybe I'd hop out as soon as we stopped for traffic lights.

But Lu didn't stop for any lights. After jumping three reds in a row along City Road, she tore through a crossing on Upper Street, sending pedestrians running and diving for cover. Other drivers worked their headlights and horns as she overtook a Parcelforce van into the face of oncoming traffic, fitted the Mustang into the tightest of gaps between two buses, and swung out to overtake again. I was wondering how she'd ever squeeze this thing through the hair's breadth entrance to headquarters – if we made it there alive – when Lu floored the brakes, took a sharp right and brought the Mustang to a screeching halt below a pub called the York.

'Like I said, I need more practice,' Lu said, killing the engine. 'Soon I'll take us all the way, but for now it's best if we leave it here.'

'Good idea,' I said.

We peeled ourselves from the car like dizzy roller coaster survivors. My hands were shaky, but not as shaky as Becky's legs when she tried to stand.

'Are you all right?' I said.

She nodded. 'Sort of.'

Along Duncan Street, shadows stretched from the walls like long spindly fingers, shrinking back when a people carrier's headlights bobbed up the slope. As it passed, a colourless face pressed itself to the passenger side window, staring out with vacant eyes –

another of the unnamed hitching a ride, a companion the driver didn't know he had.

Becky shivered, feeling the presence, and after watching the vehicle's tail lights turn off at the junction, we set off for Pandemonium House.

❧ 5 ❧
THE OVERSEERS

part from a few stragglers and passers-by, Camden Passage was quiet, and no one saw us step aside between two shops to enter the hairline crack in the wall that led to HQ.

A regular drip of water echoed along the unlit space, a space so narrow we had to edge through it sideways, shoes scraping over the gritty floor. At the far end a chink of light signalled the exit to Eventide Street, home to the Ministry's headquarters. The gap widened and brightened as we moved towards it, and one by one we tumbled out, into a starlit alleyway.

It was night in the alley – it was always night-time here. Two gas-burning streetlights by the steps below headquarters washed the cobbled ground with amber, and the old brick building stood half in shadow, half in light, with shuttered windows and upper floors so dark they seemed to merge with the sky.

Taking the steps and heading indoors, we passed through a dim entrance hall and climbed a rickety staircase to the main operations floor. An eerie wind whistled around the upstairs and candles flickered in alcoves between the closed offices on both sides of the hallway.

'Your meeting won't last long,' Lu said. 'We'll be in the waiting room when you're done.'

'And where do I go?'

'The conference room. Where else?'

My heart slumped. I'd been nervous before, but now I felt close to panic.

'It'll be fine,' Becky tried to reassure me as the girls headed off. 'Something and nothing, most likely.'

As an apprentice I'd only seen a small part of Pandemonium House: the receipts office where I transcribed the lists of soon-departeds as the telegraph delivered them, the ever-expanding records room where all numbers and names were filed, the dispatch office where girls wearing heavy headsets chattered into desktop microphones relaying calls to the field day and night.

The conference room was the operations hub, the inner sanctum watched over by the living portraits of the Overseers. To be called to this place was no small matter. I hadn't set foot inside there since the Halloween invasion, and I didn't fancy standing in the glare of those twelve solemn faces again.

Besides, there were staff here, security guards known as Vigilants, who I was sure held a grudge against me for what I'd done that night. Working alone in receipts, I'd seen – or could've sworn I'd seen – Mum's name on an incoming list. I'd stolen that list from the building, the most unforgivable thing an operative could do. As a result, our defences were thrown wide open, the enemy came roaring in, and seventeen staff were lost, taken body and soul. Could that be why I was here?

Two Vigilants were posted outside the conference room now, rifles strapped across their grey-uniformed chests. They gave me lingering dark looks when I approached, and I sensed their trigger fingers itching, but they stood back to let me inside.

The room was just as I remembered it, an immense hall of hewn stone walls with a log fire blazing in a cast iron fireplace. The elders, six to each side of the room, looked down from their portraits with ever-changing faces which faded in and out behind veils of curling mist. The conference table, smashed in two the last time I'd seen it, had been fully restored, and the crystal chandelier above it sent cascades of rainbow light through the air.

At the far end of the room were three stained glass

windows which framed a number of colourful battle scenes, fierce clashes between armoured warriors and demons in many forms, some reptilian, some feline, others in shadow-form, shifting between one shape and another.

These historic scenes weren't confined to the windows but covered the sculpted ceiling too, intricately detailed and slowly, subtly moving, vibrating from the horrors they showed. One scene in particular caught my eye. It looked familiar, *very* familiar, but I was distracted by a movement at the head of the table where a white-robed figure had just materialised.

At first I thought one of the elders had stepped down from its portrait, but all twelve judgmental faces were looking down when I checked. The pale figure stood with its back towards me, holding in one hand something metallic that reflected the chandelier's light. When it turned slowly around, I realised the object in its hand was a long-bladed scythe – but it was the sight of its face that turned my blood cold.

It was the Reaper's face, a pale grinning skull only partly shaded by the hood of its garment. Dull orbs of light shone deep inside its hollow eye sockets, the bared teeth clicked and chattered, and thunder crackled from its throat when it spoke.

'You're late, boy. You were called. Don't you know what it means to be called?'

I fell back, too alarmed to speak, my heart thudding between my ears.

'Young man,' the figure said, rounding the table towards me. 'Young man, have you any idea why you were summoned?'

I shook my head, heart in mouth. A flicker of lightning crossed the ceiling and fringed the scythe's curved edge.

'Then I'll tell you,' the figure said. 'Some here say you're a born helper. Some call you Wonder Boy. Others believe you've done more harm than good, stoking the enemy's fires and stirring the agents of darkness into the foulest of moods. Have you considered the consequences of your actions, have you asked yourself where this will all lead?'

'No. . .' I couldn't easily breathe, let alone speak. 'Whatever I've done, I'm sorry. Don't hold it against me, whoever you are.'

'And who do you think I am?'

The figure had moved nearer, within touching distance. Now it leaned nearer still until I felt its breath on my cheek.

'Don't know,' I said, but I knew I was about to find out.

The Reaper threw back its hood, lifted a bony-fingered hand to its face and with a slap and a squelch peeled the skull mask clean off. With another flurry it cast the robes aside, revealing another figure in its place – swarthy and silver-toothed, dressed in ragged black clothing and knee-high boots. To this outfit, which I knew so well, he'd added a wide-brimmed black hat worn at a tilt, which made me think less of a pirate, more of a gunslinger.

'Gotcha!' he said, creasing with laughter.

'You!'

'One of these days you won't be so easily fooled, Ben Harvester, and then how will I amuse myself?'

The Overseers certainly weren't amused, some looking on dolefully while others clucked their tongues.

'Mr October, I thought you were gone,' I said. 'Retired or dead. I thought. . .'

'That'll be the day,' he said. 'It takes more than a stray enemy fireball to keep old Dudley October down. But I must admit, it was touch and go there for a while.'

'I can't believe it's you. I missed you. It's so good to see you.'

'Yes, I imagine it is.' The silver tooth glinted. 'Excuse the reaper costume, by the way. Thought I'd ring a few changes for the field but I fear that look is badly overstated. And the scythe – imagine how newly-departeds would feel, seeing that. They need comfort and guidance, not a danse macabre.'

'Well, I prefer you this way,' I said.

'The old ones are the best, I suppose.' He glanced at the portraits, then back at me. 'As for the reason you were called here. Firstly, I thought – and my superiors here agreed – it would be best to break the news of my return to you in person rather than let you find out through idle gossip. Secondly, and more importantly, we felt the time was right to show you this.'

I followed his look to the ceiling, to the battle portrayal I'd spotted before. It pictured a transparent, slimy-bodied being with a yawning mouth as large as its head, a Mawbreed caught in the act of eating itself. I had a sudden giddy feeling because I'd seen this happen with my own eyes. More than that, I'd *made* it happen, I'd turned the Mawbreed against themselves right here in this room.

'Not particularly pretty,' Mr October said. 'Of course I was indisposed at the time so I never saw for myself what you'd achieved, but I heard about it – and my, how the staff in the clinic like to talk. But be assured of this, Ben. What you did that night has already become the stuff of our history. It's a tremendous honour for one so young to make their mark here and to have it recorded in such a way.'

Did one or more of the Overseers just smile? I couldn't be sure, but the general mood radiating from the portraits felt like approval.

'I . . . I don't know what to say,' I said.

'Say nothing. There's no time, anyway. We're running late.'

With a quick bow to the portraits, Mr October excused us from the conference room. The elderly faces were sinking back into mist as he escorted me out to the hallway past the two guards.

'So how are things with you?' Mr October said. 'I've been hearing great stories about the work your team has done in my absence.'

'Oh, things are fine,' I said.

'Feel free to elaborate. Then again, actions speak louder than words, don't they, as we've just seen. How's your dear mother?'

'Doing well, I think. On holiday now.'

'A much needed sabbatical. So much pain and sadness in her life these last few years. Keep a close eye on her when she returns, Ben.'

'I will.'

He didn't need to explain. The enemy, the Lords of Sundown, set their sights on our loved ones as much as ourselves. Family and friends were our weaknesses as well as our strengths.

'So what's this talk about new enemy activity?' I asked. 'Joe Mort mentioned it, and Sukie told Becky. . .'

'Rumours,' Mr October said. 'But behind most rumours there's often a grain of truth. The enemy are never still, and our intelligence does suggest they're stepping things up. I wasn't speaking in jest before. Your good work has put them in a flutter.'

We stopped at the waiting room door.

'Girls?' Mr October called, peering inside. 'Meeting's over. Care to join us?'

They looked up together. Becky's face was a picture of surprised wonder while Lu's greeting, a polite little nod, told me she'd known all along but had been sworn to secrecy. The four of us trooped up the hallway, past records, past dispatch. As we reached the receipts office a joyful shout went up inside.

'Mr October!'

Sukie looked up from the desk as we entered. Because of her telepathic skills she must have been among the first to know. She was in her middle teens and had a stormy appearance, all back-brushed hair and black clothing. A slight cast in her eye made her seem to be looking in two directions at once.

'I've been dying to share the news,' she said. 'Hardest thing I've ever done, keeping it all to myself. It wasn't the same without you.'

'Good to see you too, Sukie. So how's tonight's schedule looking?' Mr October said.

'It's all here.'

On the desk before her was a pistachio green Olivetti Lettera 22 typewriter and two stacks of typed cards, one of which Sukie passed to Mr October. We always kept two sets, one for the field and one for filing, all carefully transcribed from the lists pumped out by the ancient Stern & Grimwald telegraph machine across the room.

Whenever I entered this place – and I often worked long hours here – I became tense, willing the telegraph not to make a sound, not on my shift. When it did, often waking with a spark and a bang, the lists it spat out were significant. While the numbers explained how the soon-departed would go, the exact nature and cause of death, no one but the Overseers knew where the names came from. All we knew was that this cramped book-lined candlelit room was where they arrived.

Mr October tweaked the hat back on his head and skipped through the cards one by one.

'Oh my. That's tragic. How awful. Oh dear. And there seem to be a few weather-related incidents tonight – falling trees, collapsed chimney. . . What's all that about?'

'Forecasts of a tornado,' Sukie explained. 'Could touch down anytime tonight or early morning.'

'Then let's look lively,' Mr October said. 'Sukie, would you mind taking these to Miss Webster in records and working a little overtime? I'll keep Ben with me on the rounds.'

'Be glad to.' Sukie collected her cards and stood up at the desk. 'Love the new hat, by the way,' she told Mr October. 'Reminds me of Jack Palance in *Shane*.'

'Pick up the gun,' Mr October growled, narrowing his eyes.

Sukie laughed. 'You've seen that film too.'

I smiled, clueless as to what they were talking about.

'It's a Western,' Sukie explained, reading my mind, and reading Mr October's she said, 'It's in service.'

'Lu, better go prepare the rickshaw,' Mr October said.

'It's in service,' Lu said, looking in confusion at Sukie. 'There's a loaner, a Mustang convertible around the corner on Duncan Street. I haven't tried bringing it through the walls yet.'

'Nice,' Mr October said, ushering us out. 'Back in the 1960s I drove a Mustang myself.'

'Did you work for the Ministry then?' Becky asked.

'I've always worked for the Ministry,' he answered mysteriously. 'Frankly, I'd be unemployable anywhere else. But shall we begin? This first call on our list looks like a toughie.'

❧ 6 ❧
77772

That first call was a 77772, a complex case involving a black dog named Della, a boy named Alex, an Iceland delivery truck and two hundred and thirty-six cyclists who'd descended on central London with banners and loudhailers to reclaim the streets.

'Give London back to Londoners!' their red, white and blue banners proclaimed. 'Motorists, on yer bikes!' 'Two wheels are better than four!'

By three o'clock they'd brought the city centre traffic to a standstill, and with rush hour approaching, the gridlock would only get worse. The boy Alex, walking his dog east on the Strand towards Aldwych, slowed to watch the cars and buses trying to cut around the slow-moving blockade.

The drivers were livid, jamming their horns and shaking their fists. Occasional gaps on the road ahead gave some an opportunity to cut around the protesters and into space. As they floored their accelerators, skirting the parade and bumping along the central reservation, the last wasp of the year was dying, spiralling down from a great height towards earth.

How the wasp had survived so long in the biting climate was anyone's guess. Usually by this time of year most queens were hibernating, the rest of their population gone for the season. Earlier today, this particular wasp had feasted on a spillage of fruit six blocks away outside a restaurant on Villiers Street, and the bellyful of overripe plum and peach flesh was now fermenting away inside it. This was one drunken wasp, as drunk as any wasp had ever been, staring down the barrel at the worst hangover of its life, mad as hell and looking for something to sting – just for the hell of it – before meeting its maker.

It passed the Savoy Theatre, hovered a moment above a steak house door on the Strand's south side, then crossed the street, bearing down on a taxi driver's plump forearm as the driver reached out to adjust his off-side wing mirror. Sighting its reflection in the mirror a split second before it could strike, the driver batted the wasp away with a hairy hand.

The wasp sighted something else across the street, a splash of bright yellow, and set sail for the colourful scarf wrapped around the neck of the boy named Alex.

Something about that poster-bright yellow stirred a rage in the wasp unlike any it had ever known. Its wings felt leaden, everything in its field of vision was swimming and turning double, but it fully intended to leave this world with a bang, not a whimper.

Alex was straining two-handed at Della's leash when the attack began. It was the last thing he expected, and at first he couldn't imagine what the angry buzzing at his throat might be. He reacted instinctively, dropping the leash and flashing both hands at the aggressor, left then right.

It was the moment Della the dog had been waiting for, a chance to stretch her legs and let rip. She'd had enough of plodding along at human pace, choking on her confounded collar. Solid muscle from nose to tail, part Staffordshire bull terrier, part whippet, she was made for running. As Alex dealt the wasp a glancing blow, sending it past the doorway of a digital photo print shop, Della took off into the street.

She'd made it safely to the other side before the boy could open his lungs to call after her. By then the 77772 was in progress, and far across town in the receipts office at Pandemonium House the telegraph machine was chattering.

The first motorist to see the dog coming was Eric Skiller, a fifty-year-old electrician on call to a block of flats in Plaistow where an overflowing bath had led to a power outage. Passing the procession, Eric noticed a fast-moving black shape cutting in from the left and immediately went for the brakes.

The driver behind him, Jeremy Fenn, a freelance journalist leaving the city for the weekend, saw the brake lights in front too late. Pedestrians turned at the sound of the collision, loud as a bomb, as the aftershock rippled through both cars. While the journalist's MG stalled and stopped, Eric Skiller's blue Ford Transit jerked forward and kept going, the impact from the rear propelling it straight at the cyclists.

Some of them saw him coming. Not many were able to steer clear. They'd been creeping along four and five abreast, and when the Transit shot towards them they all tried to take off in different directions at once. One collision led to another as the tangle of pedals and handlebars and arms and legs spread through the blockade. Somewhere between sixty and seventy were caught in the pile-up while two cyclists near the front managed to pedal away at full pelt to avoid it.

These two were both on our list.

One, Roger Finney, 26, smacked the side of an Iceland delivery truck that was travelling on a free-flowing westbound lane. The other, 28-year-old Timothy Matterson, disappeared straight under it. While Alex picked his way across the street to re-attach Della's leash and walk on, witnesses were yelling and running to help, but no one could help these two now.

To avoid the gridlock, Lu had parked the Mustang on Bedford Street, colliding with a City of Westminster waste bin as she did. After Mr October made a quick change, becoming the grey-eyed empathiser I'd first met at Highgate, a limping old man who attended the most sensitive cases, we walked down to the Strand. Police and ambulance teams were already there, debating where and how to cordon off the scene. It wasn't easy to tell where it began and ended.

We checked the damage from a distance. Most of the protesters were unharmed, a few nursed cuts and grazes, but Matterson, the first on our list, was still jammed beneath the truck's wheels with his tan-booted feet sticking out.

'Very soon-departed,' Mr October announced. 'We'll deal with this one first and catch the other at the hospital later.'

Finney, who'd slammed side-on into the truck, was being loaded into an ambulance in front of us. He was still breathing when they drove him away, but according to his card he wouldn't be for much longer.

'So this is a 77772?' Becky said. 'Amazing how much the numbers tell you.'

'Technically speaking, it's two 77772s, or soon will be,' said Mr October. 'A very particular set of circumstances. If the restaurant staff hadn't put out the crate of rotting fruit when they did. . . If the wasp hadn't survived another few hours. . . If the boy hadn't been walking his dog in that very spot at that time . . . it wouldn't have been this way at all.'

'But their numbers were up,' I said.

'True, there's nothing anyone could've done about that. When someone's number comes up, there's no argument.'

I thought about the chain of events as we stood among the lights and noise. Big Ben struck four-thirty as Timothy Matterson's ghost rolled aside from the Iceland truck and stood to watch the ambulance workers extricating his body from under it. They didn't know he'd gone yet. They didn't know what we knew and they couldn't see what we were seeing.

The cyclist looked up in a daze, probably still feeling the tremor of the thump of the vehicle's front end that killed him. His eyes found us in the crowd and flickered with a kind of recognition.

'Oh,' his expression seemed to say. 'Oh, it's you.'

And, stepping around the ailing wasp twitching in the gutter by our feet, Mr October moved towards the cyclist's ghost and went to work.

✦

The forecasts weren't too accurate. None of our calls that night were weather-related. Not directly, anyway.

The 4275 in Edgware was standing in the wrong place at the wrong time when the chimney collapsed. A TV engineer, repairing an aerial on the roof, lost his footing on loose tiles and fell against the stack, which came apart like a sandcastle. This didn't rule out weather-related wear and tear on the tiles or the brickwork over time.

'Never assume anything,' Mr October said later. 'Sometimes the numbers tell us a great deal, but it's possible to read too much into them. We can never be sure until we've seen for ourselves.'

The 4275 wasn't happy. He'd only stepped outdoors for a moment to check on the work in progress, but that was the moment the chimney stack came down on him. He argued his case well, I thought, but in the end he went on his way with a shrug and a shake of the head.

Next up was a natural causes in Leyton, an 8847 in Ministry speak. The house was a typical two-up two-down on the W15 bus route with floral curtains and a tiny square of untended lawn at the front. Many 8847s passed away in care homes and on hospital wards, but others refused to give up the homes they'd lived in all their lives. Mary Butterfield, 91, had lived most of hers here. She'd left this world moments before we walked to her door.

Mr October wiggled his fingers and touched the door in two separate places. The door, which had been locked when we arrived, clicked open.

The chintzy interiors, all pink and brown flowers, smelt of cat pee. Alerted by a hum of flies down the hall, Mr October told us to stay back.

'Could be something you'd rather not see,' he said, heading to a room at the end. Seconds later he called, 'It's all right. All clear.'

The handful of flies were confined to the kitchen,

darting between trays of cat litter and half-eaten dishes of Felix. A tap was running. Lu turned it off and made a face as she looked around.

'Why do flies exist?' she said. 'What's the point of them?'

Not an easy question to answer. I let it go.

'In here,' Becky called.

She'd found the old lady in the living room in a reclining armchair, an unfinished cup of tea on her side table, a novel entitled *The Murder of Roger Ackroyd* in her hands. Her forefinger marked a page close to the end.

'It's the page where the killer's name is revealed,' Mr October explained. 'You see? No two natural causes cases are ever alike. Her poor worn-out old heart simply gave up when she found out whodunnit. The excitement was all too much.'

The excitement still gripped Mary's face. Her mouth gaped open in an O of surprise, and her unseeing eyes were wide with astonishment. As Mr October closed her lids, I thought of the ancientspeak book he'd given me – a book of words with the power to build up or destroy. Words with the power to kill.

A breeze passed through the room, ruffling Mary's clothing. The living room windows were shut, the curtains still, but this breeze hadn't entered the room from outside. It was coming from Mary herself.

Becky let out a little cry, feeling the old lady's presence. On the side table, the reading lamp dimmed briefly before glowing three times brighter, and then Mary's loose-fitting clothes lifted and flapped around her as something inside her began to make its way out.

This was a new thing to me, the part Mr October called separation. Most souls had already separated when we turned up. Not this one, though. Another Mary was entering the room, the hidden one who'd been with her since she was born, through two long-lasting marriages and on through the days she'd lived alone with her cats in this house.

The wind lashed our faces, a warming gust. Specks of soft light were being blown together into a shape beside her chair. The shape was mostly made of light, but tiny parts of Mary were visible too – a wrinkly hand, a wisp of white hair, a patch of navy blue pattern on her shin-length dress.

Soon the rushing wind fell to a breeze, a draught, and there stood Mary Butterfield, eyes glazed, frowning as she tried to adjust to where she was. She looked at herself in the armchair, then at us, aghast.

'What's the meaning of this?' she cried in a voice strident enough to peel paint. 'What are you doing in my house? I've a mind to call the police, I have. Get out, get out!'

'Ho hum,' Mr October said. 'It's going to be one of those.'

━━◆━━

After Mary, we followed the cards to a 126329, which Mr October described as 'most unpleasant' and which I'd rather not go into in detail. This was followed by another natural causes in Bow, then a visit to London Hospital for the cyclist Roger Finney, dead on arrival, and our last call of the shift, a 6575 at the Isle of Dogs.

At first we were confused by the 6575. On paper it looked straightforward – a thirty-eight year-old male dead as the result of a fall. Open and shut. But not many things in our line of work were open and shut.

It began with a late afternoon party, a few drinks to usher in the weekend on the top floor of a three-story block near the river. To avoid complaints from neighbours, Peter Van Dornen had invited everyone in the building. They wouldn't moan about the noise, he reasoned, if they were guests.

Friends arrived, neighbours invited friends of their own, and by six o'clock the modest one-bedroom flat was hot and heaving. Several party guests spilled out to the balcony to take the air, unaware that the bolts securing the iron safety railing were worn and loose.

The booze was running out, and the host decided to run down to the corner shop for supplies. Returning, straining from the weight of the four bags he was carrying, Peter Van Dornen stopped below his balcony to catch a breath. Something small but solid pinged in the darkness close by. Bottles clinking in the bags, he supposed, but in fact what he'd heard was the balcony's first falling bolt striking the pavement at his feet.

'Hurry up, Pete,' the guests called from three flights above, leaning over the rail, empty glasses in hand. 'We're dry. We're depending on you!'

Two or three of them pressing against the rail wouldn't have made such a difference. Twelve was more than it could take. Peter Van Dornen heard a second metallic object bounce off the ground. The next and last thing he heard was screaming.

Incredibly, only one partygoer took the plunge.

The rest, tugging and clinching like a rugby scrum, pulled themselves back as the railing gave way. The falling man, a strapping muscular type with a bulldog face and no neck, lived in the flat below Van Dornen's and later hobbled back to it without so much as a bruise. He wasn't on our list, but Peter Van Dornen, who broke his fall, was.

Just before Lu brought the Mustang screaming round the corner onto Ferry Street, Van Dornen left his broken body to go down to the river. In a kind of trance he watched the city lights dancing across the black water. He didn't look up when we joined him, or when Mr October laid a hand on his shoulder.

'You know, I'll miss this,' he said. 'I worked so hard to get here.'

Mr October's voice was low and soothing. 'You will and you did. But it's better this way.'

'Better?' I said, but Mr October's look told me not to interrupt.

'You know all about me, don't you?' Peter Van Dornen said dreamily.

'We do,' said Mr October.

'Then you'll know the doc gave me three months to live, and I'd planned to see the world, all the sights, do it all while I still could. Only my closest friends knew. Tonight was supposed to be the start, the big send-off before I set sail.'

'Not quite the send-off you had in mind,' Mr October said. 'I'm so sorry.'

'Don't be sorry,' Van Dornen said as Mr October prepared to walk him away. 'Those three months were a sentence. Now I'm free.'

Soon after, another light flashed across the Thames like a brief burst of flame, and he was gone. That was the end of the shift for Becky and me, but for Lu and Mr October the night was just beginning. More calls to make, more numbers to reel in. Always the same.

They dropped us at Liverpool Street and we took a bus home.

It was after nine when I got in. Ross had been over, leaving a note – sorry he'd missed me – and another food parcel in the fridge. I sat up, too tired to settle, and ate the spare ribs he'd brought in front of the TV, skipping channels.

Later, I lay awake in bed going over the evening's events, from the multi-cycle pile-up to Peter Van Dornen's farewell at the Isle of Dogs to the bus ride home with Becky.

'The enemy were dead quiet tonight, weren't they?' she'd said towards the end of the journey. 'There's usually some sign they're about, hiding in a crowd or under a bridge, but I didn't feel them anywhere and they didn't contest one soul. What are they waiting for?'

My thoughts exactly. Where were they now, and why the silence? The question was still ringing in my ears when I fell asleep.

It was still dark when I woke to the burr of the living room telephone. Groaning, I turned over in bed, wrapping the duvet around me.

The phone rang and rang. The bedside clock said seven. Who called at this hour? Then the phone stopped. Then it started again. Suppose it was Mum with news of her homecoming? I dragged myself out of bed and hurried to answer.

'Hello?'

It was Becky, jabbering away so frantically I couldn't make out a word.

'Slow down,' I said. 'Take a breath. Then try again.'

'The tornado they forecast touched down,' she said. 'Right here on our house, ten minutes ago. Can you come over, Ben? I really need to see you.'

7
EYES OF THE STORM

Becky lived on Parkholme Road, a good ten minutes walk from my place. I made it there in three.

Turning past the Prince George on Wilton Way, the first thing that struck me – the strangest, most obvious thing – was how peaceful the shady tree-lined street looked. The freak tornado had checked in only briefly, leaving behind a swirl of gritty brown air. Apart from the haze and the two fire engines parked outside there weren't many signs it had been here at all. All the houses were untouched except one.

And that one was half demolished.

Becky's was the left half of a semi-detached building around the corner past the pub. Most of the windows had been blown out and the roof looked as though a giant's fist had punched through it. The front yard was clogged with tiles, bricks and dust, and a tree had flipped forward over the wall, crushing an electric car parked in front. The property next door had suffered barely a scratch, losing a few tiles and gaining a coating of dust.

The Sanbornes' front door was open, giving a view of a hallway strewn with rubble, everything smashed to bits. A framed picture of Becky hung askew on one wall, the portrait I'd done of her during my first week at Mercy Road. Through the gaping front window I saw a shattered upside-down TV, a gleam of broken glass and crockery, a mountain of furniture piled up like so much landfill.

Suppose Becky and her folks were trapped indoors? She hadn't said so on the phone, only that she needed to see me. But she'd sounded panicky, rushing her words, and I hadn't heard everything clearly. Perhaps I'd missed the most important thing.

But now I heard voices and footfalls tramping around the wreckage inside, and a group of shadowy figures turned into the hall from a room further back – Becky's family and the firefighters escorting them out.

Seeing me on the path, Becky ran straight outside. Her face was pale with shock and plaster dust, her forehead and hands were criss-crossed with scratches and her knees were gashed and bleeding. She looked up and down the street in disbelief.

'So it was only us,' she said. 'They didn't come for anyone else.'

'They?'

'It, I mean.' She clearly wanted to say more but her parents were at the doorstep. 'The tornado.'

If Becky was shaken, Mr and Mrs Sanborne looked as if they'd stepped off a white-knuckle fairground ride. They looked a little alike, the way couples who've stayed together long enough eventually do, with similar rounded faces and colouring. They both had the same wild, haunted eyes.

'Mum, Dad,' Becky said, trying to sound cheerful. 'This is Ben, you know, who I told you about, who did my picture.' To me she said, 'It's just about the only thing that wasn't destroyed.'

Mr Sanborne nodded in my general direction. 'Good to meet you, Ben. Wish I could've said that in different circumstances.'

Mrs Sanborne forced a tense smile. 'Oh . . . hello,' was all she managed.

We hadn't met before and we weren't exactly meeting now. They didn't see me clearly, and no wonder. All they could see was the eye of the storm that had rampaged through their home.

'Please, folks,' the firemen called. 'Keep moving,

out to the street. It's not safe.'

'Where will you go?' I asked Becky as we went.

'My aunt in Hoxton will make space for us tonight. After that I don't know. We haven't had time to think.'

The good news was that the Sanbornes' car wasn't the one under the tree. Theirs was a midnight blue Astra parked on the opposite side of the gate. They moved towards it leadenly, like sleepwalkers.

'I'm going with Ben,' Becky announced as her dad unlocked the car. 'I'll catch up with you later, OK?'

'Fine,' Mr Sanborne grunted, not hearing.

Mrs Sanborne stared shell-shocked up the drive, close to tears. 'Look at our home. Everything's gone. Everything.'

'Mum, did you hear me?' Becky said.

'Do anything you like, sweetheart. You know where we'll be. You have Aunt Meg's number.'

Mrs Sanborne fell inside the car and stared blankly ahead while her husband fired the engine. Leaving their shattered world behind, the Sanbornes drove off up the street, passing a TV news crew vehicle as it sped to the scene to record what was left.

It was still early, first light, and on Broadway Market the Saturday traders were setting up their food and trinket stalls. Seated by the window in the Broadway Café, we ordered traditional breakfasts and watched the street.

'So tell me,' I said. 'They. What did you mean by they?'

'It's like this.' Becky leaned forward, elbows on the table. 'Like you said about your mum. Once you're involved in this thing, the Ministry and everything, you're in it up to your eyes. And it isn't only you they want – it's everyone around you, everyone that matters to you.'

True, but that didn't answer the question. 'A tornado hit your house, though. Didn't it?'

'Yes and no.'

'That makes no sense. Either it did or it didn't.'

She went quiet while the waitress brought coffee and hot chocolate and rounds of hot buttered toast. A whiff of bacon from the kitchen woke my appetite.

'Yes,' Becky said when the waitress had gone. 'A tornado touched down. Something like a tornado. But did you see the place, and no other house on the street even touched? How random is that?'

'So what did you see?'

She stirred her chocolate. 'It's hard to be sure. It came and went so fast. I was up early, making tea in the kitchen, when I saw this thing coming in low over the rooftops, darker than the sky and heading our way. Kind of like what we saw at the cemetery, only bigger and with a more definite shape. It was shaped – I know how this sounds – like a face.'

'A face?' I nearly gagged.

'That's how it looked. If I could draw things like you, I'd do you a picture. Basically, though, it was cone shaped, wider at the top than the bottom, but made out of smoke and dirt, or whatever these things carry around with them. If a thing like that can have an expression, I'd say it was angry.

'So I called Mum and Dad to look, and I ran to my room for a better view. The house was trembling, all the trinkets and knick-knacks on my shelves were rattling. The face was like a massive shadow over the street, and I swear there were eyes or something staring out of it, triangles of bright red light. I didn't dare go to the window. If I had, I wouldn't be here now telling you this.'

The waitress delivered our breakfasts, and I looked at my loaded plate, the kind of fare Mum used to serve on Mare Street before she took ill.

Suddenly I didn't feel all that hungry.

'And then. . .' I prompted.

Becky went on, 'Then everything went black. I felt a tingling here and here. . .' She touched her face and the back of one hand. 'That was from the shower of glass when the window blew. I'm lucky it wasn't worse, but most of the glass was sucked outside. There was a change in the air pressure, like on a plane when you're descending too fast and you're carrying a cold and blocked sinuses and you're sure your head's about to explode? You know?'

'I've never flown.'

'But you can imagine.'

'I think so.'

'It's like having all your teeth drilled at once. My head was splitting. The wind threw me up at the ceiling, and I whacked my shoulder, which still hurts like hell, and all my things – CDs and books and old dolls – were flying around and past me. I was screaming so hard it feels like I swallowed a load of razor blades, and I heard the roof cracking, bits tearing and splintering off. My bed went airborne, the frame hit the wall and the mattress went out the window. And I thought, there goes my soft landing, if I ever come down.'

'But you did come down. You walked away. That's incredible.'

'Yeah, but I didn't come down straight away because something was pinning me against the ceiling.'

'The storm. The air pressure.'

'No, something else. One of them.' She sniffed and wiped her moistening eyes. 'And it spoke to me, I heard its voice – it was as close to me as you are. It sounded like someone gargling marbles, if that makes any sense, but I couldn't understand a word. It reminded me of those lyrics, you know, the songs they play in the waiting room.'

'Ancientspeak.'

'Yeah. Not the same but similar, like in the wind at Abney Park. Then it used a language I did know. It spoke my name. And it spoke yours.'

I dry-swallowed and reached for my drink. 'What did it say?'

'Hold on, I'm telling you. It was more like a thought in my head than a real voice, because I heard it clearly even with everything crashing around me and stuff flying everywhere. It said, "We come from the place of two suns to settle a score. Abhorra is in mourning because of your actions, and you will repay the Lords of Sundown in kind." Something like that. And then it went on, "The outer dark will become your inner dark. Gateways will open, and you will know the meaning of loss when bedlam brings down your house."'

Becky looked at me squarely, picked up a chip and nibbled it.

'Then it let go,' she said. 'And I fell like a sack of spuds. Gashed my knees and all the air went out of me, but when I looked up it was leaving, it was over. And somewhere in the house Mum was screaming.'

'Synister,' I said, gazing out at the market stalls. I'd heard that gargling voice too not long ago.

'Huh?' Becky said.

'Nathan Synister, the scarecrow, second in command to Lord Randall Cadaverus. He attacked me that day by the canal, remember?' My fingers absently brushed the scar on my cheek, a pattern of symbols Synister's claw had etched across the skin. It was a scar only the gifted could see, invisible to others, and its message declared war on the enemy's enemy, which meant anyone who dared side against the Lords of Sundown, which meant us.

'Yeah, I remember,' Becky said.

'Sounds a lot like him.' I said. 'Nobody talks

like that. I mean, "When bedlam brings down your house." Mr October calls him pompous.'

'Scared the life out of me, all the same.'

'And he means every word. Those aren't empty threats. I've been expecting him.'

Becky looked away, suddenly pensive. 'There's another thing, Ben, something else that thing said. Something I left out from what I just told you. I'm not sure I should tell it, though.'

'Well, now you've said *that*, you *have* to tell it.'

'But it's hard.' She was toying with her food, prodding it with her fork but not eating. 'Promise if I tell you, you won't go off on one.'

'I can't promise anything.'

'I knew you'd say that.'

'Look, what's this about?'

'It's about your dad.'

A nervous knot tightened in my gut. 'Oh?'

'And about the East Coast rail crash.' She shifted uneasily on her seat. 'Brace yourself, Ben. According to the voice I heard, the crash that killed your father wasn't an accident.'

The beginnings of a migraine lunged at me as Becky continued. She didn't have to explain, though. The rest was only detail. Whichever way you looked at it, the outcome was the same.

Dad hadn't just died four years ago. It was worse than that.

While he sat in coach C of the 11:30 a.m. Edinburgh to King's Cross train, watching the country rush by on his way home to Mum and me, Nathan Synister's agents were on a sabotage mission. If the line-side signalling hadn't been sabotaged, if the minds of both drivers hadn't been occupied by the enemy, causing them to ignore repeated warnings to stop, the disaster might have been averted.

I pictured Dad in the window seat, turning over in his mind all that he'd say, how he'd apologise for his stupid mistake, the one-night stand that tore the family apart, how the scene would play out from start to finish when we opened the door at the house in Swanley to find him standing there. They never gave him that chance.

Seconds later the two speeding trains were welded together by a white-hot ball of flame, a funeral pyre visible for miles, while Synister's minions went cherry-picking souls from the burning wreckage. But somehow in the chaos Dad's soul had escaped.

Everything hurt. The diner's electric lights seemed to dim. A ball of pressure was growing inside me, radiating outwards. I wasn't aware of the plates and cutlery rattling on the table between us or the crack snaking up the wall by Becky's shoulder. For the next few seconds I didn't know she was there. I was seeing red, only one thought in my mind.

They murdered him. They murdered them all that day.

'Ben!'

Becky's cry brought me back. She came swimming into focus, along with the rest of the diner and the owner and waitress staring anxiously across from the counter. There was a thin trickle of red below Becky's left nostril, a nosebleed. Feeling it at her upper lip, she took up a napkin and dabbed away at it, studying me with an expression somewhere between pity and fear.

'Sorry,' I said. 'Did I do that? I didn't mean to.'

'I'm sorry too, Ben. I shouldn't have told you.'

'But if that's how it was, I had to know.'

'Suppose so,' she said. 'I know you can't always control it, but you need to learn. You have to turn your hurt against *them*, not against the ones who care about you. Sometimes you worry me.'

'Sometimes I wish I didn't have this gift. I

wish I could wish it away.'

'But you can't. It's part of you.' The bleeding had stopped and she folded the napkin, hiding the red splotches. 'For a second I thought the tornado was coming again. Everything was shaking. Didn't you feel it?'

I didn't. A blank spot. A missing puzzle piece.

Becky pushed her plate away. 'Don't think I can eat this now. Shall we just pay and go?'

'Yeah, let's.'

This news had killed my appetite too. While we fumbled for change at the counter Becky shot me a look. I knew that look well and I knew what she was about to say even before she spoke.

'Now we have to tell Mr October.'

ROGUE'S GALLERY

Becky gave her account in the personnel office, a dingy grey room with filing cabinets along one wall and a steel table at which we sat with Mr October. Three plain Manila folders from the cabinets were spread out on the table before us.

Mr October listened closely while Becky talked, his features skipping between three personalities, one shocked, one sympathetic, one wise and all-knowing. His face steadied and below the black hat's brim his frown lines resembled a capital Y.

'These are trying times,' he said, 'but I have to admit I'm not surprised. At least your family is safe, Becky, and you know your father escaped from them, Ben, which is some small consolation. But this is another kettle of worms entirely.'

Mr October drew the files towards himself but didn't open them yet.

'You've seen and heard the enemy screaming and yelling,' he said, 'doing the blood and thunder thing – you've witnessed them doing their worst. What you haven't seen is the enemy doing its best. Believe me, they can be very crafty, very persuasive.'

'You mean how they feed thoughts into people's minds,' I said, 'like the girl at the tube station yesterday.'

'Yes, exactly like that.'

'Well, if that method works so well, why would they do it any other way?' Becky said.

Mr October said, 'As long as they're yelling and smashing things in front of you, you won't hear them sneaking up from behind. The real damage is done in small ways while you're preoccupied with the bigger events.'

'Like the Whisperer,' Becky said. Seeing Mr October's vacant look she added, 'A new boy in our class. He's kind of suspicious.'

'Hmm. I haven't heard about him. So they're infiltrating the schools now, are they? Keep me posted.' He turned to the files. 'In light of this new information and the intel reports we're receiving, it's time you both saw this.'

He opened the first folder, fanning its mess of papers across the table. Among the piles of memos, notes and report sheets were photos and artists' impressions of a variety of faces.

'Ethan Hill,' Mr October said. 'A mole inside the Ministry until ten years ago. Leaked vital information which led to the deaths of Lu's entire family in a 66231 at a level crossing, and an accomplice of another low life – we'll get to him presently. Lu wears her sadness well and rarely speaks of it, but her pain runs deep. Because of Hill's actions we were unable to save her family. They're still lost in the great In-Between.'

Some of the mug shots showed a weasel-faced man with spectacles, others a monstrous white-eyed demon with a screaming mouth of jagged teeth. Still others pictured a withered gaunt man with Rasputin beard and hair.

'So many faces,' Becky marvelled. 'And all of them his?'

Mr October returned the documents to their folder. 'Yes, and no doubt there are others not on record. Next. . .'

He opened the second file. More of the same, except that here the majority of the faces were almost human, and were all the more disturbing for that. In one, the long-faced subject's eyes, their pupils vertically slitted like a cat's, radiated pure dark malice. This, I thought with a shudder, was the real face of the enemy.

'Meet Luther Vileheart,' Mr October said. 'Like

Ethan Hill, a former Ministry employee. He deserted us even more recently, four years ago. His activities weren't uncovered until the damage was done, and Becky's story confirms what we've long suspected.' He laid a hand on my forearm, briefly becoming the kindly grey-eyed old man, the empathiser. 'Ben, we believe Luther Vileheart supervised the fatal accident which took your father. Yes, he was acting on orders, but only after stealing the list of crash victims from these premises and trading them for a place in the enemy ranks. In return for those names they gave him a position of great power and standing.'

Mr October paused, allowing me to swallow this bombshell. Then he said, 'You should know this because what we'd feared and expected is happening now. The war is becoming more personal.'

'It's already personal for me,' I said.

'Don't let it be. Try not to let it be. With grief comes anger, which is only natural and normal and no bad thing, but you mustn't let the anger control you. If you do, the enemy will consider it a weakness and try to exploit it.'

I glared at Vileheart's faces until Mr October hastily covered them and put them away.

'Are you OK?' Becky watched me worriedly but

not with the fear she'd shown earlier. Her nosebleed hadn't started again.

'I will be. I'm still taking it in.'

Mr October said, 'You must remember that nothing you do can bring him back. Your mother is your priority now.'

'I know.'

'Good, then let's move on. Last file. There are many more where these came from but these are our three Most Wanted, and here's our number one,' he said, opening the third folder. 'A nasty little specimen. We go further back in time with him – he fled from the Ministry in the late 1960s, and like the other two he's still at large. This is Professor Adolphus Rictus.'

Now we were looking at a feral being with a clenched ratty face, beady dark eyes and a chilling grin that stretched from ear to ear. In some of his file photos, in demon form, he looked oddly similar but with shiny reptilian skin and the creepy grin widening further.

'A slippery little oik,' Mr October said. 'Rarely seen but always present. Worked undercover for the enemy here, and for six decades went undetected. He was on our medical team. There were times when the books became unbalanced and the numbers of departeds didn't match the names on our lists, and no one knew why. After Rictus defected, the numbers came back into alignment. We discovered he'd been fashioning a surgical method, right here under our noses using our own facilities, to extract living souls and transport them to the dark territories known as Abhorra. He's since shared this dangerous medical knowledge with others – the Mawbreed, for example, although their ways are even cruder than his. Some of our own employees were among his many victims.'

With a sigh Mr October put away this last pile of paperwork. 'Read the dossiers in your own time, learn how these scoundrels work – familiarise yourselves with their ways and disguises.' Finally he turned to me. 'And just because they're making this a personal issue doesn't mean we will. We can't allow anything to undermine our good work.'

I nodded but didn't reply.

'You're gifted with considerable powers, young man, powers you're still coming to terms with. They're not to be used for revenge – the Ministry doesn't condone it. Is that understood?'

'Yes.'

But it wouldn't be easy, knowing what I knew now about the order Nathan Synister had given and

Luther Vileheart had carried out. It wouldn't be easy at all.

Mr October was watching my hands, which were drawn into pale-knuckled fists on the table. Slowly I unclenched them and sat back and breathed out.

'That's better,' he said, looking up at a knock on the door. The door opened a crack and Sukie peered cautiously in.

'Sorry to disturb,' she said, 'but the telegraph's going crazy, right off the map. Whatever's going on, I think we'll need extra hands.'

'We'll be right along,' Mr October said. Leaving the three Most Wanted files on the table, he stood to follow Sukie out.

The day hadn't begun well, what with the cone-head tornado all but flattening Becky's house and then the revelation about Dad's fatal crash. You wouldn't have imagined things could get worse, but it was all downhill from there.

As we entered receipts the telegraph greeted us with a terrific smack-bang. Sparks and spurts of blue flame leapt around its metal housing, which had gained several new scorch marks. The printed list it was delivering curled all the way to the floor. We kept our distance, expecting another blast, but the machine let out a mournful whale groan and stopped.

'Needs oiling,' Mr October said. 'Ben, when you have a free moment, check the *User's Quick-Start Guide* and get that sorted.'

'Will do.'

Collecting the printout, he unrolled it in front of him like a scroll, and his face clouded over as he skip-read the details. The ever-present wailing wind rose and fell and the candle flame that lit the office began to twitch wildly.

'Oh no,' Mr October sighed. 'Oh dear.'

While Sukie prepared the cards, rolling the first into the typewriter, he turned the list around for us to see.

'Huh?' I said.

'What's it mean?' Becky said.

'Why?' said Mr October.

The first few printed blocks on the list were strictly routine, not particularly eye-catching. A natural causes, non-specific, in Forest Hill. Another 3624 on the Northern line at Clapham South. A second natural causes across the common on Lavender Hill.

What followed was highly irregular – more than twenty names and reference numbers crammed together in tightly spaced blocks, a large number to arrive all at once even during peak hours. While the telegraph told us three things about most cases – who and how and where – there were other things it couldn't tell. It couldn't predict exactly when a soon-departed's time would come, how many minutes or hours they had to spare, and it couldn't answer Mr October's question.

Why?

It was a question I had to ask too as I scanned the list again. It wasn't just the length of the list that left me speechless, but the connection between the soon-departeds it named. All of them – every one – were at the same address.

✦ 9 ✦

BAD SATURDAY

The wind wailed on. The candlelight sent eerie patterns scurrying around our faces. The question still hung in the air.

Why?

Why were so many called at once?

Why would anyone want this?

Every number at that address was a 4914667, a bad number in anyone's book. The telegraph never lied, and if it spat out a 4914667 then that's what we had to face.

About the time we were standing in receipts, digesting the new list, a man in his early twenties was stepping off an overland train in Stratford, cutting a path through the crowds between the station and the shopping centre and heading for quieter streets.

The lone figure moved with a long, loping stride, head down, a purposeful look on his well-groomed face. He may have slowed a moment to take in the big sky, the tall buildings and towering cranes. A fine morning, he may have thought, blue and bright, not a typical grey November morning at all.

The sky over Stratford was marked by aircraft trails and a passing cloud threw a shadow across the man's face. Hitching up his weighty backpack, he continued on, crossing a car park to the entrance of a four-storey apartment block where he touched a key fob to the security panel by the door.

Inside the lobby, baskets of flowers hung at the windows and yucca plants stood tall in corners. To the left were two steel lift doors polished to a shine, and at the far end a door led to the stairwell. The man called the first lift and studied his reflection in the door while he waited.

Far across the city, Big Ben was about to strike one.

In the receipts room, the telegraph machine had just finished pushing out its long curling list. In the same moment Mr October collected it from the floor and straightened up to read it, the apartment building in Stratford exploded.

'Why?' Mr October repeated, but no one spoke. The enormity of it had stolen our voices, and no one spoke at all until we were on the road with Lu tearing the Mustang through a sequence of red lights on Hackney Road.

'Oh my. . .' Mr October groaned. 'How long before the rickshaw comes back from service, Lu?'

'Two days or so. Maybe three.'

'Ah, that's good.'

'You don't like my driving?' she said, nearly rear-ending the 48 bus she was overtaking.

'It's improving,' he said generously. 'But do try not to draw attention.'

'Me? I'm always discreet.'

'Of course you are.'

Seated in the back next to me, Becky rested her hands on her bandaged knees, watching the road with misty eyes.

'It makes no sense,' she said to no one in particular. 'Why would a well-to-do man like that walk into a building with a pack full of explosives and take so many innocent people with him?'

'How do you know he was well off?' I asked.

'He lived there too, didn't he, and those apartments aren't cheap.'

'Suppose someone put the idea in his head, like that 3624 at Old Street.'

'Anything's possible,' Mr October said. 'The thought could have been instilled years ago by something he read or overheard. It could have come from a family member, a friend or total stranger, and been slowly growing and growing until it reached fruition today. Or it could have come to him recently, out of nowhere and fully-formed, while he sat in a college class or rode a bus home.' He braced himself as Lu took a corner at terrifying speed. 'We'll never know. We ask these questions because we need to make sense of our world – but I've been here a long time and it never made much sense to me.'

'So what about him?' Becky said.

'Who?'

'The assassin. The bomber. Are we supposed to help him after what he did?'

'His name's on our list.'

'So what?'

'Our job is to send the departed along,' Mr October said. 'What happens to them after that is out of our control.'

Becky was clearly unsatisfied with this and sat in silence the rest of the way. It wasn't an easy question, though. Questions like that could make you crazy if you thought about them too hard and too long.

A dense mushroom cloud hung over Stratford, rising from the apartment block's blackened shell, smothering the sky and sucking light from the air. Emergency services were working flat-out around the building when we turned into the car park. The last fires were under control, but the block looked as brittle as charcoal. One firm push and it might crumble apart.

'It looks like the end of the world,' Becky said, and I thought, for the people inside, it is.

Other teams, drafted in at short notice, were on their way. The first of them were already here. We parked beside a black SUV as Joe Mort and three junior field agents stepped from it. Joe nodded hello and put on sunglasses to shield his eyes from the gritty air.

'Like a desert storm,' Joe said, brushing dust from his usually immaculate sleeve. 'So how's things, old timer? Good to see you back in the saddle.'

'Oh, could be better, could be worse,' Mr October said, watching the rescue teams. 'But not much worse.'

'Shame you had to come back to this,' Joe said. 'Biggest salvage operation we've seen for a time.'

The other members of Joe's team were Wes

Carlisle and Curtis Noonan, whose keen eyes and sharp suits were a match for Joe's, and new recruit Kate Stone, a chestnut-eyed girl with spiky brown hair who wore a black jumpsuit and Doc Martens. Kate looked about the same age as Becky and me and had been enlisted by Joe on Sukie's recommendation. Joe Mort's was a pretty slick team.

Together the teams crossed the car park. Mounds of wreckage discharged by the blast covered the ground in front of the former apartment block – chunks of masonry and timber, furniture and electrical goods, a smouldering teddy bear, a melted computer, and two thirds of a hand-painted banner which read, 'Give London back to Lon—'. The rest had been burnt away.

Sirens wailed. Black ash and soot drifted down. The fumes of burning metal and gasoline clogged my throat and I had to shield my eyes against the dust as we neared the building, clambering up and over piles of rubble.

Another three Ministry vehicles swung in quick succession into the car park, headlights flaring in the fog. Between them they carried twelve occupants, eight of them armed Vigilants, whose presence here could only mean the enemy were active on the scene.

If the Lords of Sundown had seemed quiet lately then perhaps this was why. They'd been saving themselves for today, for something big.

We crossed the forecourt to the blown-away security entrance. Exposed girders and cross-beams and lengths of melted cabling jutted from the walls. Emergency teams swarmed everywhere, blocking entrances, their walkie-talkies buzzing, their boots grinding over cinders and glass.

'How are we supposed to get in?' I asked Mr October. 'I mean, without being seen or stopped?'

'There's always a way,' he said. 'We had a case last month when a light aircraft hit a building on the Thames. That was a tragic accident, of course, but we gained entry quite freely that night, as we will now.'

'But how?' Becky said, eyeing two cops who were marching towards us, yelling and waving.

Mr October looked them straight in the eye and lifted a hand, snapping his fingers together: clickety-clack.

As he did, everything stopped. The rescue workers froze in mid-stride. The mushroom cloud, the million clumps of ash drifting down, an arc of water the fire brigade were directing at an upstairs window – everything held its place and stood still.

For a moment I thought Becky was frozen too, for she didn't move a muscle when Mr October called, 'Now!' and waved us forward. She stared at the scene with unblinking eyes.

'It's OK,' I told her. 'I've seen this before. It's just one of the things he does.'

We wound our way around a crush of fire workers who were suspended halfway inside, halfway outside the lobby, and stepped in through the hole in the wall where the door had been.

It felt like the dead of night inside, everything scorched and reeking of burning. One lift door was blistered black from top to bottom, the other was missing. Joe Mort waited by the stairwell while we found our flashlights and Mr October dispensed breathing masks from a supply inside his coat.

'The stairs are the only way up,' Mr October told the assembling teams. 'Keep your wits about you. There may be Deathheads or Mawbreed here. Everyone ready?'

'Ready,' we murmured, disjointedly.

I looked back across the lobby, drawn by the sudden return of noise outside. Shouts and running footsteps and crackling walkie-talkies signalled the end of the big freeze, but no one would stop us now.

Our lights searched the darkness as we started up, Joe's team leading. The stairwell stretched above us like the building's great choking throat, ash-black snow whirling in the beams. At the first turn of the stairs we stalled, hearing whispers and howls far up in the darkness, and one guttural sound that began as a growl and ended as a long drawn-out belch.

'Mawbreed,' said Lu.

Everyone tensed. The Vigilants gave me purposeful looks as they locked and loaded their rifles.

'How come they're here so soon?' said Kate Stone. 'Did they know in advance?'

'Maybe they saw the list,' Becky said.

'How could they? It's classified.'

'Maybe it was leaked. Lists have been leaked before. Haven't you heard?'

'Infernal Enquiries will look into it,' Mr October said. 'Joe's team, take this floor. We'll take the next. Rusty? Check the third,' he called to the third team leader, a square-jawed military type with crew cut ginger hair. 'Vigilants – start at the top and work your way down. When you're done, convene in the lobby.'

'Yessir.'

'Check.'

'Copy.'

'Let's kick some enemy butt,' enthused Rusty, chomping at the bit.

'A little propriety, please,' Mr October said, and we continued upstairs towards the unknown.

Moments after Joe's agents turned off along the first floor, the muffled thud of an explosion echoed up the stairwell behind us. On the second level we passed a wall sign that read: APTS 5-8. Mangled pieces of a fire door lay in a tarry smoking pile where the stairs turned up another flight.

There were four apartments on our floor, two on each side of a hall space where a large central section of floor was missing. Steel rods and copper cables poked up from the hole. All four apartment doors had been extinguished, leaving four yawning cave mouths. As far as I could tell above the noise of sirens outside, the enemy were inside at least two of them.

Mr October indicated the space where the floor had been. 'We'll have to edge round. Becky, we'll take the two on the left. Lu and Ben, check the others.'

There was little more than a half metre of floor on all sides. All that remained was a crumbling ledge skirting the walls, which creaked and shook as I followed Lu towards apartments 7 and 8. I shuffled along with my nose skimming the wall. Lu was more agile, springing to the first doorway in six strides. Something splintered under my feet and fell tinkling down through the building's dark.

'Steady,' Lu said. 'Just a few more steps. What are you afraid of?'

'Falling. Dying.'

'That won't happen. You're not on the list.'

'I wasn't on the last list. What about the next one?'

She didn't answer that, instead training her flashlight through the cave-like opening. There were rapid scuttling sounds somewhere inside.

'The good news is, it still has a floor,' Lu reported. 'Otherwise it's a hell of a mess.'

As I caught her up, a shrill cry went up in the apartment across the hall and a blast of orange light filled its doorway. Framed against it, Becky's silhouette pressed its hands to its ears. The flame brightened, then faded.

'Ah, it wasn't too bad,' Becky called. 'Mr October just took out two demons with one fireball. You should've seen it!'

'Lucky shot,' Mr October replied. 'There are still three separated souls in here. Let's get down to business.'

Seconds later another, smaller white light flared inside Apartment 5, a sure sign that the first newly-departed was safely away.

But we had work to do on our side too.

'After you,' said Lu.

'That's OK. After you.'

'No, you.'

Stepping inside Apartment 7, I was a bundle of nerves. I knew I couldn't do what Mr October did. I'd tried a few times without success, and still had no idea how to throw a fireball. I couldn't generate a spark. If whatever was inside this room came thundering at us, I'd have to find another way. I'd have to think fast.

If the entrance to the apartment resembled a cave mouth, we were now in the cave that used to be someone's home. Until an hour ago George Pride, 43, and his partner Philippa Moss, 38, had lived here blissfully unaware that the clock was ticking and their numbers were about to be called.

Now it was a place of calamity, everything gone or in tatters and filled with the same cloying smoke as everywhere else. Outside the blown-out windows the brown haze surrounded the block like a cape, holding the darkness inside. Our lights travelled from wall to wall, then settled on a moving mass on the floor near a door on the right. That door was still intact.

'Are we too late?' Lu said. 'What do you think?'

I didn't want to, but I had to look. George Pride's body lay flat-out, done to a crisp. The movement and sounds came from the thing coiling itself around him – a Shifter in snake form, three times the size of George himself.

It seemed to be growing even as we looked, swelling along its entire length. The demon's scales were a shiny bottle green and its golden eyes had a sleepy, overfed look.

Lu's hiss was a match for the snake's. 'Quick. . . It's trying to digest him.'

His soul, she meant. 'What can we do?' I said.

'It's what you can do that counts. You need to stop it before it finishes, but hurry. He's nearly gone.'

The snake raised its head, baring long inward-curving fangs. The noise from its throat warned us not to interfere. The creature's eyes didn't flicker when another shout and another fireball sounded across the hall. Its hiss became a whisper, a chilling voice.

'You can't help this one, Ben Harvester. First come, first served.'

Great, I thought. It knows my name too. They

probably all did by now.

The creature tightened its hold on George Pride and tilted back its head as if preparing to strike.

'Now,' Lu said. 'Think, Ben, think.'

'Think what?'

'Like you thought about the Mawbreed that time.'

I knew what Lu meant, but this was different. Every situation was different. Sometimes the pictures came easily to mind, sometimes they took ages or never came at all. This one was still piecing itself together when the snake erupted, too gorged to keep its gourmet dinner down, and showered the room with a spray of digestive juices.

We spun around, hiding our faces.

'Oh yuck,' Lu said. 'That's gross.'

The short silence that followed was broken by a roll of thunder and a bark of voices on an upstairs floor. The conflict was still raging up there, but the one in this apartment seemed to be at an end.

There was another movement now among the snake's steaming remains, George Pride's newly-departed soul slowly picking its way out of the mess and standing upright. A burly man with singed grey hair matting his scalp, he wiped slime from his forehead and blinked into the flashlight beams, trying to recall who he was and what he'd seen.

'I know why you're here,' he said at last, oblivious to the mess at his feet and looking anxiously at the door on his left. 'Philippa. . .' he murmured. 'Oh God, Philippa was here too.'

'Where?' Lu said.

'The bedroom. We were getting ready to go out for the day when it happened.'

'I'll check,' Lu said. 'Stay here please, George. Ben will look after you.'

He gave me the once-over. 'You're just a kid. How can you know what to do?'

'I have a good teacher,' I said. 'Will you step this way?'

When I opened the door he went without question, not glancing back until the last second when an anxious look entered his eyes, an afterthought. He should have waited for Philippa. They should have gone together. But he couldn't turn back now and I was glad when he continued on, feeling his way forward until the light covered him.

It turned out to be a good thing that George went when he did, not knowing what I was about to find out. Closing the door on the rectangle of light, I turned to see Lu returning from the bedroom, shaking her head.

'She's gone,' she said. 'Her body's still there – parts of it are. But the rest of her isn't. They took her.'

After that, we swept Apartment 8 to find no one home. It may have been unoccupied at the time of the blast but it was hard to tell from what remained. There were no departeds or demons inside, though, and we returned to the ledge to a thump-thump of Vigilant rifle fire high in the building. Mr October and Becky were waiting for us over by the stairwell.

'How did it go?' Mr October called.

'Only one. And one got away.'

'Oh dear.'

'We scored five,' Becky boasted, and then added more thoughtfully, 'but there were three we didn't get to in time.'

We waited in the lobby for the others. Teams trooped down in twos and threes, some hobbling from injuries, others from sheer exhaustion. One Vigilant had been sliced at an angle, right collarbone to left hip, his uniform seeping dark red, but he'd live. All were present and otherwise correct.

'Look,' Kate Stone said suddenly, pointing outside.

Rescue workers were moving away from the forecourt – not just moving away but legging it, yelling and waving each other on. Something was about to give.

'Time to go,' Mr October said.

'Check.'

'Yessir.'

'Move out!'

'Not a successful salvage operation,' Mr October said as Lu reversed at speed across the car park, gears shrieking. 'Not by any stretch. We saved seventeen, but they took thirteen, including the bomber. Seven survivors in total.'

'So the list *was* leaked,' Becky said, eager to prove a point.

'We don't know that yet,' Mr October said. 'But soon we will.'

Becky put on her belt and turned with me to watch the fragile black building in the fog while we drove away. I suppose we were waiting for it to fall, collapse in on itself like a burnt-out matchstick house. But it didn't fall as long as we looked.

✦10✦
MISS WEBSTER

t the end of that shift Mr October produced two T-shirts from the depths of his coat, one for each of us, black with white lettering.

'A memento of today, a day you'll never forget,' he said.

The logo on the T-shirts read: I SURVIVED BAD SATURDAY.

We were given the next day off whether we liked it or not. Sundays could be as busy as any other day, but Mr October refused to let us back to the field so soon after our involvement in today's traumatic events.

'You've seen more in the last forty-eight hours than most junior agents do in a year and you need time to regroup,' he said. 'Sorry, that's Ministry policy for all new recruits. You could twist my arm and come in for a little clerical work, but salvage ops are out of the question.'

Becky didn't care much for clerical work, preferring to be out there, hands on, helping where she could. In the end she decided to be with her parents in Hoxton, whereas I jumped at the chance to come in. The receipts office was my home from home.

I spent late Sunday morning there with Sukie, testing her telepathic powers while the telegraph machine was quiet. Sukie had the desk. I stood with my back to the shuttered window, keeping my hands behind me where she couldn't see.

'How many fingers am I holding up?'

Sukie didn't look up. 'Three.'

'And now?'

'Seven.'

'And now?'

'Six,' she said through a yawn.

'Amazing. How do you do it?'

'Dunno. I don't even think about it.' She ran a hand back through her black mane. 'And that won't fool me either.'

'What won't?'

'Doing a church and steeple.'

I quickly let my hands go and parted the shutters to look down on moonlit Eventide Street through the mist my breath made on the glass.

'Let's try something else,' I said. 'What am I thinking?'

'Do we have to?' Sukie said wearily.

'I'm curious, and besides, nothing's happening right now.'

There was a polite knock at the door. The door creaked open and Kate Stone from Joe's team looked in.

'Oh hi,' she said with a shy smile. 'Need any help in here?'

'Not really,' Sukie said. 'Slow morning.'

'It's just, I'm barred from the field after yesterday on account of my age. They said I could do filing and such, but I feel like a fifth wheel around here.'

'You should be at home,' Sukie said, 'or out with your mates. So should Ben for that matter, but I can't get rid of him.'

She winked at me. Only kidding.

'Yeah, but my mates aren't the same anymore,' Kate said with downcast eyes. 'They've been kind of offhand with me since I started here and it's getting worse. So I suppose I'll just go home.'

'Could be something for you in dispatch,' Sukie offered. 'One of the girls is thinking of clocking off early, so try asking there.'

'Thanks. I will.'

She slipped away, closing the door softly, a sheepish girl compared to the one I'd seen at the bomb scene. Perhaps, like Becky, she preferred the live experience of the field, and by the sounds of it she too was having a hard time at school.

'So where were we?' Sukie said. 'What you're thinking, right?'

'Never mind. We don't have to do this.'

'No probs. We have time to kill. You're thinking Kate Stone is cute.'

'No, I'm not.'

'You're wondering why your heart beats faster when you see her,' she said.

'Shut up. This wasn't a good idea after all.'

Sukie laughed. 'And you're blushing.'

She was right there too, but I didn't need a psychic to tell me that.

'Only teasing,' Sukie said. 'But I can't help knowing these things. You're also thinking about your mum, worrying because you haven't seen her for two weeks. She'll be fine, though. Don't fret.'

'I'm not fretting.'

'But you are.'

I went over and perched on the desk, and we sat for a time, watching and waiting on the telegraph.

'You'll never understand it,' Sukie said. 'I don't understand it myself, like I don't understand your gift, either. I can't open doors in space, for example, and I definitely can't blow things up. It's like we're all different parts of a body, each of us with our own skills and our own special parts to play. And I suppose Mr October is like the body's heart or head . . . one or the other.'

She was interrupted by a muffled bang and a gust of smoke that announced the first batch of names. For the rest of the shift we took turns in transcribing the telegraph's lists and delivering the cards to Miss Webster for filing.

The records room was a colossal white space that grew with each newly-added name. Miles high in the rafters, bat-like guardians flew in circles under a pale ceiling of cloud. On the countless floors and up and down the great spiral staircase, filing clerks went about their business, scaling ladders, opening and closing cabinets, checking and re-checking records.

When you first entered this place, Miss Webster's booth was the merest speck in the distance, far across the marble floor. The walk towards it seemed to take hours, and when I finally got there Miss Webster was her usual crotchety self. The spiders that flitted about her permed hair had been busier than ever, and their network of webs covered her face like a caul.

'Good afternoon, Miss Webster,' I said.

'What's so good about it?' Miss Webster said. 'They all look the same to me.'

'More names for your ledger,' I said, pushing the cards across her counter.

'So I see. I'm not blind.'

'But you'd see better if you brushed some of those cobwebs away.'

'I'll brush you away with the back of my hand in a minute,' Miss Webster said. 'Off you go, back where you came from.'

'No change there then,' Sukie said when I returned. 'Surly old witch. Still, I suppose it's understandable, her being the way she is.'

'What's understandable?'

'Oh – but of course you don't know.'

'What don't I know?'

Sukie turned her kinked gaze on the telegraph, watching intently as if expecting it to kick off again. When it didn't, she relaxed and turned to me.

'Well, you haven't been here that long, so you can't know everything. Miss Webster's worked in records thirty-odd years, maybe nearer forty. Before that she was in dispatch, and before that . . . she goes back a long way, anyway.

Her brother once worked here too.'

'I didn't know she had a brother,' I said. 'Hard to imagine her having family.'

'Well, she did. Terence Webster, a junior on the medical team in the 1960s. Very up and coming. What he didn't know – nobody knew at the time – was that he was working alongside a traitor. He was a junior on Professor Rictus's team.'

'Rictus. . .'

'You know about him?'

'One of the Most Wanted,' I said, remembering his startling ear-to-ear grin bearing twice the usual number of teeth.

'Terence Webster was one of his first victims,' Sukie said. 'Had his soul ripped right out while he breathed. Professor Rictus stole scores of others from employees and soon-departeds the Ministry were supposed to help, but he flew the coop before anyone found him out.'

'So I heard. He uses some kind of medical procedure, doesn't he? I've seen Mawbreed and Deathheads take living souls too. . .' I glanced at the floor where a Deathhead had pinned me the night I discovered how powerful my own gift could be. 'They're bad enough, but Rictus sounds worse.'

Sukie agreed. 'Most victims don't last long. Without their personalities, they can't. Their bodies become empty shells until they stop working, which could be minutes later, or hours, or even days. That's how Miss Webster's brother was when she visited him at the clinic – still alive, but sort of not alive. She never recovered from seeing him like that. She stayed on here, doing her bit for the war effort, but she's been bitter and broken-hearted ever since.'

'Poor Miss Webster.' I never thought I'd say that, but I meant it.

'Don't get me wrong,' Sukie said, 'there are times when I feel like punching her lights out. Then I remember. It's easy to think some people are made that way, but you never know. I just wish she wouldn't take it out on us.'

The telegraph sputtered away for a minute and stopped abruptly, leaving four new numbers and names. Three of the four were natural causes cases, or soon would be.

'A quiet Sunday,' Sukie said. 'After yesterday's bombing I guess everyone's staying safe at home, watching the news and taking no chances. Well . . . better get these processed.'

'I'll do it,' I said.

'You did the last lot.'

'I don't mind.'

Now I knew about the sadness in Miss Webster's life, the loss we had in common, I supposed it might be easier to face her. I was almost looking forward to seeing her again until the moment I arrived at her booth.

'You again.' She scowled over the tops of her pince-nez spectacles. 'Talk about bad pennies. Don't give me any lip, Harvester, I know you and your kind and I will not stand for it. Hand me those cards at once and make yourself scarce.'

'Yes, Miss Webster. Here you go. Have a good day.'

She didn't reply. Snatching the cards from my hand, she flicked a small white spider from the tip of her nose and returned to work on her ledger.

Sukie left early, answering a call from dispatch. A thirty-four-year-old man had collapsed in a crowded buffet at Brent Cross shopping centre. An enemy presence had been reported in the vicinity and Sukie was called in to flush the enemy out by tracing its thoughts.

'See ya, Ben,' she said as she left. 'Keep your eyes open and don't do anything I wouldn't do.'

After she'd gone I took over the desk and sat alone with the rushing sound of the wind. Pulling two volumes of the *Apocalypti Phrase Book: Unexpurgated* from the shelf above the desk, I fished out the typed pages I kept hidden behind them – the account of my adventures as a Pandemonium operative.

Whenever I had the time I'd work here on the Olivetti, typing as fast as I could to keep the report up to date. Things had been so busy lately I was falling behind. Rolling a clean sheet of paper into the platen, I typed:

I do not think Kate Stone is cute.

Then I backspaced and hit X enough times to cross out the line and went on:

The night has a thousand eyes.

Time sped up. The candle burned down to a stub while I typed. I took a new candle from the desk and lit it from the old one's flame and snuffed out the old one and replaced it in the candle holder. When the telegraph made a noise like a backfiring exhaust, I cleared the typewriter and waited. It was the last chance I had to work on the journal during that shift.

Seagulls screamed in the distance as I crossed London Fields. The daylight was draining and the park was cold and barren, the barbecues extinguished until next year and bare trees standing tall over golden carpets of leaves.

I slowed past Dad's bench on the path but didn't stop to sit. A chunk of the money we'd been left in Aunt Carrie's will had paid for this bench, and it was money well spent, Mum had said, our way of keeping Dad close. I left the park near the sign on Lansdowne Drive and was waiting to cross the street when something on the other side caught my eye, making me draw back.

Two undercover agents were watching me from the corner of Shrubland Road. Long-coated, hands pocketed, with faces that were impossible to identify, shifting rapidly from one set of features to another. When one of the men lifted a gloved hand to his inside pocket, my breath seized up. It was the kind of movement gangsters and spies made in films when they went to take out their guns.

Instead the agent removed a small flask and offered it to his partner, who unscrewed the cap and took a sip before handing it back. They were pretending not to see me, so, pretending not to see them either, I ran to Middleton Road, glancing without thinking at the wall of graffiti.

Someone had scrubbed the older artwork from the wall's right side behind the scaffolding, replacing it with a stencilled scarecrow figure not unlike Nathan Synister, black and white except for the eyes, which were red. A speech bubble beside the scarecrow's mouth said:

WE HAVE A LIST TOO
AND YOUR NAME IS ON IT

That message was meant for me, no question, and if I dared look again tomorrow there'd be another just like it. I fled indoors, up the cold stairwell to our balcony, where I stopped and leaned across the rails to look down.

The two agents hadn't followed me this far, or if they had they were well hidden. The street was empty, the first afternoon shadows crawling across it as I fished out my keys and let myself in.

In the kitchen, I lowered the blinds to shut out the view of the graffiti wall and paced around, wondering how long they'd been watching without me knowing. Tomorrow I'd report what I'd seen at headquarters. Before that, I'd call Becky to warn her. Her aunt's place in Hoxton may be under surveillance too.

The phone rang in the living room. Perhaps Becky already knew. I hurried through to answer.

'Ben? It's me,' a breathless voice said.

Not Becky's voice. It took me a moment to place this one. I'd almost forgotten how she sounded. 'Mum!'

'Got it in one. You'll never guess where I am.'

'Where?'

'Gatwick airport. Just came in. Put the kettle on, darlin'. I'll be there before you know it.'

❧ 11 ❧
DONNA HARVESTER

A taxi dropped her out in the dark. Meeting her on the unlit stairwell to help with the luggage, I didn't see her clearly until we were indoors in the hall.

She had a lean, tanned, healthy look and her hair had lightened to near-blonde in the sun, but her sombrero didn't go with the winter coat she'd worn for her homecoming. She took off the sombrero and dropped it on her suitcase and opened her arms wide.

'Darlin',' she said.

'You look great,' I said. 'Five years younger. No, ten!'

'Flatterer. You should've come with us. You would've loved it.'

'Next time,' I said.

We settled at the kitchen breakfast bar with cups of tea and the duty free chocolate she'd brought. Her bandaged right arm looked half as swollen as it had been before she left, and she didn't wince when she moved it.

'Did Ross take good care of you?' she asked.

'Yeah, he was fine. Checking up on me all the time.'

'And school's been all right?'

'The same. Nothing changes.'

'You certainly don't. Never have much to say for yourself, do you?'

'I'd rather talk about you.'

'Well, what would you like to know?'

She began by describing the self-catering apartment she'd shared with Ellie, its veranda looking out over palm trees towards mountains and sea. In the evenings they'd sat out drinking sangria and watching the sunset, and because Mum rarely drank normally, she went to bed early three nights in a row and woke with a hangover on two consecutive mornings.

'Bad old me,' she laughed. 'Served me right.'

She told me about the bars and restaurants they'd been to and the day trips they'd taken, the green caves they'd explored and the active volcanic region where men poured pails of water into holes in the ground and steaming geysers jetted many metres into the air.

'And that was only week one,' she said.

'Wow! So what did you do in week two?'

She lifted her cup, gently blowing air across the hot tea. She took a sip and put the tea down and studied the bubbles on its surface.

'Money,' she said absently.

'Sorry?'

'It's what Dad called the bubbles. Bubbles on your tea, he said, means money's coming your way.' She smiled. 'Actually I didn't see much of Ellie that second week.'

'How come?'

'We just had different plans. She had to run around to appointments about this timeshare idea of hers, and I . . . well, I had more time for myself, that's all.'

But that wasn't all. I could tell by the way she wasn't looking at me there was more.

'So what else?' I said. 'What happened last week?'

'It's a little awkward. . .'

'Bad news, you mean. It's not about your illness, is it?'

'No, no, nothing like that. I feel fit as a flea. I'm just not sure how you'll take it.' She laid a hand over mine on the table, took a long breath. 'I met someone, Ben.'

At first I didn't get what she meant. 'Oh. Who?'

'Someone,' she said vaguely. 'Someone special.'

'You mean a man.'

'That's right.'

It felt like a sting. I pulled my hand out from under hers and folded my arms on my chest. Mum didn't speak, giving me time to digest this.

'What about Dad?' I said.

She looked away. 'Dad's gone.'

'Only a few weeks ago.'

'Four years ago, Ben. The rail crash was four years ago.'

But she'd seen him only last month in the conference room, the night we'd all said goodbye. She'd wept while I opened a door to let Dad out of this world. Had she forgotten already, or was she trying to blank it out? I stared at her, mystified.

'So who is this fella?' I said after a lull. 'And what's so special about him?'

'Don't be like that. You're so full of anger.'

'Is there any wonder?'

'You needn't be angry about this. Let me explain.'

'Then explain. I'm not stopping you.'

But the sparkle she'd come home with had gone. I'd wiped it away, I'd hurt her, and I didn't like myself for it.

'Mum, I'm sorry,' I said. 'It's just. . .'

'That's all right, honey.'

'It's just a shock, you know, hearing it.'

'But it isn't what you think. It's not like we're engaged. I didn't lose my head or do anything foolish. It was all very proper, really.'

'Proper?'

'We'll talk about this later, if you like. When you're ready to listen.'

'I'm ready now.' I really wasn't, but I didn't want to see the pain on her face again so I tried to make more of an effort. 'Tell me about him, how you met and all that.'

'Are you sure?'

'I'm sure.'

'Well. . . Ellie had gone for the day, and after breakfast at the harbour I took a short walk, then went shopping at the HiperDino supermarket down the hill from where we were staying. A child ran up the aisle, banged into me here.' She rubbed her right elbow. 'It was an accident, but the pain spun me right around and I dropped my basket and everything in it went flying across the floor.

'That was when he turned onto the aisle. He saw I was in trouble and came to help. He picked up my things and got me through the checkout, but my arm was throbbing so badly I thought I would faint, and I'd left my medicine at the apartment, a long way up a steep slope. I couldn't make it back.

'So he settled me at a café across the street and ran to the pharmacy for painkillers, then sat with me till I felt better. It was only then that we got to talking. He seemed very easy-going and polite, very charming. He's English, from London, in fact. Quite well off, but I didn't know that then. After an hour – and the time just flew – he called a taxi to take me home. He insisted on paying, wouldn't let me argue, and before I left, he gave me his card. In case of emergency, he said. I didn't plan to call. I didn't think I should. Later, though, I started wondering where I'd seen him before. I was sure I had but couldn't place him. But when I woke up that night I knew.'

'You'd seen him on one of your day trips,' I guessed.

'No, earlier, in London. Just around, here and there. I didn't know him.'

'But you rang him.'

She nodded. 'Only to thank him for helping, not expecting to see him again. So when he invited me to dinner at a little restaurant he knew above the harbour, I thought twice about it. But then I said yes.'

'Did you think about Dad?'

'Of course. I always do.' Mum flushed. 'But let's get this straight. There's nothing for me to be ashamed of and no reason for you to worry. It's just that sometimes when we're sad, Ben, like we've been sad about your father, we need company – someone to listen. There's nothing wrong with that.'

'OK, Mum.'

'Besides,' she said, 'I had a feeling he was sad about something too, but he never spoke about it and I never spoke about Dad. We had a great evening, and by the end I felt, well . . . better. Loads better. Ellie saw it in me as soon as I came in. Of course, I had to tell her everything.'

'And what did she say?'

'She said, "Hon, you deserve some happiness. You've had enough hard times."'

'So you saw him again after that, I bet.'

She managed a smile. 'Every day.'

She brought holiday snaps to show me, shots of the geysers in the volcanic desert, a picture postcard view from her veranda, Ellie looking sleepy and overfed at a harbour-side restaurant table. At the bottom of the pile were three night-time photos of a smart young couple standing together on a harbour, the sunset behind them, looking as happy as any couple could. The man had a rugged handsome face, slicked-back dark hair and a confident smile. He wore a Hawaiian shirt and his arm was draped round the woman's shoulders. The woman, in profile, looked up at him with doting eyes and her hair glowed in the evening sun. The pose was similar in all three snapshots, but in the last the woman looked straight at the camera.

I almost didn't recognise her. In this man's arms, in these photos, Mum was transformed, almost a stranger.

'His name's Tom Sutherland,' she said. 'I know this is difficult for you, Ben. I understand how you feel. But no one can ever take your dad's place, you know that.'

'That's true,' I said. 'No one ever will.'

She went quiet then and put the prints away.

'Anyway, you might feel more forgiving when you see him for yourself,' Mum said. 'I've invited him to dinner tomorrow night. He's so looking forward to meeting you.'

Monday. Not the best of school mornings. Miss Neal ill-tempered again, the class unusually quiet, and at the back of the room Simon Decker muttering to himself, seemingly invisible to all except the two of us.

Kelly from the gang of five, who'd claimed a seat at his desk, glared at me as if she were his bodyguard when I looked their way, and when I turned to face the front Miss Neal glared at me too.

'Pay attention, Harvester,' Miss Neal said. 'You know what'll happen if you don't. Have you ever noticed how nicely attention rhymes with detention?'

'Sorry, Miss.'

'You will be. And the same goes for you too, Miss Sanborne.'

I could've pointed out that Becky hadn't raised an eyebrow or made a sound all through the lesson, but speaking up would only make things worse for both of us.

'It can't go on like this,' Becky said later, over coffee and bacon rolls at the crypt. 'I'd rather bunk off school. I'd rather be in that shoebox flat of my aunt's than here.'

A trio of sirens screamed above us on the street. The police had stepped up their presence all over town since the bombing. They were everywhere now, at rail and underground stations, on every other street corner. There were even two plain-clothed officers on Middleton Road this morning when I left for school, or perhaps they were the same undercover agents in disguise.

'Any news from your mum?' Becky said after the sirens faded. 'When's she due back from her hols?'

'She got back last night. She's looking really well.'

'Oh good. I've been thinking about her a lot lately. She went through so much that night at headquarters, I thought she'd never get over it.'

'She doesn't remember a lot,' I said. 'It's funny, because when I first told her about the Ministry she wasn't happy, she didn't want me involved, but in those last few days before her holiday she hardly mentioned it, and now she doesn't remember seeing Dad that last time. She knows he's gone, she wouldn't have paid for that park bench if she didn't, but she doesn't know how she knows. I can't explain it.'

Becky looked up, struck by a thought. 'Wait, I'm not sure . . . but maybe I can explain. Something happened that night, during the siege. . .'

'A lot happened that night,' I said.

'I mean while I was looking after your mum, after you'd filed your dad's card. A woman came in the waiting room, very striking, dazzling green eyes. She wore a coat with a houndstooth pattern. She smiled and took your mum's hand and looked into her eyes a moment but she didn't speak. Your mum said, "Thank you," and relaxed, very peaceful, like a weight had left her, and after that the woman went out. Dead strange, really. So I don't know, but I wonder if that woman did something to help your mum forget.'

'That *is* strange,' I said. 'Any idea who she was?'

'She gave her name but for the life of me I can't remember it. She's obviously part of the set-up there – I've passed her on the floor a few times – but I don't know what she does. Anyway, it's good to know your mum's doing so well.'

'Yeah, and she came home with big news too.'

'Oh? What news?'

Becky listened, fascinated, while I explained. The chatter of coffee morning pensioners reverberated off the walls like ghostly voices.

'Well, personally I don't think it's so bad,' she said when I'd finished. 'What are you worried about?'

'Dunno. I just am.'

'But you do remember what your dad said, the last thing he ever said to your mum.'

'He said it was time to let go and move on.'

'Maybe that's all she's trying to do. Even if she's forgotten everything else, it could be she remembered that one thing. It's what he wanted.'

'It's just so soon.'

'And if she met someone a year from now you'd still say the same.'

Who knew how I'd feel a year from now? But I said, 'Yeah, probably.'

'Then aren't you the one who needs to let go?' Becky said. 'It won't be easy. It won't be easy for your mum, either. But now she needs a friend to help her move on. Trust me, I know. Mr October says I'm a sensitive, highly compassionate, and he's never wrong.'

'But the bloke's coming to dinner,' I said, almost shouted, drawing stares from nearby tables. 'She expects me to be there. I'll miss my shift.'

'We'll survive without you for one night.'

'Suppose I don't like him? Suppose he doesn't like me?'

'Give it a chance,' Becky said. 'It may not be as

bad as you expect. And don't be so selfish, you.'

'Selfish? Me?'

'Think of your mum. You want her to be happy and well, don't you? Why should her being happy make you so miserable?'

I stirred my coffee, watching the money bubbles.

'Let's talk about something else,' I said.

Five minutes later, we were back in school, caught in the crush on the corridor. As we passed the cold spot, someone in the crowd stuck out a leg, sending Becky flying.

Her hands and knees smacked the floor and her face creased in pain. Raymond Blight, the most likely suspect, stood smirking by the lockers as Becky picked herself up and dusted off her hands. The fall had re-opened the wounds to her knees, and red roses bloomed through both bandages.

I stepped towards Raymond. 'You did that on purpose.'

'Did what, fish?' He puffed out his cheeks, making a fish face, and waggled his hands at his jaw like fins. This was more or less Raymond's level.

'Don't get involved,' Becky said, retrieving her bag from the floor. 'He's not worth it.'

'He really isn't,' I said, but the red mist was gathering. I'd had enough of all the bad air coming our way, enough of Raymond Blight. I took another pace forward. The school bell sounded, running through me like a toothache, and the anger Mum had seen in me was here again, focusing on Raymond Blight.

'You'll not push her around anymore,' I told him. 'Her or anyone else.'

'You don't scare me.'

'What did she ever do to you?'

'She doesn't have to do anything,' Raymond said.

I would have gone for him, given him something to be truly scared of, if the others hadn't stepped in then, two from each side blocking my way.

Among their number were Ryan and Matthew, Becky's old mates, and two others not even in our class. None of them moved or said anything, but all seemed to be of the same mind.

You shall not pass.

They stood there shoulder to shoulder, forming a wall, staring me down with vacant eyes. Huddled safely behind them against the lockers, Raymond

Blight leered, and next to Raymond, Simon Decker stared off down the corridor, almost imperceptibly moving his lips.

THE MAN WHO CAME TO DINNER

Mum had spent the whole day cleaning. I came home to a hum of air freshener, a gleaming kitchen and a spotless bathroom. She'd even been in my room, which now didn't resemble my room at all. Surfaces were uncluttered and shelves neatly stacked, everything in its place. I wasn't used to this kind of order. I'd never find anything now.

'Since you're home early you can help move the living room furniture,' Mum said, more energised than weary from work. 'There's only so much I can do one-handed.'

'He's coming to eat, not inspect the place. Why move the furniture?'

'Tonight we'll dine properly. Not off our knees in front of the telly and not in the kitchen. We'll move everything back and pull out the nice table we never use. Do we have enough chairs?' she asked herself. 'Ah yes, there's a spare in my room. Be a love and fetch it.'

'Shouldn't it be just the two of you?' I said, carting the chair downstairs. 'Just you and him?'

'Don't be silly. This is your evening too. Did I say how much he was looking forward to meeting you?'

'Several times.'

'It won't kill you to have a night in, will it?'

'Suppose not.'

'Now set that down and help me with this,' she said as we entered the living room.

'No, I'll do it. You have a rest.'

She perched on the spare dining chair while I pushed the heavy sofa tight against the window and the two armchairs to each side of the room. Earlier, unable to move them by herself, Mum had cleaned around them, and dusty grey outlines remained where they'd stood.

'I'll see to that,' she said, on her feet again. 'Then we'll set up the table.'

I stood back while she vacuumed up the dust bunnies. The maisonette hadn't been this clean since we moved in. Everything sparkled as if a veil had been lifted. With the table in position she brought polish and place mats, the best silver cutlery and candles.

'There,' she said. 'Now I'll check the roast, then

get myself showered and smartened up. He's due in an hour.'

Taking a last look around the room, I sensed a difference, not in the re-arrangement of furniture and shiny surfaces but something else – something missing, or new, or out of place. It was probably only a detail, nothing important. The previously wonky art prints on the wall were now straightened and the keepsakes and ornaments stood where they always had.

But then I had a slow sinking feeling. On a shelf above the TV was a framed photograph, a holiday snap of Mum and Tom Sutherland on the harbour at sunset. What I was missing was the photo of Dad it had replaced – Dad wearing a Superman T-shirt and blowing a kiss to the camera in the garden in Swanley, looking happy and content before his troubles began. His photo was nowhere in sight. She'd swept it away.

'Something wrong?' Mum said.

'No, nothing. You did a good job, that's all.'

'Ah, thanks, hon.'

It was only a small thing, but to me the missing photo was significant. If she'd hidden it because seeing it made her sad, I would gladly keep it in my room. I'd ask her about it sooner or later but I wouldn't say anything tonight in front of our guest.

But I was restless now, my nerves on springs. Upstairs in my room, I thumbed a couple of DC comics without reading them, then put them aside and crossed to the window to check the street.

The wall across the way stood in darkness, its graffiti messages invisible. I was glad about that, but not so glad to see the two figures standing in front of the wall, their long shadows stretching across the road towards our block.

They were probably the same two from yesterday, still on duty, still keeping watch. From this distance they appeared to grow from the darkness itself, creeping out in human shape. When they both looked straight up at my window I swung aside and fell back against the wall, holding my breath.

When I dared to look again a car's headlights were turning in from Lansdowne Drive. The two watchers had moved on, but they could be in hiding anywhere now. The bedroom door flew open behind me and I nearly screamed.

'So what do you think? Will I pass?' Mum said, fussing her hair, wiggling her hips in a smart black dress. She sucked in her tummy and looked at me as if everything depended on my opinion, but I was still preoccupied with the watchers outside.

'You look amazing,' I said. 'I hardly recognise you.'

'Well, thanks a lot.'

'That came out all wrong. What I meant—'

'Never mind. Are you ready? Is that what you're wearing?' A host of anxious questions hung about her lips.

'You think I should wear something else?' I said. I hadn't thought of changing.

'No, you'll do. He'll probably find the school uniform charming. Oh good grief. . .' she gasped as the intercom buzzed. 'On your best behaviour now. No backchat.'

'It's my evening too,' I reminded her.

Mum rolled her eyes. 'Smart mouth.'

She hurried to answer the door.

My initial thought, seeing him for the first time, was that he looked nothing like Dad. Tom was as handsome as his photograph and wore a smart, charcoal suit jacket and pale chinos. He was handing

146

Mum a bouquet of flowers when he heard me on the stairs and looked up.

'Well, hello. You must be Ben. Glad to meet you, sonny.'

'I'll put these in water,' Mum said.

I came down and shook his hand, and I tried to smile but I didn't speak. Until Mum returned from the kitchen I felt stranded. A large brown paper bag Tom was holding rustled at his side.

'Aperitif?' Mum said, ushering us to the living room. I'd never actually heard her use that word before, and I wondered if she needed to try so hard. 'Shall we go through? Excuse the mess.'

'What mess?' I said, and her look said that was quite enough, thank you.

'Very nice,' Tom said, scanning the room. If he noticed the new photograph he didn't comment. 'Did I mention I grew up not far from here? It was a different area then, though. Quite trendy now, isn't it?'

'Well, I suppose,' Mum said, bringing two sherries and a tumbler of lemonade on a tray. 'We were lucky to find something so close to the park.'

She placed the tray on the table and Tom turned to me, smiling, showing me the bag.

'For you.'

'Oh, that's nice,' Mum said. 'You shouldn't have.'

'What's in it?' I said warily.

'Let's see, shall we?' He winked at me and reached inside the bag. 'Careful how you handle this. It bites.'

He took out a miniature cactus, unusual but quite beautiful, no more than six centimetres tall with red and gold markings and pale silvery bristles as fine as baby hair. Delicate, creamy-white flowers grew from its prickly pear-like stems. A protective cylinder of plastic surrounded the plant.

'You'll want to remove this to let it breathe,' Tom said. 'I'm no expert on cacti, but this is one of the most striking I've seen. Just a token from a farm on the island. Do you like it?'

I nodded.

'Say thank you, Ben,' Mum said, and to Tom she said, 'Never has much to say. It's that age, you know.'

'Thank you.' Frowning at her, I lifted the container for a closer look. A faint sweetish scent drifted from it. 'It has a funny smell,' I said.

Tom nodded. 'I noticed that too. Like ripe bananas. A pleasant enough smell, though, unless you can't stand bananas. You might like to draw it sometime. Your mum tells me you're a keen artist.'

I wondered what else she'd told him, but the shapes and contours of the plant were irresistible. I would've wanted to draw it even if he hadn't suggested it.

'So I brought you these too,' he said, this time lifting from the carrier a large Moleskine sketchbook and an elegant varnished wooden pencil case with hand-carved swirling patterns on its lid.

'It's made to order,' he said. 'Crafted by a friend of mine. If you look closely you'll see it's personalised – made just for you.'

I set the cactus down and took the box from his hands, running a thumb across its textured surface. At first I didn't see what he meant, but then I found the two words hidden among the delicate swirls: *Ben Harvester*.

'Amazing,' I said, flipping the lid. A set of twelve yellow-bodied pencils nestled inside, every weight of black from faintest to heaviest. 'This is the best. These are the best. I always wanted a Moleskine too, but they're dead expensive. Thanks.'

'That's more like it,' Mum said. 'Ben, run these things up to your room while I check our dinner. Tom, you haven't touched your sherry.'

'A bit of a nag, isn't she?' he joked as I went out.

'You ain't seen nothin' yet,' she said, and they laughed and tapped glasses.

Upstairs, I peeled the plastic surround from the cactus and placed the plant on the shelf between a Hulk action figure and the knick-knack tin containing my four-leaf clover chain. Inside the tin, the clovers were still healthy and green, but I couldn't imagine why. By rights they should have died off weeks ago. It had to be some kind of magic.

Hope, faith, love and luck, I thought, remembering Becky's explanation of what the four clover leaves signified. I wondered where she was right now, perhaps bracing herself in the Mustang's back seat while Lu sped her and Mr October across town.

Coming down the stairs, I saw them together in the living room doorway, holding hands and gazing into each other's eyes. I hung back in the hall and cleared my throat, and they coughed and pulled apart.

'It's ready,' Mum said, hurrying out to the kitchen. 'Are you hungry?'

I shrugged.

'I could eat a horse,' Tom called.

'That's a shame. We only have chicken.'

Dinner was served. I hadn't been looking forward to it, I wasn't good around strangers, but the talk was light-hearted, no difficult silences, and now and then Tom would say something to make Mum laugh and she'd go off into an embarrassing schoolgirl giggle while I studied my plate.

From their conversation and the looks that passed between them I gathered they'd already spoken about Dad, though Mum had told me they hadn't. They didn't mention Dad now, but he seemed to be in the air, not far from their thoughts. At one point I asked Tom about his family, if he had one, and a strained look crossed his face before Mum quickly changed the subject. That was when I knew, or thought I knew. He understood what it meant to lose someone too.

'Hope it was all right,' Mum said at the end of the meal. 'Roasts are my speciality, but I can do other things too.'

'It's a treat,' Tom said.

'Our usual idea of a treat is a takeaway from Hai Ha's,' I said, and Mum rolled her eyes.

'Well, it's been lovely,' Tom said, raising his glass.

'To our fabulous hostess. And a pleasure to meet you, Ben. I hope we'll become good friends. Next time we'll do this at my place. In fact, how are you both fixed at the weekend?'

'I'm busy,' I said.

Another of Mum's reprimands came my way in a look. 'He's always off doing something. But there's no reason why he can't change his plans just this once.'

Just this once. But I'd already changed my plans for tonight and I couldn't keep missing shifts. I looked at the window, hearing a raven caw-cawing past.

'We can work something out,' Tom said, 'even if it's only for a few hours before you get back to whatever you'd rather do. Shall I have my driver pick you up, say, Saturday noon?'

'Your driver?' I looked at him, gobsmacked.

Mum smiled and arranged her cutlery on her plate. She knew much more than she'd been letting on. The gifts he'd brought were nothing to Tom Sutherland, a spit in the ocean. He was loaded. Really nothing like Dad at all.

'A driver,' said Mum, 'and a big house in Belsize Park. You should come along, Ben. No one's forcing you but I'm sure you'll enjoy it. Personally, I can't wait to see it.'

'No pressure,' Tom said. 'It's only a thought. But you'd make your mum happy by joining us, and her happiness is what counts, right?'

'Yeah, I suppose,' I said.

'Oh no,' Mum said suddenly. 'But I have a hospital appointment on Saturday morning. I'd completely forgotten my clinic starts again so soon.'

'No worries,' Tom said. 'We'll drive you. We'll pick Ben up later on our way back.'

'Are you sure it's no bother?' Mum said.

'None whatsoever,' Tom said.

I had a strange sense of a door closing firmly, taking the light with it and shutting me out.

'But I always go with you, Mum,' I said. 'The hospital's *my* job.'

'You've always done a fine job too,' she said, 'but you can help in other ways, Ben. Give yourself a break for once, no arguments now.'

And that was the end of that.

Later, after Tom had left and I'd moved the furniture back into place, Mum gave me a goodnight hug, holding me in such a way that I found myself looking straight at the photograph, so I closed my eyes.

'Don't worry,' she said. 'It's going to be fine, I'm

going to be fine, and you don't have to do anything to prove you love me. Let Tom help out if he wants to.'

'You're serious about him, aren't you?' I said.

'Oh, it's a bit soon to say serious. But I enjoy his company, and he makes me feel good.'

'Well, it shows.'

'Thank you, darlin'. That's quite a compliment, coming from you.'

Perhaps it was too soon, but it seemed to me that Tom Sutherland was already replacing Dad in her life – and now in this one small way he was replacing me too. The clinic was always an ordeal, the hospital full of departed and soon-departed souls and demons and chemical smells that made me gag, but getting Mum through it was one way I'd been able to help, and now I couldn't even do that.

❧13❧
THE GREAT GIG IN THE SKY

Winter seized the week. Temperatures dipped and freezing fog settled over the streets in the mornings. On the way to school the air burned my eyes and my head swam as if I had a cold coming on.

The atmosphere at Mercy Road was equally frosty. Teachers rebuked us for things we hadn't done and classmates either made smart remarks behind our backs or ignored us completely. Even Mel Kimble, who I used to think was OK, turned up her nose when we passed.

'What's wrong, Mel?' I asked, Tuesday afternoon, as Miss Radcliff's French class wound up for the break. 'Why's everyone being like this?'

'It ain't us, it's you,' she said, not looking at me. 'You're like a private club, you two, and nobody likes that here, innit? It's you two against the rest of us.'

At least she was talking, but not for long. Mel was quickly shushed and dragged away by two of her friends before I could ask anything else.

As they went, someone tapped my arm from behind, and I turned to find two of the gang of five, Kelly and Ryan, facing me. Their blank faces put me in mind of the unnamed dead in taxis and buses, and the usually hostile Kelly remained calm when she spoke.

'Mel's right. It's not us, it's you.'

'Becky was everyone's friend before you came,' Ryan said.

'She could still be your friend.'

'Nah.'

'Not likely,' Kelly said. 'Not as long as you're here. Everything's changed because of you. You brought something bad here, a bad influence, know what I mean?'

Looking past them at the small dark-haired boy innocently packing his bag at the back of the room, I had a good idea where the influence really came from.

'Can I just ask one thing?' I said, still eyeing Decker.

They shook their heads and strode away.

'What about you?' I said, catching Fay De Gray as she left her desk.

As usual Fay looked stunned to be spoken to,

unable to meet my look. Watching the floor, she edged sheepishly around me towards the door.

'Can't talk to you either,' she said. 'We're not supposed to.'

'Says who? What do you know, Fay? What's scaring you?'

That was as far as I got with her. Shaking her head, Fay ran from the room.

At her desk, possibly overhearing all this but looking on without comment, Miss Radcliff massaged her temples and squinted as if feeling the onset of a headache.

Because of the biting weather we took the bus to Islington after school. Progress was slow on the icy roads – we could have walked it in half the time – and I sat upstairs with Becky in a kind of shock, hardly speaking.

'Can't take much more of this,' was all she said until we left the bus on Upper Street, where she dragged me aside to speak her piece. She'd obviously been giving this some thought, and she built up a head of steam before she finished.

'It's no use asking anyone there for an answer,' she said. 'We both know why it's happening. It's because of what we believe in and what we are. Well, I can't see everything you can, Ben, and I can't do what some field agents do, but I still feel things, I know when someone's hurting and when they need help, and I know it's the right thing to do. And sometimes knowing you're right is all you've got, even if it turns everyone against you. I've found my place, we both have, and we can't let them mess it up for us.'

At first I thought "them" meant the other pupils, but she meant more than that, I realised now. The kids didn't know what we did outside school, and they didn't know what someone – something – else was doing to them.

'I'd say that's a good summary of our situation,' I said.

'I should think so. It took me all afternoon to come up with it.' As we hurried between the empty shops and frosted café tables on Camden Passage she added, 'We can't say we weren't warned, that's all.'

A wave of dizziness nearly floored me as we set off

between the brick walls. The entrance felt tighter, more claustrophobic than ever, and the bricks chafed my cheek as I squeezed through. Exiting the passageway onto Eventide Street, I doubled up, hands on knees, certain I was about to black out.

'What's wrong?' Becky said. 'Something happen back there?'

'Just a cold starting. Maybe flu. I'll be fine.'

'Take your time.'

The alley came slowly into focus. The feeling passed, but my legs were still rubbery. I straightened up, looking past Becky at the vehicle parked by the steps below Pandemonium House.

'I see Lu's rickshaw is back from service,' I said.

'Yeah, good thing too. She tied the Mustang around a lamp post last night. Fortunately no one was with her and she jumped out in time, so no one got hurt.'

'What happened?'

'She hit black ice and went into a skid. That's what she claims, anyway, but you know how she drives. The Mustang's at the repair depot, but I'll bet they don't let her out in it again, at least not until she's passed her test.'

We headed indoors, into the whistling wind. On the way upstairs Becky said, 'Another thing you missed last night. Mr October stumbled and fell three times. He wasn't good on his legs all night, actually. I can't see that old man's body lasting much longer.'

'He came back to work too soon. He'll find another personality to replace it – he has lots more. But I'll miss that old codger when he retires. He was the first one I met.'

The sounds of a disturbance met us at the top of the stairs. A muffled voice called, 'Look out!' and a huge thud vibrated along the floor, followed by a tinkle of breaking glass.

Sukie peered out from receipts, a stack of typed cards in her hand. She was watching the dispatch room door, where the sounds were coming from.

'Oh hi,' she said, unusually surprised to see us.

'Hi Sukie. . .' I said. Another shout, another dull thud. 'Any idea what's going on?'

'Yeah, of course.'

But of course Sukie knew everything.

'As a matter of fact, I don't know everything,' she said. 'I'm not hearing much at all today. Something's not right. Feels like the signals are blocked. Could be I'm being screened.'

We looked at her nonplussed.

'Screened?' Becky said.

'Tell you later. It's kinda complicated.' She was still focused on the dispatch room. The disruption inside had died down, replaced by a mechanical whir and drone.

'What's that?' I said.

Sukie touched a finger to her lips. 'Mr October, I think.'

'What's he doing?'

'Quiet. Just wait.'

She glanced irritably back inside the office as the telegraph kicked off again, spitting and growling.

'Brilliant, and I only just finished this lot,' she said. 'Ben, would you be a honey and take these for filing while I process the next batch?'

A door slammed open, making all three of us jump and nearly spinning the cards from my grasp as Sukie handed them over. The mechanical drone stepped up in volume and, seated at the controls of a red mobility scooter, Mr October trundled from the dispatch room into the hallway, bumping the walls left and right. His elderly face was even paler and wrinklier than his off-white suit and the top of his bald head glowed, reflecting candlelight.

'What are you gawking at? Don't you have work

to do?' he grumbled. 'Don't look at me, this isn't my idea. The elders thought I should give it a go after last night, and there's talk of having a stairlift installed – health and safety nonsense and all that. Frankly, I feel insulted. I'm perfectly capable, and besides, it's Lu's job to get me around. It's a lot of fuss and bother over nothing.'

He promptly went into a coughing fit, pressing a handkerchief to his mouth. As the coughing eased he composed himself again, looking at me as if surprised to see me.

'Ah, Ben. I see you have a new batch for filing. What's our programme?'

I read him the numbers off the cards while Becky followed Sukie inside receipts. A couple of 8847s, a 10176—'

'Another of those,' he said. 'How odd. They're very uncommon. What else?'

'A 12123 in Camden, a 1732 in Stockwell. . .'

'Come, walk with me a while. I'll keep you company on the long trek to snarky Miss Webster's booth.'

'We're worried about you,' I said, waiting while he reversed and turned the scooter into position. 'I mean, worried about this shape of yours, this personality's health.'

'You worry too much, but that's your way, that's why you're here.'

'I heard about you falling. Have you fallen before?'

'More times than I can count. And you know something? Every time I fell I got back up again.'

'One of these days you won't.'

'Still argumentative,' he said. 'Well, when that day comes I'll admit defeat and hang up my boots. Or hat. Whichever.'

'Couldn't you do the same job in a different body?'

'All of my personalities are separate and distinct,' Mr October said. 'In here – ' He tapped his chest. '– there are warriors and magicians, scholars and teachers, ravens and snakes, but there's only one empathiser, and he – which is to say, me in this form – is the one best-suited to the task.'

'So when he wears out, what then?'

'Oh, he'll have a successor. Who knows, it might be you, or even Becky, who's skilled in this area too. At that time, this old man will retire and I – which is to say, another part of me – will take on another role. But don't trouble yourself. I may be old but—'

'You're very resilient.'

'True, and I'll wager I have a good few decades in me yet.'

In the enormous records room a strange tension gripped the air. The filing clerks were always busy but today their actions seemed nervously driven and, miles high in the mist, the guardians flew in agitated patterns. I hadn't seen anything like this since the Halloween siege. Were they expecting another attack?

I crossed the floor at a shuffle to let Mr October keep up.

'Confound this thing,' he said, stopping the scooter and leaping up, into the frame of the black-hatted pirate, a stronger and more capable body for the long walk ahead. 'Time's of the essence, and see what they give me for transport! Between you and me, Ben, I sometimes wonder if the Overseers are losing touch.'

'I don't get what's happening here,' I said, looking around the white space. 'Is something going on I should know about?'

'They're on alert,' he said. 'It seems the Bad Saturday list was leaked after all. Our Infernal Enquiries team have confirmed that the names on that list reached enemy hands about the time we received them. Hence, the books are unbalanced and the numbers are presently out of alignment.'

'Then someone, a traitor, gave up the list?'

'The investigation's ongoing. For now, we're assuming there's an enemy agent in our midst or a disaffected Ministry operative about to defect. He or she may not have joined the other side yet but could be about to do so.'

We walked on, watching the rush and tumble around us until Miss Webster's tiny booth, jammed between two skyscraper cabinets, finally came into view.

'One leak, one crack in the order of things, and look at the fallout,' Mr October said. 'Seems to me there's a pattern to the enemy's tactics this time, something shrewder and more insidious.'

He would have said more but we'd arrived at Miss Webster's booth, where Mr October doffed his hat and flashed his silver tooth. 'Afternoon, Miss Webster.'

She gave her customary scowl. 'Afternoon, is it? It's all right for those who get out once in a while to see for themselves what time of day it is.'

'The cards, Ben,' Mr October prompted, and I set them before Miss Webster and stepped back before she could snap at me too.

'May I say you're looking lovelier than ever today,' Mr October told her.

The compliment passed her by. 'And may *I* say you fool no one,' Miss Webster said. 'Just because you have the gift of the gab doesn't mean you have anything to say that's worth hearing.'

'Of course not, Miss Webster.'

She sniffed and plucked a small tangle of cobwebs from her chin. 'And another thing. . .'

'Yes, Miss Webster?'

'I'd suggest getting rid of that awful hat. Makes you look like Jack Palance in *Shane*.'

The strained mood in records was spreading through HQ. Parties of armed Vigilants patrolled the operations floor as we collected Becky for the rounds, and there were more guards outside, two posted at the entrance, teams assembling in the alley, boots snapping over the cobbles.

Lu, already in position at the rickshaw, watched in bemusement.

'What's all the fuss?' she said, and Mr October said, 'I'll explain as we go.'

When Lu took off, charging through the invisible gap into darkness, the giddiness rushed at me for the second time. A vertical slit of light at the end widened and spread as if a door were opening, and then we were in London again, veering right along Camden Passage.

'You felt it again, didn't you,' Becky said. A statement, not a question. 'Are you sure you're up to this? If you're coming down with something. . .'

'I missed one shift last night. I'm not about to miss another.'

'Is there a problem?' Mr October said. 'What are you two rabbiting on about?'

'Nothing,' I said. 'Just an odd feeling when we came out.'

'And the same before, when we went in,' Becky added.

'Hmm. I see.'

He studied me for a long moment before turning to watch the street. He seemed lost in thought, perhaps preoccupied by the security breach and the state of alert back at Pandemonium House.

The dead rocker had wandered a good distance from the scene of the motorcycle smash that ended his fifty-two year innings on planet Earth. An icy patch of road and a steep wall on the Blackwall tunnel's western bore were to blame. Prior to the accident he'd been tooling along high as a kite on prescription medicine, according to the 534227 on his card, which may have had something to do with it too. No other motorists were involved.

This newly-departed was Pat Malone, a man with a long black ponytail, a lined and puffy drinker's face and big saucer eyes. We found him staring up in dismay at the O2 theatre, then at the ticket in his hand. His leather jacket and blue jeans were shredded and bloody.

Mr October began to change, clothes rippling about him, features skittering like bugs, but halfway through becoming the empathiser he seemed to rethink and switched back to the pirate guise.

'I've a hunch he'll be more comfortable seeing me like this,' he said. 'Observe his general demeanour and take note of why he's here. See the ticket he's holding. His disappointment is understandable – not only is he dead but he's going to miss the concert too.'

'The gig, man, not the concert,' Malone said. 'And it ain't just a gig – it's the Stones.'

'Ah, the Stones.' This meant something to

Mr October, who'd been around for many a long year and heard and seen so much. 'Yes, I used to like their particular brand of beat combo music myself back in the day.'

'It's rock 'n' roll, man. Beat combo music? Where you bin?'

'Now what was that song of theirs I used to enjoy?' Mr October hummed a short refrain.

Malone's face lit up. 'You can't carry a tune but that's 'Paint It Black' sure enough,' he said, but he quickly became distraught again. 'They'll play it tonight for sure. If I could only hear it one more time. I mean, how many more chances would I have had to see 'em again? How much time do they have left, anyway?'

Mr October removed his hat and dusted it off and combed back his hair with a hand. 'One never knows.'

'Couldn't you wait?' Malone pleaded. 'Just until after the show. You could come for me later, couldn't you? I swear I won't try to run. I'd meet you here right after. What do you say?'

Mr October checked the card and became quiet for a time, considering the possibilities.

'Come oooon,' said Malone. 'Just a few hours

is all I'm asking. I'm dead, I ain't disputing it. I just wanna see the Stones!'

We awaited Mr October's decision.

Finally he turned to Lu and said, 'Call dispatch. Ask for one – no, make that two junior agents to keep Mr Malone company until we return, in case there's an enemy presence at the concert – gig.' To Malone he said, 'This is quite irregular, but I do believe it's possible to bump you to the end of our schedule.'

Malone's eyes filled with delight and gratitude.

'As a matter of fact,' Mr October said, 'I wouldn't mind catching a few minutes of the Stones myself if we're back in time.'

'Man, you don't know how much this means.'

'Oh, I do.'

Malone narrowed his watery eyes at Mr October. 'Who are you anyway, mate? Haven't I seen you before?'

'Yes, but I'm surprised you remember. It was so long ago and you weren't in the best of shape. Your first motorcycle accident on the road home from Brighton, where you'd been appearing as an extra in a moving picture called *Quadrophobia*.'

'*Quadrophenia*. Sure I remember.'

'You were in the ambulance on the way to the

hospital, and you opened your eyes very briefly and there I was, attending to your fellow passenger, who sadly wasn't as fortunate as you. The staff couldn't save him that night, but they worked hard to bail you out.'

Malone was walking on air when we left. A lone figure standing beneath the O2, he watched the rickshaw pull away and raised a hand in a V for Victory sign.

'It's only rock 'n' roll but I like it!' he called.

Because of the late change to our timetable, because Mr October wished to see the Rolling Stones, we were early for our next call at Canary Wharf.

Ordinarily, being early was a good thing. The Ministry encouraged punctuality. But this case turned out to be different, presenting us with what Mr October called 'a moral dilemma'.

The 9664, Clare Turnbull, 37, stood at the edge of her office building's roof, swaying on flimsy legs in the wind. A crowd had gathered sixteen floors below and police were ordering them across the street while calling through amplified speakers for Clare to move back from the edge and come down.

At the start of all this they'd come to arrest her. Now they were here to save her. When we came up to the roof, Clare Turnbull was still very much alive.

The numbers said she was a financier accused of siphoning small funds from many different accounts into one large off-shore account of her own. She must have heard at the last minute that detectives were entering the building, too late for a clean getaway, time only for Clare to take the lift as high as it would go, then run up the last flight of stairs to the roof.

It was freezing up there. My teeth chattered and Becky hugged herself, her scarf tugged up over her nose and mouth. We kept to the far side of the roof from Clare while Mr October discreetly became the elderly man in white.

'Looks like the old softly-softly for this one,' he said. 'No sudden noises or moves now.'

Becky muttered something inaudible, then tugged down her scarf and repeated it.

'We could save her, couldn't we? Never mind the police. We could do something right now.'

'You misunderstand,' Mr October said. 'Our business can seem brutal at times, but here's her card, her name and number. She's on the same list as everyone else, and as you well know the telegraph doesn't get these things wrong.'

Becky was horrified. 'She's still alive and breathing, though. We could bend the rules a bit, couldn't we?'

'I'm afraid not. Our rules never bend, they only break.'

'But you bent them for that bloke, that rocker, twenty minutes ago.'

'He's a newly-departed. All I did was rejig the schedule to accommodate him. Not the same thing at all.'

'So you mean to say whatever happens, whatever we do, she's bound to fall?'

Mr October nodded and said gravely, 'That's what it says here.'

'Then why not just push her, get it over with?' Becky demanded.

'Now you're being facetious. We can't do that for the same reason we can't save her,' Mr October replied. 'Regulations. We can't intervene in the natural order of things.'

Becky found this as hard to take as I did. Her shoulders sagged and she looked away past the Gherkin at the bright full moon sitting low in the sky behind a mask of cloud. A seagull's silhouette crossed the moon's surface, gliding, wings unmoving.

'Look,' Becky said, 'imagine we were like . . . like a film crew or something shooting by a river or a lake and we saw some kid drowning. We'd drop the camera and try to save them, wouldn't we? We'd do what we could. We wouldn't just stand there recording it all.'

Mr October wiped his weary face. 'What's written will come to pass, and in such a case you'd find that the child you manage to save is not on the list, and the child you try to save but who drowns *is* on the list. I don't wish to sound callous, but that's how it goes.'

'In other words, we do nothing at all,' Becky said, outraged. 'And nothing we do makes any difference. But you still have to try. In fact, what the hell, I'm *going* to try. I'm going to talk her out of it. . .'

'Becky. . .' Mr October said, but she was already marching away on her mission. She'd only taken a half dozen paces, though, when it happened. Destiny struck.

The seagull came out of nowhere, diving out of the gloom above the rooftops. Perhaps it never saw Clare Turnbull standing on the roof in its line of flight, or perhaps it veered so close out of curiosity, attracted by her outstretched arms, which she held out for balance in the wind. For all the gull knew, she could have been offering up food from her frozen hands.

It didn't strike her. From our vantage point it seemed to miss her by a fraction, brushing past her billowing hair. Clare flashed out a hand, sensing the movement, reacting to the rush of air from its wings as it curved east. That was all it took to unsettle her, and then she was pinwheeling her arms frantically to bring herself back.

In the last moments before she went, her instinct seemed to be telling her not to go, not to fall but hold on for dear life, because whatever came next if she lived – newspaper headlines, scandal and jail time, the end of one life and the start of another – had to be better than no life at all.

But she fell. Her name was on the list and the telegraph never lied. She fell, and screams and howls rose from the street and drifted up on the wind and across the roof as Becky turned back to us, hanging her head.

Behind Becky, in the exact spot Clare had just left, a busy constellation of dim lights danced and flickered, arranging themselves into a sequence of different shapes, a bird treading air, an angel with outstretched wings, then finally a wingless figure, Clare Turnbull herself.

Clare's separated self sat on the edge, looking out

on the glittering city. Her shoulders were shaking, not from the cold but because she was sobbing.

Mr October squeezed Becky's hand. 'You see? It's hard, but there's nothing anyone could have said to help her – not until now. But now the time for talking begins.'

He started across the roof, shuffling along on his walking stick, the city lights twinkling around him as he prepared to send Clare Turnbull to her own great gig in the sky.

14
THE SCREENING

The call came in towards the end of the shift. A rusty-sounding bell trilled at knee height in front of the passenger seat, and Mr October opened a concealed compartment, lifting out a strange-looking antique telephone. It was a black two-piece candlestick phone, the kind you see in old gangster films, with a rotary dial and a wire snaking back inside the compartment.

'Hello?' Mr October said, holding the earpiece to his ear. He listened for a moment with a stern expression, nodding but not speaking.

Sensing the importance of the call, Lu slowed to a trot along the Ball's Pond Road, awaiting instructions.

'The rickshaw phone only rings when a matter is urgent,' Mr October said, hanging up. 'Lu, turn this thing around! We're to drop Miss Sanborne here and return immediately to headquarters.'

'What's this about? Shouldn't I be coming too?' Becky said. 'We're all on the same team, aren't we?'

'This doesn't concern you,' Mr October said. 'Besides, you've done your stint for tonight. It's better if you go home.'

'In case you've forgotten, Mr October, I don't have a home anymore.'

'I hadn't forgotten. My apologies. Be with your parents, then. They need you more than we do at this point.'

'Then why take Ben? He hasn't done anything wrong.' Becky gave me a quizzical look. 'Has he?'

As far as I knew, I hadn't, but Mr October was giving nothing away.

'I sincerely hope not,' he said.

'It's OK,' I told Becky. 'We'll sort it, whatever it is. Do like he says and go to your aunt's. I'll see you in the morning.'

She climbed reluctantly down to the curb, and while Lu doubled back on the street I twisted around to watch Becky's forlorn figure dissolving in the lights behind us.

'Any idea why they called us in?' I said.

Mr October said, 'All I know is that it's an Infernal Enquiries matter, and they said to be sure to bring you.'

'Uh-oh.'

'I'm sure it will be fine. You're one of our rising stars – no one so young has ever made such an impression on the conference room – and they know not to jeopardise your education.' Watching the traffic, he added with a sigh, 'The Stones will be onstage about now. Ah, well.'

The earlier journey from headquarters had left me with a just-bearable pulse behind my eyes all evening, but when Lu returned through the walls I thought my skull might explode. Leaving the rickshaw on doddery legs, I had to take a minute on Eventide Street while my head slowly cleared.

'Easy,' Lu said, taking my arm and helping me along.

Several other Ministry vehicles were parked around the alley, half a dozen SUVs, a Ford Anglia, a late 1950s Plymouth and a Mr Whippy ice cream van playing the *Magic Roundabout* theme. An ice cream van? I would've thought that odd if I didn't spend most evenings riding in a single-seater rickshaw with two other passengers and room to spare.

There was a lockdown in place in the building, an air of confusion, and Vigilants were posted outside every office on the main operations floor. Clerical staff ran back and forth carrying files and field teams stood around muttering among themselves. Joe Mort gave us his customary nod, and Kate Stone smiled, then shyly looked away as we passed. A woman in a black and white houndstooth coat watched us with striking green eyes. Could she be the one Becky had told me about, the woman who'd held Mum's hand in the waiting room? This wasn't the time to ask.

'We should be in the field now, no idea what's cooking,' Joe said, and further along the hall team-leader Rusty complained, 'We're wasting time when we could be bustin' enemy heads. What're we waiting for?'

The Vigilant outside receipts was one of the pair who'd brought me in on Halloween night, the less approachable of the two. He had the same fixed expression as his colleagues, and he wasn't moving from his post for anyone, not even for Mr October.

'Sorry, sir,' he said. 'Orders is orders. You're not allowed to pass.'

'Ludicrous,' Mr October said. 'Can't you hear

the telegraph, you numbskull? Do you have the faintest idea what that means?'

'Sir, that doesn't concern me. It's not my job.'

'Well, it should concern you. And don't give me that "sir" business, either.'

'No, sir.'

'You're preventing Ministry staff from doing their duty,' Mr October seethed. 'Don't think for a second it won't be noted. I intend to report this matter to the elders.'

'Yes, sir.'

'Who's responsible for this palaver, anyway? Who called the lockdown? Speak up, man.'

'The elders, sir,' the Vigilant said. 'And even you have to answer to them.'

'Insolence,' Mr October said, losing patience, momentarily morphing back and forth between the pirate and a personality I hadn't seen before, a wild-eyed man of the wilderness, blond-bearded and bare-toothed, his face burning with terrible fury.

The appearance of this one, a madman at boiling point, chilled my bones even though I saw him only briefly. Kate Stone, seeing him too, clapped a hand to her mouth. The Vigilant fell back, thumping the door, and a hush descended on the hallway as if everyone, even those who hadn't seen, could feel it.

'Who was *that*?' I asked as Mr October recomposed himself.

'Forgive me,' he said. 'He was, indeed is, a fearsome Norse warrior. Sometimes I almost forget he's there, as he doesn't often appear. I'd rather try to reason than resort to thuggery, and he's anything but reasonable, to say the least. Shame, though, I didn't have time to let him loose before I was struck by Synister's fireball.'

I blinked at him. 'Nathan Synister did that to you?'

'Let's just say I owe him one.' Now he turned to the Vigilant at the door. 'Are you letting us in or not?'

'Sorry, sir. Ordinarily I'd follow your orders, or those of any field team leader, but as this comes directly from above. . .'

'Mr October?' someone called down the busy hallway. 'Conference room, please. The elders are ready.'

'Ben, go to the waiting room,' he said, changing for the meeting into a well-groomed city slicker type in a midnight blue suit. 'No point in dilly-dallying here. I'll get to the bottom of this.'

Behind the receipts office door, the telegraph rumbled on.

Sukie was already in the waiting room, as were several other lost-looking staff. Lulling ancientspeak music played through wall-mounted speakers, a kind of bossa nova jazz featuring a singer who sounded like Astrid Gilberto, who Mum liked, but whose lyrics were indecipherable.

'You were here when the lockdown began,' I said, taking a seat with Sukie. 'Didn't anyone explain it?'

'Nope. The Vigilants came and threw me out of receipts and I've been here ever since. I should've clocked off hours ago.'

She stared glumly at the floor, elbows on knees, chin resting on her fists.

'Why did they call me back?' I said.

'They recalled more than half the staff,' Sukie said. 'It's outrageous. There are souls in limbo out there and we're sitting on our hands.'

I remembered a remark she'd made earlier, before our rounds. 'You usually know what goes on here, don't you.'

'Yeah. Usually. Just not now.'

'What did you mean, about being screened?'

She looked at me, or past me. The cast in her eye

made it hard to tell which. 'It's like when the magic goes. When the gift disappears. Y'know?'

'Not exactly.'

'It's happened to me before, mostly in crowded places, sometimes on duty and sometimes not, but it's never been this extreme or lasted so long. It's been on and off since I came in today.'

'So you're not hearing anything . . . other people's thoughts.'

'That's right. The signals are scrambled.'

Leaning closer, I said, 'Can't you read mine from here?'

She shrugged and stared across the waiting room, chewing her lip.

'Just try,' I said. 'Concentrate. What am I seeing?'

To help her along, I formed a clear and simple picture in my thoughts: Dad's bench in London Fields with the brass name plaque and dry autumn leaves blustering around it, deep red and golden-yellow.

'It won't work,' she said.

'But you can try.'

She did try, closing her eyes and concentrating.

'Nah, it doesn't work,' she said, 'because it never does when you think too hard. You know how it is.'

'Not really.'

'That's because you're still learning. It's like anything, like cycling or swimming or painting. Once you know how, you just do it. And once you start analysing what you're doing and how you're doing it, you lose it.' She sighed and looked at the door. 'Funny, all those other thoughts sometimes drive me nuts and I wish they'd stop . . . but I miss them when they're not there.'

The door opened. At the threshold stood Mr October in mid-transformation, part city slicker, part pirate, holding a parcel of dog-eared papers under his arm. After a moment his features calmed and he adjusted the brim of his gunslinger's hat, looking in with a straight face, no silver-toothed smile in sight.

'Looks bad,' said Sukie.

'Come with me, both of you,' Mr October said. 'The meeting was brief but illuminating. Someone around here has some explaining to do.'

The hallway was clearing, field teams drifting towards the stairs and clerical staff back to their offices. Some glanced my way and shook their heads disapprovingly, causing a nervous sweat to crawl over me. The stubborn Vigilant guarding the receipts office door now stepped smartly away without being asked.

The office looked like a hurricane had stormed through it. Security had torn it apart in the raid, leaving only the typewriter and the telegraph machine untouched. Papers were scattered far and wide, books had been dumped from shelves to the floor and more papers and books were heaped on the desk. The telegraph was quiet now, but the list it had produced earlier looked long.

'Deal with that, Sukie, while we discuss,' Mr October said. 'There's no time to process these names before the field teams move out. We'll relay everything through dispatch.'

'Will do.'

Sukie cleared a mess of paperwork from the desk and settled down while I moved to the window. The Vigilant peered in from the doorway with eyes as cold and dead as a shark's.

'So here's the situation,' Mr October said, untucking the parcel from under his arm. 'During a thorough search of the premises, our security people came into possession of *this*. . .'

'And what's that?' Sukie said, not looking up from her prodding, two-fingered typing.

'A manuscript found concealed behind volumes of the *Apocalypti Phrase Book, Unexpurgated*. Ben, would you care to explain?'

My stomach clenched when he showed me the typescript, on the cover page of which I'd typed *A Dispatch From The Ministry*. I couldn't deny it was mine, but I didn't say anything.

'It doesn't bear your name, but it's clearly yours,' Mr October said, 'and it's obvious that you typed it right there on that machine. Note the slightly raised lowercase "i" and the clogged aperture of the uppercase "Q". . . They're like fingerprints. I know that machine's quirks well.'

I stared at the floor, avoiding the Vigilant's look.

'We haven't read it thoroughly,' Mr October said. 'Presently, we will. But how and where it was written isn't the issue.'

'It's only for me,' I said. 'No one else was meant to see it. I only wanted to record things . . . to try to make sense of everything I've seen since I've been here. It doesn't give any secrets away, honest.' I added quietly, 'No one would believe it, anyway.'

'Sukie, were you aware of this?' he said.

'Well, I know it's been on his mind,' she said, removing one typed card and rolling in a new blank. 'It does name names, and it does tell our location, and it says a few things about how our operation works.'

'You've seen it?' I said, embarrassed. It was as if she'd read my private diary, which, in a way, the typescript was.

'I've read your thoughts, so of course I knew where you hid it,' she said. 'But, Mr October, I believe Ben did mean it to be private, which is why he kept it here to make sure no outsiders would see it. He hasn't even told Becky. He wouldn't have shown it to anyone, anyway, without your permission, and not until—'

'Yes, yes, yes,' Mr October said. 'That's all well and good and I'm sure, Ben, you meant no harm. What's of greater concern is the list of names our Infernal Enquiries team found tucked between these pages. I'm talking about the Bad Saturday list.'

My mouth fell open. Sukie looked up from the typewriter, stunned.

'Well, I didn't know about *that*,' she gasped.

Mr October frowned. 'And why not? You're supposed to know everything that happens here, every stray thought, every daydream.'

'Usually I do. Mostly I do. Just not today.'

He narrowed his eyes. 'Care to explain?'

Sukie fingered her temple as if she could feel my headache. 'It's like I told Ben. The other thoughts aren't there, or at best they're sort of woolly and scrambled. Could be there's a screener in the area.'

'Someone blocking you,' Mr October said.

'Yeah, like someone shutting off the signals, tuning them out.'

'And why would anyone do that?' I asked. I must have been punch-drunk from that last disorientating journey between the walls, because none of this was making sense.

Mr October said, 'To enable someone to plant evidence without Sukie's knowledge. Someone with a grudge against you. Someone *in* the department but not *of* the department.'

'Which they couldn't have done without screening me first,' Sukie agreed.

A terrific noise from the alley rattled the window. A convoy of field teams were leaving, their vehicles speeding to the wall with engines revving and headlights ablaze. One by one they vanished into the gap, a crack fine enough to be invisible from here.

Sukie gave a little gasp and turned so pale I thought she was fainting. She sucked air and waved a hand as if to say, 'It's all right, it's OK,' before she began to breathe more easily.

'It's over,' she said. 'It's coming back, I just wasn't

ready for it all to come at once. Give me a minute. The screener must have gone, or stopped or something.'

'Everyone's gone,' I said, checking the now deserted alley. 'It could've been any of them.'

'Another turncoat in our midst,' Mr October said. 'You see, Ben, I've told you how devious the enemy can be. If they're not whispering in your ear they're stifling thoughts and stealing them. Sukie, are you able to continue? Dispatch are waiting.'

'I'll do it,' I said. 'She finished her shift ages ago. I'll take over now.'

'I'm afraid you can't.' Something in Mr October's posture, a slight lowering of his head, told me there was worse news to come. 'It's procedure.'

'But I'm here now, and Sukie – look at her, she's all worn out. What procedure?'

He spoke as if a great weight were pressing down on him. 'It's the Ministry's way, Ben. The elders think only in terms of evidence, what can and cannot be scientifically proven. There's no room in their philosophy for hope, faith, love and luck. They only believe in what they can see. In fact, without proof, without evidence, they believe in nothing at all. Which is why, it grieves me to say, they've called for your immediate suspension from duty, effective until this matter is resolved.'

'Suspension. . .' I could barely repeat it. I couldn't believe what I was hearing.

Sukie stopped typing long enough to curse under her breath, then went back to work.

'Procedure,' Mr October said. 'As soon as the elders have proof of your innocence and the guilty party is found, you'll be reinstated. As things stand, they simply won't allow you to continue. Rule 39b, subsection C of the operations manual states, "Any member of staff under investigation or linked in any way to an ongoing investigation shall be considered exempt from duty. . ." And so on. A lot of hot air, in my opinion, but there it is.'

'So what happens now?'

'Now you must leave.' Mr October looked down at the floor, remorseful.

'The Ministry needs me,' I said. 'And I need the Ministry. . .'

'I know. But their decision is final.'

As I started across the littered floor, past the desk, Sukie grabbed my hand.

'It'll work out, you'll see,' she said. 'We believe in you.'

Mr October fussed my hair and tucked the confiscated typescript back under his arm. 'They'll have their evidence and choke on it,' he said. 'In the meantime, be on your guard, young man. This may be a part of a larger plan.'

I nodded and kept walking, just about holding myself together, but my throat felt likely to burst. I didn't look back when I left the office, so the last thing I saw was the face of the guard at the door. It was the first time I'd ever seen a Vigilant smile.

❧ 15 ❧
STILL LIFE

They did *what*?' Becky said when I broke the news the next morning. 'That's bang out of order! They can't suspend you.'

'They already have.'

'But the Ministry needs you.'

'That's what I said. They didn't agree.'

There were delays on the icy roads this morning, no school buses yet, and we were among the first to arrive on Mercy Road. The school yard was empty with a chill wind blowing across it, but we kept our voices low as we turned in at the gates, stepping carefully on the frosty ground.

'So this Vigilant,' Becky said, 'you say he's one of the team who arrested you that night?'

'Yeah. Do you know him?'

'Not really. Vigilants are kind of unknowable, aren't they, but I think he's called McManaman. I'll keep an eye on him, try to find out what he's up to.'

'Don't,' I said quickly. 'Leave it to security.'

'He *is* security.'

'Then leave it to Mr October. Don't get involved.'

'I *am* involved, Ben. You should see where I'm living.'

'I know, I'm sorry. Would you like to talk about it?'

'I don't mind. Could be worse,' she said. 'Mum isn't sleeping, but she's in much better spirits now. She's stronger than she looks. Everything we lost, she said, it's just stuff, material stuff, and who cares as long as we're all here and safe? And Dad's had the bit between his teeth ever since he had a run-in with the insurers. Would you believe they tried to make out the tornado was an act of God?'

'They never.'

'Honest they did, but Dad wasn't having it – there's no act of God exclusion on our cover, he reckons, so they have to pay up. They'll also pay our accommodation costs while the repairs are done if we leave Aunt Meg's for a bigger place. Mum's not sure – she doesn't want to move again – but you'd never believe how cramped it is. If we'd had anything left to bring from the house there wouldn't be room for it. The only things we saved were some books and clothes and that portrait you did of me.'

We were lingering outside the main entrance.

It would be our last chance to speak openly for a while.

'One more thing,' Becky said. 'About your journal, Ben. Why didn't you tell me? It wouldn't have gone any further.'

'I never meant to show it around. Besides, it doesn't matter now they've confiscated it. I'll probably never see it again.'

'I'll put in a word for you. And suspension doesn't mean forever. Just lie low for a while and try not to worry. It'll blow over.'

We started indoors. The school felt as vacant as it looked from outside, and the stale-smelling interiors sounded hollow as we walked through. Close to where the two corridors met at the heart of the building, Becky stopped dead in front of a message board.

'They must be kidding,' she said. 'If it's not one thing it's another. Unbelievable.'

We looked at each other, speechless, then back at the notice tacked to the board, which said:

Due to the inclement and hazardous weather conditions, pupils are required to remain on school premises during breaks and at all other times. This is to ensure the safety and well-being of all. This notice will be strictly enforced. – A.M. Hatcher, Principal.

'I used to think Mr Hatcher was OK,' Becky said. 'You could have a laugh with him and all that, but not lately, and if he wrote this he's been brainwashed like all the rest. If we can't go out to the crypt, we can't talk about you know what, so we can't talk about anything that matters all day.'

'You're kind of talking about it now,' I said. 'To hell with it, I'm going.'

'Do that and you're in deep trouble,' a voice boomed at my shoulder.

I turned slowly, cautiously around. A tall, raw-boned man with a salt-and-pepper beard and a permanent frown, Mr Hatcher was looking at me as if I were something he'd scraped off his shoe.

'If I hear one word, just one word to that effect,' he said, 'you'll be in my office faster than a speeding bullet, lad. Is that understood?'

'Yes, sir,' I said, wondering how one word could tell him so much. 'It's just. . . I mean. . .'

'Speak up.'

'It's just that we never go any further than the tea rooms over there. It's only twenty steps away, probably, and there's never much traffic outside the rush hour.'

'That's as maybe, but there are other dangers

you'll be aware of if you follow the news.' He was talking about the bombing, the growing fear there may be more to follow, and a police siren raced past outside to prove his point. 'In any case, I didn't spend my precious time composing this notice just to have students ignore it. You'll disregard it at your peril, Mr Harvester.'

'Yes, sir. But I only—'

'End of.'

He moved along. I looked around for Decker, but Decker was nowhere in sight.

'It's getting so you daren't even think,' Becky said. 'It's like the whole world's against us.'

'I know.'

'So what will you do?'

'I'll go anyway. What's there to miss? I'm sick of this stinking place.'

'Calm down.'

'Why?'

'Just be quiet,' she said.

'Why should I?'

'Because there's a ghost over there near the cold spot. Look.'

The shadows she was pointing to were somehow deeper than elsewhere, and I noticed a kind of streaky half-light that didn't seem to come from any particular room, but I wasn't altogether sure what else Becky was seeing.

'Could be it needs our help,' she said. 'I get the impression it's scrabbling around all fours, like it's looking for something.'

'Hold on. Someone's coming.'

We moved to the cold patch and waited. The office receptionist strode by, nose in the air, giving us a wide berth as she passed.

'Now do you see?' Becky whispered.

A trace of movement near my feet could have been my own shadow for all I knew. 'Not really.'

'That's odd. But the others who came here, your dad and the fire children, were as clear as day to you. So why not this one?'

'Maybe it wants something from you, not me.'

She shivered at the thought, or perhaps because of the chilly air. 'It's moving again. . .'

'What can you tell me about it? Can you describe it?'

Becky half-closed her eyes. 'It could be either a man or a woman. Hard to say because it's so old and withered and scrawny . . . malnourished, like it's been locked away for ages without food or light. And its fingernails are all cracked and bloody. I think it's been trying to dig its way out . . . or in.'

'What does it want?'

She hushed me, checking around to ensure no one was within earshot before she spoke.

'Who are you? And what can we do? Is there something you'd like to say?'

But then the bell went off, loud as a fire alarm, and the first school bus party came stampeding indoors, their shouts and footsteps ringing off the walls.

Becky sighed. 'Great timing. They scared it away. Did you hear what it said? I couldn't make out a word, and it seemed. . . I'm not sure. . . I think it burrowed straight down through the floor.'

The new school rule amounted to a lockdown – lockdowns were following me everywhere this week – so we didn't have another chance to discuss what she'd seen. No one spoke, anyway, in Miss Neal's class, and at first break I sat with Becky in the school canteen, sipping tasteless tea and feeling watched. The other kids wouldn't sit near us but their critical eyes never left us.

It was frustrating to leave so much unsaid, not to be able to speak of work – the work she could still look forward to and which I already missed – or to wonder aloud what the ghost was doing in the cold spot and why the school attracted so many of them.

'Later then,' Becky said at the end of break, meaning after school and before she left for Islington.

As things turned out, we never had the opportunity to talk again later because I was destined for another showdown with Mr Hatcher.

❖

So far that day the sickly light-headed feeling hadn't bothered me, which was something to be grateful for, I supposed. But in Mr Redfern's afternoon art class in the upstairs room with the best light in school, it came back with a vengeance, and something else – something strange and terrifying – came with it.

Today we had a still life session. Tables were pushed together to seat six to eight, and for those of us who'd forgotten to bring our own objects to draw – nearly all of us – Mr Redfern took a selection from the cupboard behind his desk.

There was a basket of wax fruit, a lump of fossilised stone with whorled eye-like patterns, a Wedgwood vase embossed with angels, and a grinning garden

200

gnome with a red-painted coat, white beard and pointy peaked cap. These were placed one to each table while Mr Redfern assigned us places to sit. I got the basket of fruit, Becky the vase. The gnome on Decker's table had a grin that looked weirdly unhinged.

'You'll think the subjects are dull,' Mr Redfern said before we began, 'which they are, but this isn't entertainment. It's about training your eye to see. Take in what's in front of you all at once, then look again closer, notice the details, the lines and contours and imperfections that go to make up the overall. Then think about which media to use. Would the stone look best in charcoal or pastel or paint? Your choice.'

An uneasy hush settled over the room. Mr Redfern retired to his desk and we set to work, heads dipping over sketch pads.

For the wax fruit I chose wax crayons. I began by roughing out the general shape in pale colours, outlining within that shape the individual fruits, but from the start I had trouble keeping it all in focus. The mound of bright apples, bananas and pears seemed subtly different each time I looked, as if they were being rearranged in the basket by unseen hands.

After five minutes the texture looked right but

not much else did. The bananas were banana shaped but the apples and pears could have been anything. You couldn't tell which was which. Every change I made, every line I added only made matters worse, and at times I had to look away to clear my head.

Soon others at the table were taking more interest in my work than their own. Even Fay De Gray watched with big baffled eyes. They all knew art was my subject, something I was supposed to be good at, and I knew what they were thinking, Ryan and Curly and all the rest. They were taking a kind of pleasure in seeing me get it so wrong.

In my sketch pad the fruit had become a blistered, rotting mass, all weeping and putrefied. Snorts and giggles broke out around the table, and now others at other tables were gawking too. There were always off-days, days when I didn't see clearly and the image I wanted to capture stayed just out of reach, but I'd never made such a hash of anything as this.

The others left their tables and came over to gawp. The picture was slipping further away from looking like fruit at all. Another line here, a patch of shade there, and suddenly it became something else – an abstract mess of colours all melting together, something a blindfolded chimp could've done.

You would've thought I'd never held a crayon before, that I wasn't in charge of this one now. The crayon snapped between my fingers as it whipped across the page, gouging the paper as it went and skidding on across the desk. I wasn't in control of it, but something was – the freezing cold something clutching my hand.

I dropped the crayon and jumped clear of the table. The rest of the class gathered around, looking from me to the vandalised sketch pad in amusement. Even Mr Redfern had made his way over and shook his head like a bystander at a traffic accident.

'What on earth is *that* supposed to be?' he said.

Whether he meant to or not, he'd just given 8C permission to gloat. They didn't hold back, and laughed freely, nudging each other and pointing.

He did that. *Him.*

A dull ache pulsed behind my eyes. The lights in the room seemed to brighten and streak. Through the crowd I saw Fay De Gray's astounded face, and Becky, close to tears, sharing the humiliation. The pressure gripping my fingers was only just starting to fade, but something else was taking its place. Bunching my hands into fists, I turned and looked around for Simon Decker.

He was the only one still seated. Alone at his table with the grinning gnome, he put down a red pencil and peered up with innocent eyes that seemed to say, 'What?'

That was all it took.

I threw myself through the crowd and straight at him, fists flying. The first blow landed cleanly, catching Decker so sweetly on the right cheek it swivelled him around on his chair. The next split his lip in two places as I carried him the rest of the way to the floor. I'd landed a good few more shots before Mr Redfern dragged me away by the scruff of the neck, clamping my arms behind me until my shoulders locked, just as the Vigilants had on the night they arrested me.

In the reception area outside Mr Hatcher's office, I sat on a moulded plastic chair next to Simon Decker. Decker stared off into space, working his way through a stack of paper towels from the washroom, mopping his busted lip and bloody nose. I didn't recall connecting with his nose but I supposed I must have. I'd been blinded by the red mist at the time.

We'd been here for twenty minutes, time enough

for me to cool off, but I still felt like one of those geysers in Mum's holiday snaps. Sooner or later the pressure inside had to find a way out.

If Hatcher asked me to explain why I'd done what I'd done, I wouldn't know where to start. But I couldn't tell the truth. I'd have to invent something. He'd looked at me in a funny way. Something like that.

A buzzer sounded on the desk. The receptionist reached in slow motion for her phone, listened a moment and then looked over.

'Mr Hatcher will see you now.'

Decker frowned at the red-stained paper towel in his hand, dropped it in the waste bin beside him and took up another towel. As we stood to go in, he turned to me with an anguished face, and to my amazement I heard him speak for the very first time.

'Why do you hate me so much?' he said.

FEVER

I could have given him a list, even if hate wasn't exactly the word. The changes we'd seen around school, the strange air, the constant needling and threats of detention – all of this I blamed on him. For all I knew, the lockdown was an idea he'd put in Hatcher's head – and I was certain of it after the meeting.

Decker didn't make a sound all through it, but his lips were never still. Hatcher had to be blind or spellbound, because if he noticed what Decker was doing he didn't comment. It seemed Decker was pulling the strings, feeding Hatcher his lines – and Hatcher had plenty to say.

I was a bully, he said, prone to aggressive and disruptive behaviour, disrespectful to staff and fellow pupils, attention-seeking, argumentative and sullen. My homework was often late or incomplete, shoddy and badly organised, showing a lack of attention to detail. My concentration was poor, my communication skills less than poor, and my general lethargy in class led him to suspect I was staying out late on school nights. None of which would look good in the next school report.

'One more thing,' he finished, 'and taking everything into account, it won't come as a surprise. You're suspended for the rest of the week.'

And as Decker whispered on, I couldn't help wondering if a few carefully directed thoughts of my own might seal up his mouth for good.

Becky had left by the time Mr Hatcher dismissed us. I walked home through De Beauvoir Town, kicking a plastic bottle along the gutter, slowing to watch a raven sail above the houses. I willed it to swoop down and become Mr October, who'd show me a way out of this mess, but the raven flew south and shrank into the distance.

Mum would throttle me, or at the very least ground me, and if she didn't hear the news from me it would find her on the grapevine eventually. I was grateful to find she wasn't home – I hadn't a clue what to tell her. In the kitchen I found a hastily written note she'd left, which said:

Honey, sorry to miss you. We're going walking on the Heath this afternoon, which will be freezing but the exercise and fresh air will do me good. After that Tom wants to take me to a little restaurant he knows – sounds very posh, the menus are all in French! But he speaks several languages so will save my blushes there.

Oh, and he has a little something he'd like to give you on Saturday after my appointment. I know you'll love it, but don't ask. I'm sworn to secrecy.

Won't be too late but I've put some goodies in the fridge for your tea. Enjoy!

Love, Mum. xxx

The thought of food made me queasy, and I wasn't all that curious about Tom's gift either. Was he being generous or was he trying to buy affection, pampering the kid to please the mother? Either way, I didn't particularly care.

Darkness was falling. As I went around the maisonette, turning on lights to keep the shadows at bay, the fever closed over me again. My balance was so rocky I had to feel my way along the walls. In the bathroom, I doused my face with cold water, then cried out in alarm at the stranger staring back at me from the mirror.

That couldn't be me. Those eyes like dark smears and the greying corpse-like skin couldn't be mine. I turned away to clear my head and looked again and touched the glass, and in the mirror the tiled walls tilted sideways. On rubbery legs I stumbled along the landing to my room and plunged headlong into the dark.

I was asleep before I knew it, but the sleep was shallow and restless, and twice I woke in a cold sweat, convinced I wasn't alone in the room. If I dreamt, I remembered only flashes – Simon Decker's cold gaze and split lip, the Vigilant's smile, Nathan Synister's leathery scarecrow mask and his clawed finger pressing my cheek.

The sickness deepened. The night stretched out. The room began to feel like a coffin. At one point I woke with my face buried in the boiling pillow as a car's sound system shook the building. Later, I came round to the thump of a door and a soft tread of footsteps on the stairs. Just before eight in the morning a hushed voice spoke from the doorway.

'You can't go to school like this,' Mum said, and by the time I looked up she was gone.

The nearest thing to a thought in my head came hours later, this time at noon with icy daylight squeezing between the curtains.

As she gets better, so you get worse.

At various times snacks and drinks appeared on the night-stand – sandwiches, soup, tumblers of fruit juice – and were taken away untouched. Then I felt Mum's weight on the bed as she dabbed my forehead with a cool flannel. I couldn't open my eyes.

'Mum . . . what's the time?' I yawned.

'Five after three, darlin'. Friday afternoon.'

Again she left and again I drifted. What she'd said didn't register until my next waking spell. I'd lost two whole days.

I finally made it downstairs that evening. Mum was in the living room, pondering a crossword puzzle in a glossy magazine. She looked up to see me swaying at the door, grabbing the door frame for balance, and threw the magazine aside and came to take my arm.

'Here,' she said, 'sit down.'

'Not used to standing,' I said.

'That's no surprise. It's been a while.'

She eased me into an armchair. I fell back, breathing heavily, the room and its furnishings slowly revolving around me.

'Wait there,' Mum said.

'I'm not going anywhere.'

She brought hot milk from the kitchen and perched on the sofa opposite me.

'This is all wrong,' I said. '*I'm* supposed to be looking after *you*.'

'Sometimes even carers need caring for,' she said. 'What good would they be if no one looked out for *them*?'

'Did I miss anything? It's weird, losing so much time.'

'Ellie came last night to keep me company, and your friend Becky phoned, quite worried about you. Also, I called the school to explain your absence, and they said—'

'I've a good idea what they said.'

'So what happened? They said you'd been in a fight, a very one-sided fight by all accounts. Doesn't sound like you at all.'

'It was nothing.'

'Three days suspension is not nothing, Ben. Is this true?'

'Suppose so, but there wasn't much to it. This new kid's been on my case ever since he joined the class, and I lost my rag with him, that's all.'

'So much worry,' she said. 'I remember you

going through a . . . difficult stage after Dad left, skipping school, threatening to run away from home. It's understandable when you're unsettled and unhappy and life seems so unfair. Are you unhappy now?'

'I'm fine,' I said.

'I'm not sure you are. You know you can talk to me if something's upsetting you. This isn't about my new . . . situation, is it?'

'Situation?'

'Because of Tom. Because if it is we need to work it out. I won't have you wasting away. You look dreadful.'

'It's the flu or something. And the fight was a one-off. It won't happen again.'

'It better not. You've never been in trouble like this,' she said.

Damn right, I thought. Trouble every day, everywhere. You don't know the half of it, Mum.

'What about tomorrow?' she said. 'Shall I just cancel our afternoon at Tom's? He won't mind. We'll do it another time.'

'Dunno how I'll feel tomorrow.'

'Let's see after my clinic, then. Who knows, the present he's got for you might make you feel better.

Shall I give you a clue? You've always wanted it but we could never afford it.'

Money again. Money in the air every time Tom Sutherland's name came up. Money on the skinning surface of the hot milk in my mug.

'He's trying hard,' Mum said. 'He wants you to like him.'

'He doesn't have to try and he doesn't have to buy me things. We've only met once and I haven't made up my mind about him.'

That took the wind from her sails, and she smiled, but not with her eyes. She needed my approval, my blessing, and I couldn't give her that yet. I missed Dad too much, but I felt bad for hurting her again. It had never been so hard to say the right thing.

By the time they returned from her Saturday clinic, I'd decided to tag along to keep Mum happy. Still a little shaky as I came off the stairwell and out to the path, I took one look at his car and nearly keeled over.

The white Cadillac limousine, long and sleek and gleaming, more than whispered money – it screamed it. A gang of hoodies had gathered round to admire it, checking their reflections on its polished surfaces. A rear window purred open and there were Mum and Tom, smiling out at me.

'Hop in, make yourself at home,' Tom said. 'How are you, sonny? Your mum tells me you've been out of sorts.'

'A bit better, thanks.'

'That's good.'

The limo's interiors smelt of new leather and were spacious enough for a coach party. I settled at one window, Tom at the other, while between us Mum shivered with pleasure.

'Isn't this something?' she said. 'I've never been so spoiled. Don't forget your seat belt, Ben.'

'Say hello to Hector,' Tom said. 'Hector, here's Ben.'

'Pleasure,' said Hector. The driver, fiftyish with an olive complexion and bristly silver hair, nodded at me in the rear-view mirror.

'So how did it go?' I asked Mum.

'The clinic? Couldn't have been better. The nurse was amazed! Said she'd rarely seen such good progress. I'm her star patient.'

'Brilliant news!'

'There are still some questions about my white

cell count, though, so they'll keep a close eye on me and of course I'll have to keep attending.'

'Still, it sounds really promising.'

The limo was already moving, but I hadn't realised until then. It was like moving on air, not a hint of a bump or a dip on the road. The hoodies, who'd lined up at the roadside to watch us go, turned away towards London Fields.

'Glad you could make it, Ben,' Tom said. 'Just say if you need anything. We'll do our best to make you comfortable. Here's a little thing to keep you entertained on the way.'

Mum's eyes twinkled as Tom reached for whatever it was on the seat beside him. She knew what was coming, but I still wasn't especially interested, at least not until he held out the gift, and then my jaw hit the floor.

'Take it,' he said, passing me a copy of *Detective Comics* issue 27 in a sealed plastic wrapper.

On the front cover the caped crusader swung from a rope above Gotham City, one arm locked around the neck of a criminal in a green pin-striped suit. *Starting this issue,* the cover said, *the amazing and unique adventures of The Batman!*

My hands trembled as I held it. The comic looked

new, unopened and unread, but it couldn't be an original. Mint originals were rarer than rare, highly sought after by private collectors and selling for astronomical prices. A genuine 1939 *Detective Comics* #27 in top condition would be worth more than most houses, many times more than the Cadillac we were gliding along in.

'Don't worry,' Tom said, 'I know what you're thinking. It's a 1970s reprint, although even those are hard to come by these days. I'm not crazy, I see the attraction – I have a soft-spot for hero and villain stories too – but I can't see how any comic could be worth millions.'

'Millions?' Mum was mortified.

'Over two million US dollars for the last rare one in March. Now which issue was that? Jog my memory, Ben.'

'*Adventure Comics* number one. The first ever Superman story.'

'And this is the first ever Batman and Robin,' Tom said knowledgeably.

'Only Batman,' I said. 'Robin came a year later in issue thirty-eight.'

'Yes, of course.'

'And how much is this reprint worth?' Mum asked.

'Oh, nowhere near as much,' Tom said. 'Only a thousand or so.'

She stared at it aghast. 'Good God. You said it was valuable, you never said *this* valuable. Tom, it's too much. Ben can't accept it, can you Ben?'

'No,' I said, reluctantly offering it back. 'Mum's right. I'd be scared to touch it.'

Tom Sutherland spoke calmly but with a firmness that put an end to the argument before it could begin. 'Donna, I insist. What's wrong with giving the boy something he's only ever been able to dream about? Open it, Ben, read it. That's what it's for. I'll be disappointed if you don't.'

He could be persuasive, I had to give him that. At the same time I had the uneasy feeling the gift was being forced on me. This comic, even a reprint, should be in a glass cage in a museum, not here in my sweaty hands.

The ride continued. I eased the comic from its wrapper, half-expecting a peal of thunder when I turned to the first page. *The Bat-Man*, it said. *The Case of the Chemical Syndicate*. Six brief but dazzling pages followed, ending with the revelation that Bruce Wayne had been the Bat-Man all along.

Tom and Mum chatted quietly as we went. Mum

giggled from time to time and I concentrated on the comic to filter them out. How would Dad feel if he could see the three of us now – Mum and this wealthy stranger, me with the hugely expensive comic on my lap and the whiff of luxury all around?

And I thought, he'd feel as easy about it as you do.

This wasn't me. It wasn't us. Mum had struggled hard and long to make ends meet and deserved a better life, but this one didn't fit her any better than Mr October's reaper costume fitted him.

The next time I looked up, we were coming down Haverstock Hill with the tube station on our left. Across the street below a cluster of bistros and shops was the bench where I'd sat one afternoon with Mr October after a call around the corner on Belsize Grove. The newly-departed, a 43765, had suffered from a heart condition and died of fright.

On the same side of the street was the telephone box Mr October had used that day, changing inside it for the next leg of his shift. Past the phone box, two shady figures with indistinct faces darted into a grocery store as if to avoid being seen. I stared after them, but they hadn't reappeared when Hector turned off the hill onto Downside Crescent.

Tom's place on Lawn Road was concealed behind a tall yellow stone wall which ran the entire length of the block. A security gate opened as if by magic as Hector pointed the Cadillac towards it and closed after us as he drove through. Sliding the comic back inside its wrapper, I sat up to look around.

'What about this,' Mum said, squeezing my hand. 'I'm so excited. It's a palace!'

The limo crunched over a gravelled forecourt, parking in front of a grand three-storey building with pillars flanking its stepped entrance and French doors letting onto balconies at every level. Despite the overcast day the house sparkled, reflecting light. Even a rare first edition issue 27 couldn't buy a home like this.

'Thank you, Hector,' Tom said, not waiting for the driver but opening the door himself, taking great care to guide Mum out by her good arm.

Stepping outside, I felt I'd just entered another world. The nearby streets were incredibly quiet, troubled only by birdsong and a rustle of trees. It was like being in the countryside, miles from anywhere.

A dark bronze sculpture stood on the forecourt, a reclining male figure. 'A Henry Moore,' Tom said matter-of-factly, seeing me stop to admire it.

'An original, unlike your comic.'

There were more precious works indoors – marble statues and busts and paintings. An eye-popping image of black and white waves overlooked a great stone staircase. A Bridget Riley, said Tom, and I didn't bother asking if that was an original too.

Like the records room at headquarters, the entrance hall and downstairs rooms seemed larger than they should be, their high ceilings and stone floors amplifying our footsteps as we went. At the rear of the house we came to a bright shimmering space where turquoise water lapped the white-tiled sides of a heated indoor swimming pool.

On the pool's far side, French doors looked out on a well-maintained landscape garden. Shrubs and dwarf trees were arranged on several stepped levels, and a narrow stream bubbled from a cluster of rocks on the right and disappeared underground on the left, dividing the garden in two. An arched bridge crossed the water towards a high walled maze, which stretched far into the distance.

'The maze is a gift to myself,' Tom said. 'It gives me a kind of peace and privacy I can't find anywhere else.'

'It's all so beautiful,' Mum said.

'But strange,' I said.

Tom looked at me. 'Strange?'

'I mean . . . the maze is so big and the next house along looks so far away.'

'Another property used to stand between here and there,' Tom explained. 'I bought the land and developed it into what you see now.'

'Seems like a great big expense,' I said. 'Buying a place just to demolish it and building a maze no one will use.'

He patted my shoulder. I flinched, but he didn't seem to notice.

'Well, I use it myself occasionally, and visitors sometimes do. In fact I've a hunch some of last month's guests are still inside, trying to find their way out.' He laughed. 'Joking aside, it is rather hard to navigate. If you like, I'll give you a guided tour before lunch.'

Mum shivered. 'It's cold out there. Suppose we get lost?'

'You won't if you stay with me,' he said, 'and you'll find the maze isn't at all cold. It has underground heating. At times you can hear the pumps working under your feet. Very faint sound, but it's there.'

He took us outdoors and across the bridge.

Silvery fish sparkled in the shallow stream. The air was chilly and a pale mist shrouded the Belsize rooftops, but closer to the maze we were met by a gush of tropical warmth. A map of the layout was fixed to a post noticeboard inside the entrance.

It was all mazes within mazes. Puzzle paths reached everywhere, some plotting courses that dwindled to nothing, others leading close to a central square before doubling back towards dead ends. The pathways quivered around the map, seeming to shape themselves into new routes even as we looked.

'An optical illusion,' Tom said. 'It isn't really moving by itself, but if you study it too closely, or not closely enough, it plays games with your eyes. My op art collection inspired the design.'

We'd just started inside when a sickening feeling of claustrophobia hit me. If anything, the headache that came with it was worse, and I had to stop for breath while Mum and Tom, walking ahead, turned left off the path and out of sight.

Against the near silence, birds twittered distantly and the garden stream babbled away. There was a subterranean rumble I felt through my legs, a thrum of heating pumps. I was wondering how far Mum and Tom had gone, whether they'd realised I was missing, when they reappeared at the head of the path.

They looked different somehow, their faces distorted and fringed with migraine lights. They hadn't changed, but the way I was seeing them had. I shouldn't have come. The sickness hadn't passed yet. In the same moment I heard Tom's worried voice – 'He's really not well, is he? Let's get him inside. . .' – the maze whirled around me and the grassy ground came rushing up.

Later, I wouldn't remember Tom catching me mid-fall or lifting me off my feet to carry me back to the house. I sank towards unconsciousness while a voice inside my head kept repeating over and over:

Something's wrong. Something's wrong. As she gets better so you get worse.

I managed to open my eyes for a second just before Tom took me indoors. I was staring straight up at the sky, and high in the mist a congress of ravens flew in formation, their dark forms spelling out words against the grey, and the words said:

**WE HAVE A LIST TOO
AND YOUR NAME IS ON IT.**

❧ 17 ❧
THE GREAT AND DANGEROUS

The doctor's name was Rosewood. He was an old friend of Tom's. They'd settled me on a sofa before a crackling fire in a large, dim living space. A mirror brightened above the fireplace when Tom opened a shutter to give his friend more light.

The doctor slipped a thermometer into my mouth and checked my glands and blood pressure, burbling in a mellow voice that nearly lulled me into a doze.

'Stand by, this may sting a little,' he said. A needle prickled the crook of my arm. 'Just a wee something to bring down your temperature.'

'Brave boy,' Mum said as Dr Rosewood packed away his stethoscope.

'Not brave, just sick,' I said. Being brave was something you had a choice about.

They moved to an adjacent room. From the tones of their voices behind the closed door I guessed the prognosis wasn't bad. Mum sounded reassured and even laughed at some remark Tom made before his doctor friend left.

I rested there until I felt brighter, more able to stand, and then crossed to the door and opened it a crack. In the next room Mum and Tom sat at a small dining table overlooking the misty garden. There were vases of fresh flowers all around the room and a spread of cakes, scones and sandwiches on the table.

They seemed unaware of me standing there and looked content and at ease in each other's company. Were they meant to be together, and would I have to get used to this? I wasn't sure I wanted to know. Hearing the door creak, they both looked up and smiled.

'Ah, the warrior returns,' Tom said. 'Here, Ben, can you face a bite to eat?'

Mum patted the chair seat next to hers. 'Sit down, hon. Dig in.'

'If this doesn't appeal I'll have the kitchen drum up something else,' Tom said. 'The chef's very good. Ran two of the best restaurants in town before I headhunted him.'

I wasn't hungry, but a glass of iced water from the table eased the parched and bitter taste in my mouth.

'Suppose I must've fainted,' I said.

Mum nodded. 'So you did. Good thing Tom saw it coming and caught you in time. We were just saying, weren't we Tom, we were wrong to bring you out so soon. We'll do this another time when you're well.'

Tom poured steaming tea into china cups. 'Dr Rosewood reckons it's the same thing he's been seeing all month, a three- or four-day bug at worst. Says you'll be fighting fit by tomorrow.'

'We'll get you home after this,' Mum said. 'That's where you should be when you're out of sorts.'

'Or Ben could rest here,' Tom said. 'There are plenty of guest rooms.'

'I'm fine,' I said. 'I can get home by myself.'

Mum was having none of it. 'Fat chance. You need mollycoddling.'

'I only need rest. There's nothing you can do at home, anyway, except sit around while I sleep.'

'Suppose I have Hector take him?' Tom suggested. 'Would that ease your mind? And if it's what Ben wants. . .'

'Sounds good to me,' I said.

Mum wagged a finger at me. 'Then be sure to call if you need anything and if you feel any worse you *must* let us know. I don't want to spend the day worrying.'

'There's nothing to worry about,' I said. 'You heard the doctor.'

'All right, you win. Have it your own way.'

Later, kissing me goodbye on the steps outside, she said, 'I wouldn't let you go if I didn't think you looked so much better. And he does look better, doesn't he, Tom?'

'Five times better, ten times.' Tom shook my hand with both of his and leaned close to speak confidentially, man to man. 'And you shouldn't worry either. Your mum's where she wants to be and I couldn't be happier to have her here. You do trust me to look after her, Ben, don't you?'

'Yeah,' I replied, watching her, not him.

'Terrific. Here, in case you need to ring.'

He pressed a business card into my hand and I pocketed it without looking at it. As I did, I noticed a distinctive smell about him, probably aftershave, similar to the miniature cactus's sweet-sour scent in my room.

'Don't forget your comic,' he said. 'I think you left it in the car.'

It was still on the seat when I climbed in. Hector turned the Cadillac around on the forecourt and Mum and Tom waved us off from the steps before turning indoors.

Let them be together, I thought, as long as I

don't have to see them together.

On the journey to Hackney I held the comic on my lap without opening it while Hector negotiated traffic. In Camden we moved slowly through a stop-start jam under the fiery gaze of the demons and Chinese dragons that clung to the walls above the shops.

'So how long have you worked for Mr Sutherland?' I asked.

'A very long time,' Hector answered.

It was our only exchange of the journey.

Twenty minutes later he pulled up outside my block on Middleton Road and waited while I unhooked my belt and slid out. The air was bracing, my breath jetting steamy trails as I leaned to the driver's door to thank him.

'Don't mention it, young sir,' Hector said. 'It's what I'm employed for.'

As he turned back to face the street, the light falling across his eyes turned his irises to vertical slits. It was only a flash, a brief impression, and Hector drove away without another word. Shuddering, trying to shake off what I thought I'd seen, I headed indoors. Now I really *was* seeing things.

I washed and put on clean jeans and my I SURVIVED BAD SATURDAY T-shirt. In the bathroom mirror I looked more like myself, pink rather than grey-skinned. It was strange how the sickness came and went. Even stranger, the scar Nathan Synister had etched across my cheek had faded almost completely. I could barely feel the marks with my fingers. I took a breath and let it out slowly. The world was steadying, at least for now.

I'd call Becky soon. We'd lost touch since midweek, and I was sure we had lots to catch up on. First, though, I wanted another closer look at the comic. As I took it to the bed and opened it, the sweet-sour cactus scent filled my nose, the smell I'd caught in the air around Tom. It still clung to the palm of my hand he'd shaken even though I'd only just washed it. The scent seemed ingrained, trapped in my pores, and remembering that handshake I stopped at the thought of something he'd said.

You do trust me to look after her, Ben, don't you?

And why exactly had he needed to ask that?

I looked at the comic. It lay open to the last page of Batman's Chemical Syndicate adventure and the first page of the second story. It wasn't the story I expected to come next. It wasn't the story that should have come next. I stared at it in bemusement until, piece by piece, everything fell into place.

Until today I'd never actually seen an issue 27 up close, but I'd read enough about it to know what to expect, and this wasn't it. The second story should be 'Speed Saunders, Ace Investigator: The Killers of Kurdistan'. Instead, leaping off the page in bold reds and blacks was something called 'The Great and Dangerous Adventures of The Lords of Sundown'.

The story, which ran to eleven pages, began with two demons sitting on rocks on a beach, watching the midnight tide. Far above them, above the headland, twin crimson moons coloured the sky, turning the sea blood red.

Tonight had been a travesty for their side in the eternal war. The fallout would soon begin. An hour ago in a hidden London alleyway a great battle had been lost at Pandemonium House. More than three hundred of their number had taken part, demons of every size and kind, and only a handful had returned safely home.

The senior demon, Nathan Synister, let out a deflated sigh, found a smooth flat fragment of bone on the ground and skimmed it across the water. It bounced two hundred and eighty six times before sinking. His red eyes, one of which never blinked since it lacked an eyelid, were troubled and far away.

'Someone must pay for this debacle,' he said. 'The Lords of Sundown have suffered setbacks before, but few as catastrophic as this.'

His companion, a junior entity named Luther Vileheart, looked up at the sound of his leader's voice.

'There'll be weeping and moaning tonight,' he agreed. 'Grieving on an almighty scale.'

'And that's just for starters,' Synister said.

'Yes, sir.'

In contrast to his leader, Vileheart had a smart, nearly-human appearance, dark featured, strong-boned and handsome – at least, handsome for a human. Under his robes he wore a black single-breasted suit and polished black Oxford shoes. A talented Shifter – like all Shifters he could transform at will – he specialised in undercover work among mortals. Only the diamond pupils of his snake eyes marked him out as a friend in these parts.

'At least we didn't leave empty-handed,' he said. 'At least we brought back a handful of souls to replace those we lost. We could've fared worse.'

'Not much worse,' said Synister. 'Look around you.'

Luther Vileheart looked.

Fires blazed across the land, and as far as the eye could see the shoreline was littered with skulls and other bodily parts, a carpet of dead, dry bones. The demons stared in silence, overwhelmed by the scale of the defeat.

Something was stirring in the far distance, close to the headland. Vileheart noticed it first, a movement so slight it might have been a death's head moth twirling inside the murk.

'See that, sir?' he said. 'It comes our way. It could be a messenger, don't you agree?'

'More than that,' Synister said as the figure slowly emerged from the darkest furthest corner of the beach. 'Unless I'm mistaken, that's our master Lord Randall Cadaverus.'

Vileheart drew breath. The horseback rider was suddenly clearer to see, black robes swirling around it as it crossed the shore. He had never met the master face to face. In fact, he'd heard that very few had looked his malevolence in the eye and survived.

As the rider drew nearer, another shape came into view alongside it. A short distance out to sea, a gilded cage kept pace with the horse, gliding just above the churning water. Inside the cage were three wraiths, scrawny and scraggy with tormented faces and trailing white hair, tendril fingers gripping the bars of their prison. All three wailed for mercy in an unsettling cat-like chorus.

'Attention,' said Synister. 'Get off that rock and stand to meet your master. And whatever you do, remember not to look at him directly.'

The rider was nearly upon them. They heard the splinter of bones under the great black stallion's hooves. They saw the steam from its nostrils tinted red against the sundown sky.

The prisoners trembled in their cage, looking down on the lapping water. It wasn't the cold, dark sea they feared but what lived inside it, the many excitable fast-moving shapes flickering under its surface.

The horse drew up before the two demons, crushing a grinning skull to dust underfoot. Its robed passenger dismounted, carrying a dark bundle under one arm, which he now set carefully on the ground. The bundle, which appeared to be composed of shadows, squirmed and twisted.

'Your maleficence,' said Synister. 'To what do we owe this honour?'

'There's no honour in defeat,' Cadaverus said. 'There's nothing but everlasting shame. The whole of Abhorra mourns tonight.'

With long tapering fingers he pushed back the hood from his face, the sight of which caused the caged beings to sob and the two demons to draw breath and avert their eyes.

'This should have been a great victory,' Cadaverus said. 'Instead we're left licking our wounds. How many losses, Synister?'

'Hundreds we know of,' Synister said. 'Many more still unaccounted for.'

Cadaverus watched the horizon, where an army of servants were digging a hole the size of a meteorite crater in the land. It would take countless nights of hard labour to fill that hole with the defeated. The fatalities were piled high as a hill.

The dark bundle stirred at its master's feet, emitting a slow hiss as it began to work itself into a shape.

'This will not stand,' Cadaverus said. 'Tonight Pandemonium House opened its defences, gifting us a chance we've waited decades for, and we let it slip away. We should've taken at least a hundred and ninety-six souls, and how many did we win in the end?'

'About seventeen,' said Synister, embarrassed.

'Yes, and those were virtually worthless too – security staff, drones, minions. What happened to those I sent you for? The ones with gifts of hearing and sight?'

'We failed,' Synister was forced to admit.

'I'd say so.' Cadaverus's aura darkened. 'The question now is, who answers for this? Who pays the price?'

Nathan Synister fell to his knees. 'Not me, your miserableness. It's true I planned the siege, but my duties elsewhere kept me away until late. By the time I arrived, matters were already out of hand. I'd delegated staff, but they were unequal to the task.'

'Excuses, excuses.' Lord Cadaverus turned next to the junior demon Vileheart. 'And what was your role in this fiasco?'

'None, sir.'

'None?'

'That is, I wasn't directly involved. I'd done some reconnaissance beforehand, and I had a minor role in guarding the children known as the Willows, the ones who perished in a house fire before we captured them.'

'And you failed at that too. The children escaped.'

'We were overpowered.'

'You outnumbered our enemy fifty-to-one,' Cadaverus seethed. 'Thank your stars, you two, I'm in a lenient mood, and be glad these three buffoons –' He gestured at the cage. '– made an even worse mess than you.'

Lord Cadaverus glared at the prisoners. Two looked up with the timid faces of woodland creatures caught in a hunter's crosshairs. The third nervously eyed the choppy water.

'Who was in charge of the conference room triptych?' Cadaverus asked. 'The stained glass windows we used to enter their headquarters?'

'We were,' the prisoners answered faintly.

'And when the appointed time came to unlock the windows and let loose our forces, who gave the order?'

'He did,' said one.

'Him,' said another.

'They did,' said the third, not daring to look.

'Your timing was abysmal,' Cadaverus said. 'Not only did you let a precious lost soul, Jim Harvester, slip through your paws, you delayed long enough to give the Ministry every chance to regroup. Gross incompetence. Where do we find these fools?'

'One simple little task and they couldn't even do that,' Nathan Synister gloated.

'Be quiet.' Cadaverus spat on a rock. His acid spittle fizzed and burned a hole straight through it. 'If I want your opinion, I'll ask for it. Don't think passing the blame will lighten your own burden.'

'Apologies, my Lord.'

Cadaverus refocused on the wraiths in the cage. 'This should have been our night of nights – Samhain, a time when darkness rises and the balance of power swings in our favour. How in the name of all that's unholy did you manage to mess that up?'

The wraiths cowered behind the bars, shaking and mewling.

'Out of my sight, the lot of you,' Cadaverus said, clapping his hands, and the cage descended into the sea, slowly enough to allow him the pleasure of hearing the prisoners beg for forgiveness one last time before they were eaten alive.

Their screams travelled the length of the shoreline, reaching as far as the gravediggers on the horizon, all of whom stopped to listen. The cage was now half-submerged, surrounded by thousands of frantic splashes. The feeding frenzy had begun.

The two demons looked on, well aware of what

237

was taking place. This was, after all, the Carnivore Sea, the smallest but deadliest strip of coast in Abhorra, on the least populated, most northerly tip of the isle. There would be other punishments, some worse than this, before the night was over. This, they knew, was only the start.

The screaming stopped. The sea was a deeper red. Cadaverus waited until the water calmed and then with a motion of his hand brought the cage back above the surface and across to dry land. The cage floated in space for a moment, then tilted sharply aside, spilling its cargo of bones through the bars and onto the beach.

'A fair and just punishment, eminence,' said Nathan Synister. 'Those wraiths undermined everything we did tonight.'

'I don't need to be told what is and is not fair punishment,' Cadaverus growled.

'Indeed not, my Lord.'

'Do you seriously believe those three half-wits are the only reason our plans went belly-up?'

Cadaverus's robes flowed around him in the airless breeze. The horse grew restless, shuffling its hooves over brittle skulls and collarbones.

'The plan was flawed,' said the junior demon, but

immediately fell silent, realising he'd spoken out of turn.

Synister stared at him contemptuously.

'A curious observation,' Cadaverus said. 'Your name is Vileheart, correct?'

'Yes, my Lord. Luther Vileheart.'

'The same Vileheart who took the life of the Harvester man among others?'

'The very same.'

'Would you care to explain the statement you just made?'

Vileheart swallowed, feeling the heat of Synister's gaze. He couldn't bring himself to look at the scarecrow any more than he dared meet the master's eye. Instead he stared at the bundle of darkness writhing at Cadaverus's feet.

'Well?' Cadaverus said. 'Where was the flaw in your leader's plan?'

'The plan was unsubtle,' Vileheart said. 'We could have taken Pandemonium House unawares, but by staging a full-frontal attack we gave them time to adapt. Some of their operatives have considerable powers, powers we underestimated, and we played into their hands—'

'Treasonable talk,' Synister interrupted. 'I'll deal

with you later, minnow.'

'Quiet,' Cadaverus said. 'Let the entity speak. Continue, Vileheart.'

'That's all, your unworthiness,' Vileheart said. 'Except to say, it seems to me there are other ways to inflict maximum damage on the Ministry and its members.'

'And they might be?'

'This is nonsense,' said Synister. 'There was no flaw in the plan. This is a flagrant attempt to subvert—'

'Silence!'

Cadaverus's patience had run dry. He twitched a tapering finger at his second-in-command, sealing the scarecrow's mouth. Synister's eyes rolled back in shock. He tugged at his sewn-up lips with the talons of both hands, but the thread which held them was unbreakable. Then, recognising the futility of fighting the spell, he sank down onto a rock in a strop.

'Now,' Cadaverus said. 'Your thoughts, Vileheart, please. . . You were saying?'

Luther Vileheart gathered himself to speak. 'My Lord, I never meant to question the wisdom of my superiors. I have the highest regard for them, but I believe we need a different approach against the Harvester boy and his companions. Rather than

bellow in their faces, we should insinuate and suggest
. . . if you follow.'

The dark bundle rolled over and shuddered,
sprouting four stalk-like limbs, which clawed and
kicked at the air.

'Fascinating,' Cadaverus said. 'An agent after my
own black heart. So what do you suggest? What tack
should we take?'

Seated on the rock, Synister let out a muted protest.
Ignoring him, Vileheart continued.

'First, your lowliness, identify our enemy's
weaknesses, their Achilles heels, if you will. Some
months ago I recognised the boy Harvester's mother
as one such weakness, a heavy-hearted woman
doted upon by her son. I approached her at her
place of work, a rather drab dining establishment,
posing as a customer and showing her an act of
kindness.'

'Kindness?' Cadaverus was stunned. 'A baffling
human trait. So what form did this act of kindness
take, and what was the reason for it?'

'It was a simple gift, my Lord. Local currency,
money, of which the woman had little. What mere
mortals call "tipping". I did this to give the woman
some hope.'

'Hope? Even more baffling. Why would you do that?'

'I've spent many days under cover among the living, my Lord, and I've learnt that nothing hurts them more profoundly than hope first given and then snatched away. In extreme cases it can destroy a person's faith.'

'Ingenious, Vileheart.' Cadaverus was greatly impressed.

With a shake of his misshapen head, Nathan Synister looked away in disdain.

'And when a mortal loses hope and faith,' Vileheart went on, 'I've observed that it's often because they've lost something else – something the species calls love.'

'Love. . .' The word lodged like a pebble in Cadaverus's throat. 'I've heard of it. And what then?'

'Then, my Lord, without love, hope and faith, our enemy have nothing to fall back on but luck. And luck can never be relied upon. Without those qualities—'

'I'd hardly call them qualities,' Cadaverus said.

'Indeed, malevolence. Without those . . . traits, it becomes much easier to capture their precious souls. Those who've lost the will to live offer little resistance.'

'And this is how it will be with the Harvester woman?'

Vileheart nodded. 'Yes. In fact I was on the verge of success some weeks ago, but then she was struck down by a sickness – a human condition. She's since been harder to reach, but if I persist. . . She's the key to breaking her son, the boy who's causing us so many headaches. I hear she has plans for travel and a vacation, and away from her son's influence it should be easy to arrange a chance meeting and enter her life with a view to destroying it.'

Cadaverus looked out at the crimson night, the twin moons bearing down on the water like furious eyes.

'Yes,' he said. 'A subtle approach. Whispering, not shouting. I see how that might work. Very good.'

Luther Vileheart bowed his head. 'I hope it wasn't too bold of me to suggest it, sir.'

'I would've been more concerned if you hadn't.'

As Cadaverus spoke, the bundle he'd brought to the shore began to sit upright, flexing its limbs and growing a stumpy head and neck. There was a squelching and grinding of sinew and muscle, and from its mouth came a haunting, baby-like cry.

The horse drew back, snorting red-tinted clouds.

Vileheart stared enchanted as the being remoulded itself first into one shape, then another, finally taking on the appearance of a human child of perhaps eleven or twelve years old. A knowing smile spread across its face as its features steadied.

'Lord Cadaverus...' it said in a scraping, whispery voice.

Cadaverus paced back and forth on the carpet of bones, filled with renewed inspiration.

'Vileheart, here is our newest recruit,' he said. 'This entity is much like yourself, a Shifter well suited to undercover work. And that's what you'll do – you'll re-enter the world of mere mortals and bring back souls that are worth a real price. A handful of Vigilants won't fit the bill. Bring me the gifted and their loved ones.'

'Yes, your unworthiness,' Luther Vileheart said.

The child nodded, a determined look in its eye, but it didn't speak again.

'As for you,' Cadaverus said, rounding on Nathan Synister. 'This is your last chance. It's all very well sending in the big guns, the Deathheads, the Mawbreed – you're old school and that's what you know. But these are new times. The war is changing. We don't want the enemy to see us coming over the hill, do we?'

With a flick of his fingers, he removed the stitching from Synister's mouth.

'No, eminence,' Synister said. 'We'll do better this time.'

'You must.'

'Yes, eminence.'

'Excellent, then we're set.' Randall Cadaverus looked past the shoreline of bones to the dark horizon, a calm settling over him. 'You know what's to be done, so take your chance and don't fail me again. This Halloween isn't over yet.'

In the action-packed scenes that took up the next few pages, a titanic struggle played itself out – the heroic Lords of Sundown versus their dark adversary, the Ministry of Pandemonium, and the Ministry were on a hiding to nothing.

One artist's plate showed a girl who resembled Becky Sanborne caught in a tornado inside her home, pinned to the ceiling by an all-conquering Nathan Synister, red eyes aglow.

'I take it all back!' Becky's caricature screamed.

'You were right all along!'

The scarecrow replied as all comic villains do. 'Heh-heh-heh. If only all my opponents were so wise!'

Another illustration showed – and here I had to pause as the full horror of it dawned on me – a man and a woman, Tom Sutherland and Mum, Luther Vileheart and Mum, walking hand in hand into a tunnel. Against the muddy walls in a thought-bubble above Vileheart's head were the words, 'Now . . . my plan is complete. The boy will never recover from this. . .'

And here I was in the next plate, straining to keep hold of Mum's wrists while an unseen force dragged her deeper inside the tunnel. 'I was wrong, we were all wrong!' I cried above Mum's screams. 'They lied! The Ministry is an abomination . . . but don't blame her. Don't take her, take me!'

I had to force myself to look at the last image. I already knew what it would be. In this one, Mum was gone, taken by the dark, and as I reached sobbing into empty space after her, the scarecrow's silhouette stood over me, barking in triumph:

'See what happens when you oppose the Great and Dangerous, taking sides in a war you can't possibly win?'

In a small box caption below this last plate, black letters on a yellow background announced: *More fantastic adventures from the Lords of Sundown next month!*

Somehow I had to make it stop. I couldn't let the story come true. If I stayed here much longer I wouldn't stand a chance, because being in this room was the very thing making me sick.

The enemy had been weaving its web, spider-like, ever since Halloween, and now we – me, Mum, Becky, everyone I cared about – were tangled so deep inside it I couldn't see any possible way out.

We were nothing but prey, and the spider was already home.

❦18❦
MAGIC AND LOSS

I flung the comic across the room. It struck the shelves, scattering action figures and dislodging the clover chain box, which hit the carpet and fell open. Inside, the clover chain looked shrivelled and black, poisoned by the same noxious air that had been poisoning me.

It had to be the cactus. What else could it be? Its sickly scent was making me gag even now. I took it to the window and hurled it as hard as I could past the balcony. Its terracotta pot disintegrated on the street and a moment later the plant became mush under the wheels of a police patrol car speeding from Lansdowne Drive, siren howling.

Downstairs, collecting my jacket on the way to the door, I remembered Sutherland's business card. If I phoned, would he let me speak to Mum? And would she even believe me? She'd been blind to what he really was ever since that first generous tip in the Mare Street café. It wouldn't be easy to convince her, but I had to try.

The number rang and rang, and the voice that eventually answered was so calm and composed it made my flesh crawl.

'Hello Ben,' Luther Vileheart said. 'Did you enjoy the story?'

'I'm going to kill you.'

'Heh-heh-heh. We'll see about that. You'll have to find me first.'

'Put Mum on,' I said. 'Put her on now, or else.'

'There's no point,' he said. 'She already knows.'

The words were knives, shredding what was left of my nerves. 'Don't you dare hurt her.'

'I wouldn't dream of it, at least not yet. We're not often in a position to take mere mortals whole.'

I didn't even want to guess what that meant. 'I'm coming over. Then we'll settle this, just you and me.'

'We're leaving,' Luther Vileheart said. 'It's too late. *You're* too late. If only you'd insisted on keeping her with you. Why did you leave her, anyway? Why give her up so easily? Just think about that, Ben Harvester, when you're mourning your loss.'

The line clicked dead, and in the silence a thousand accusing voices crowded around me. She was my responsibility – sick or not, I should have stayed, and whatever happened to her now would be down to me.

Aching all over, I dragged myself down the stairwell to the street, expecting to see a mocking told-you-so message on the wall across the way, but the wall remained blank.

A 394 bus was approaching the stop outside the park. Its route would be a slow round-about haul to Angel but it would get me there faster than I could walk, and at Angel I could catch the tube. The driver gave me a weary look as I touched my pass to the Oyster reader, then set off suddenly, spinning me halfway towards the back. I fell onto a seat and stared blindly out the window while a recorded female voice spoke the name of each stop.

The smell of Vileheart's touch still clung to my fingers. The poison had been slowly and surely administered and its side effects were still churning away in me. For Mum's sake, I had to find a way through it, ignore the aches and pains and show her – show the enemy – what I could do.

The bus jerked to a stop at Geffrye Museum. I'd been in fixes before, I'd called for help without knowing it, and Lu and Mr October had answered. 'You rang,' they'd said mysteriously, my distress signals having been logged by dispatch. So why weren't they answering now?

Where were they?

Darkness had closed over the streets by the time I left the underground at Belsize Park. I stumbled down the hill and along Downside Crescent, retracing the route the limo had taken this afternoon.

Luther Vileheart's security gate was closed, the property sealed up like a fortress. I paced the block from end to end, looking for another way in, but the walls were as tall as the maze's, too high to scale. Still, I had a strong sense of the house standing empty on the other side. If Mum were inside, I'd know, I'd feel her there. But the silence was absolute, and the little hope I'd come here with was fading. I had only one choice now, only one place to go.

Fifteen minutes later I was back at Angel, stumbling along Upper Street, half-blinded by headlights and fighting my way through the crowds. Outside the York pub a mob of shoppers blundered straight through me, shouldering me aside into a group of drinkers who stood under a pall of cigarette smoke. The one I collided with, a man with thug's eyes and clenched teeth, cursed and pushed me away.

'Watch your step, mate,' he grumbled, and the others leered as if they knew the kind of trouble I was in and found it amusing.

I turned onto Camden Passage, my heart racing so violently I thought it would burst. The Saturday trinket stalls were still busy, the casual shoppers drifting between them casting their eyes over jewellery, art and obscure, out of print books. Barrel organ music swelled as I moved aside, keeping my back to the entrance, awaiting my moment. I couldn't go through until sure that no one would see.

A man with a baby strapped to his back glanced my way as he ambled past. A trio of goth girls followed him, not seeing me, and a young couple with two squabbling kids pointed at the barrel organist's monkey to turn the children's attention from their argument. The marmoset monkey ran excitedly in and around the crowd, offering its bowler hat for change.

Here was my chance. It had to be now, while the monkey was centre-stage. Scanning the stalls one more time – no one even vaguely aware of me – I backed into the shade and felt behind me for the opening in the bricks.

The opening wasn't there.

I'd entered here so often I should be able to find my way blindfolded by now. I'd miscalculated, I'd felt in the wrong place, that was all.

I tried again, skimming my fingers across the rough surface, left a fraction, right a fraction. Still nothing. Forgetting the stalls and their visitors, I turned to face the wall, feeling with both flattened hands for the spot where the gap should be.

It wasn't there. It should be, it always had been before, but it wasn't there now.

The crack had sealed itself up. Why? Because I'd been suspended from duty? Was this how it would be until they took me back . . . if they ever took me back? Just now, that seemed a very big if indeed.

'Let me in,' I pleaded, panicking now, pounding the walls. 'Please let me in. . . Please. I need your help!'

I sank to my knees, twisted around and sat on the cold, damp ground, looking up through glazed eyes. The faces around the stalls were little more than shapes in the dark, but quite a few of those shapes were staring. Others hurried away, ignoring me, as city dwellers generally hurry from drunks and homeless folk slumped in shop doorways and alleys.

'Please. . .'

'Must be mad,' someone murmured. 'Kid's talking to a brick wall.'

Another passer-by tossed a coin at my feet, taking pity on the poor, destitute, crazy kid he'd taken me for. At that moment, I didn't feel too far away from being that crazy kid, either.

I couldn't stay but I didn't know where else to go. At least here I had a chance to catch Mr October or other staff coming or going, but that would only draw attention and I'd already risked giving the Ministry's location away. These people at the stalls would be curious now. I had to move on.

Log jams of buses crawled along Upper Street, brakes whining, engines radiating steamy heat. Lu might emerge from the traffic at any time with Mr October and Becky in tow, or perhaps Sukie would find me first, tracing my screaming thoughts through the hustle bustle. But none of them were anywhere to be seen.

The nose-to-tail bus queues rolled on. I was watching in a daze, hardly seeing the sleepy-eyed passengers crammed inside, when it hit me; I suddenly understood what I'd been missing – something so obvious I couldn't believe I'd overlooked it all the way here.

The unnamed dead were absent. The sunken-eyed lost souls on their never-ending journeys across town simply weren't there. Come to think of it, they hadn't been on the underground either, not on the busy platforms or the overloaded trains between here and Belsize Park. I was so used to seeing them wherever I went I took them for granted now.

So where had they gone all of a sudden?

A quiet voice tugged at my thoughts, trying to tell me something important. I hurried on, covering my ears, listening harder. It was Sukie's voice, a memory of something she'd said during the lockdown, the night they gave me my marching orders.

It's like when the magic goes. . .

That had to be it. The magic was dying. It must have started the moment Luther Vileheart offered me the cactus from his brown paper carrier. He'd brought me one gift and taken away another – the gift which had opened the Ministry's doors to me in the first place.

I wouldn't die without it. I'd be like anyone else. But without it I couldn't see well enough to help anyone, not even myself. Without it I couldn't help Mum.

I took off down Duncan Street. If demons were

coiled inside the shadows down there I'd never know it. If there were newly-departeds around the next corner I'd pass by without ever noticing them. Their world, the world alongside this one, had vanished. It had made itself invisible, and I was running on empty to find it again, without a clue where to start looking.

I was out there all alone in the dark.

Late afternoon rolled into night. Touring the city, sometimes on foot, sometimes by bus or train, I began to appreciate how the unnamed must feel on their travels. The journey had no beginning, no end, only a hopeless rush towards nowhere.

I needed to be where newly-departeds would most likely be, not under dripping bridges or on cold park benches, but where they could be found in numbers. Wherever they were, the Ministry's field teams would be too. But without Mr October and Lu to guide me, these places weren't easily found. The care homes would never let me inside, and there were places inside hospitals I couldn't go to alone.

A & E at the Whittington off Highgate Hill was as far as I got. I waited in a stuffy corridor, watching medical staff dash around carrying clipboards and supplies. An ambulance crew with deflated faces rolled in a trolley on which a covered body lay with drips and tubes attached. A muscly forearm poked out from the sheet they'd draped over the passenger. I didn't need special senses to know he was dead on arrival, but I saw nothing of his ghost or any Ministry agents in attendance. Another trolley brought a drunk man who held a bloodstained white patch to one eye and cursed in a thick slurry voice at the crew trying to help him.

Before long the chemical smells and the echoes of voices and metallic utensils made me queasy. I was starting away when a smudge of red hair left a side room along the corridor and made for the hospital exit. I only caught the man's face for a second, but I was sure it was Rusty, the field team leader. Passing the open doorway he'd just left, I saw a portly nurse tugging a sheet over the face of a white-haired old lady in the bed.

'Rusty!' I called, hurrying after him. We hadn't crossed paths often – he'd been in Stratford on Bad Saturday and at HQ during the lockdown – but he would know me and I might persuade him to call in. 'Rusty, hold on!'

Outside, a misty rain prickled my face. An SUV sped from its parking spot, lifting spray from the ground as it passed. That must be Rusty's team, heading to the next call on their list. I gave chase to the junction, but the vehicle didn't slow and its blacked-out windows stayed shut. Its tail lights moved into traffic and disappeared down the hill.

I kept walking the way it had gone, shivering inside my jacket. My face grew numb in the icy rain and my lips were burning. I walked six or seven blocks before losing count, continuing on in a trance.

The rain stiffened. Lights streamed along the gutter. I stopped at a street corner, lost, without a clue where I was. And I knew as I stood there, freezing and trembling, that Vileheart's plan was almost complete. I could feel Mum drifting away.

Nothing hurt more profoundly, he'd said in the comic, than hope given and then snatched away. It could destroy a person's faith and without faith I couldn't see anything, the entry to Pandemonium House would stay sealed and the Ministry wouldn't come racing in like cavalry to the rescue. I could stand here all night without seeing

Lu's face among the traffic.

The night spun out. I wandered from street to street, blind in the driving rain, sometimes ducking inside shop doorways for shelter, holding myself against the cold and shaking. In one unlit doorway something stirred at my feet, and I jumped back, remembering the bundle on the beach of bones in Abhorra, the entity taking shape. But the man at my feet was elderly, rank smelling and wrapped in damp blankets. He looked up through the dark, lungs wheezing.

'Help me, son,' the homeless guy said. The sound and smell of him told me he didn't have long. I could stand at the roadside and flag someone down, but the longer I spent with him the less chance I had of tracing Mum. The effort of speaking seemed to drain him, and he rolled over into an immediate sleep while I took off in the rain, not looking back.

The sickness churned through my insides as I followed one unfamiliar street to the next. The city had become strange and cold and alien, as if another city with different architecture and different thoroughfares had overtaken it. There were no landmarks above the rooftops, no London Eye, no BT Tower. Everything hung behind a grey curtain, lost at sea. The rain fell less heavily now, but I was moving through clouds.

I travelled another hour, maybe two, before I turned another corner onto more familiar ground. Through the sheeting rain I spotted a face I knew – an unfriendly, even monstrous face, but one I was glad to see all the same. It was the red and black face of the dragon clinging to the wall above the Max Orient restaurant in Camden.

I could've cried. After circling the city for hours in search of something I'd never find, I'd somehow landed on Camden High Street, a fifteen minute walk from the Vileheart residence where I'd begun. I had nothing left, no gas in the tank, but at least from here I could make it home, and from home I would start over again.

Heading for the lock, past the brightly coloured boots and goth skulls on the walls above the Cold Steel tattoo parlour, I had a feeling that even these streets were subtly different, altered in ways I didn't understand. Perhaps it was their emptiness. The freezing rain had driven everyone indoors and the world had gone into hiding.

A bus surged through a puddle, soaking my jeans. Cold cramps tore at my legs, and every step felt like my last. At the Regent's Canal bridge I came to a standstill, needing to rest but afraid to stop. I could seize up completely and freeze to death if I stayed long.

Watching the raindrops ripple across the black water, I realised I could walk straight home from here along the waterside, or I could leave the canal at Islington to camp outside the Ministry's wall until someone turned up. At this hour, in this weather, there wouldn't be many people around to witness the comings and goings.

I was about to move on when someone patted my shoulder. I turned to see three boys about my age but stockier, their mischievous eyes peering out from the hoods of their coats.

The taller of the three was the one who'd turned me around. His jaw rolled like a camel's around a wad of chewing gum. Behind him, the other two exchanged a look that reminded me of the Ferguson twins in 8C – a dark secret passing between them.

'Mate, can you help us out?' said the taller kid, who I guessed was their leader. 'We're trying to get home but we're broke. Can you lend us a quid?'

'Sorry, I don't have anything,' I said.

'Are you sure? Why don't you check?'

'I'm not lying.'

'Never said you was. You might be mistaken, though.'

'Sorry,' I said, turning away. 'I've got to get home too.'

I knew what was coming but I couldn't run and I didn't get far. I'd taken only two paces when the leader darted around in front of me and the others clamped my arms from behind.

'Hold him,' the leader said.

'We're holding him, innit? Check his clothes.'

'I'm checking.'

Raiding my jeans' pockets front and back, the leader came away empty-handed except for my Oyster pass, which he tossed over the bridge in disgust.

'And his jacket,' said the one holding my right arm.

'I'm checking that too. Shaddap. He ain't got nothin',' the tall kid spat.

'Told you,' I said.

'Shaddap you,' he said.

'Them trainers look all right, though,' said the one on my left. 'We could have them.'

'Get him down,' the leader said, then whispered

close to my face, 'Don't try nothin' or we'll mess you up.'

They lowered me to the cold ground, yanking my arms up behind me, jolting my shoulders. If I'd been able to move I wouldn't have put up much of a fight. The strength for fighting had left me a long time ago. I'd lost so much in the city tonight, and the city hadn't finished with me yet.

The leader began to untie my laces, smacking his lips around the gum.

'Hey you! Yeah, you!'

The shout snapped out of the dark like a firecracker. There was a sound of booted feet slapping through puddles, approaching from the lock side of the bridge.

'Get off him! Leave him alone!'

Startled, the muggers dropped me at once. The back of my head whacked the ground as they took off towards the dragon, and I lay there with the rain drumming my face. For several seconds I floated away, then fought my way back again as the boots slowed to a scrape nearby. A small figure, much smaller than it had sounded, knelt over me, easing me up to a sitting position.

'Ben?' A girl's voice, a whisper. 'You're Ben

Harvester, right? From Mr October's team. I *thought* it was you.'

She wiped matted hair from her brow and watched me with big dark eyes. It took me a long moment to place her. 'You've had a bad night, I can tell,' said Kate Stone.

'A bad day. A bad week.'

'Here, let me help.'

She re-tied my laces, then hooked a hand under my arm and got me to my feet. She wasn't tall, the top of her head barely reaching my chin, but her strength was surprising.

'Where did you come from?' I said.

'Other side of the lock. We had a 1663 around there not five minutes ago. I'm on my way home from the shift. I live over there. . .' She pointed past the dragon in the direction the muggers had fled. 'Along Arlington Road. Can you walk, do you think?'

'I'll try.'

'Looks like you've been to hell and back. What happened?'

'Long story.'

'I've got time to hear it. If you like, you could come to my mum and dad's. You could have a hot bath and we'd fix you something to eat, give you dry clothes and get you home.'

'Thanks, but I need. . . I need to find Mr October. My mum's in real trouble and I need—'

'What kind of trouble?'

'The worst kind there is.'

I told her about it as she supported me from the bridge towards the lock, and she listened intently, sighing and nodding. The story came out in a muddle and I was raving before I finished, but she seemed to get the general idea.

'This is dreadful,' Kate said. 'We have to call it in.'

'That's all I want.'

'Leave it to me.'

We turned onto empty Camden Lock Village, where a bronze lion statue spread its great paws on the ground before it and a row of brightly painted half-scooter chairs overlooked the water, their seated back ends butting up against the low wall in front of them as if they'd been frozen halfway through the journey inside it.

'Look, I don't have a direct line to Mr October,' Kate said, 'but I bet I can get hold of Joe Mort. He's still in the field, and if I can reach him he'll relay the message.'

'Would you? But it could be too late.'

'Try not to think that way. If this demon took your mother alive then there's a good chance she's still alive, OK? You have to believe that.'

'I don't know what to believe anymore.'

'Wait here,' she said. Leading me to the first half-scooter under the shelter, she wiped water from its seat with a handkerchief and settled me onto it. 'I'm going now, OK? I'm going to call. I'll tell them where to find you, so don't go wandering off.'

'I won't. I don't think I can move from here, anyway. Kate?'

'Yes?'

'Thanks.'

She smiled, dimple-cheeked. 'No problem. Just doing my job.'

She hurried away, and I listened to her boots slapping the ground until they faded. Sagging and trembling on the scooter seat, I felt a deep sleep coaxing me to stop and give in. My eyelids closed by themselves.

Perhaps I did drift off for a time, because when I opened my eyes again I didn't know how I'd arrived at this spot or how long ago.

The journey came back to me gradually a little at a

time, until I remembered the last thing: Kate dashing into the night to make the call. When had that been? Seconds or minutes ago?

'Please hurry, please come. . .' I said under my breath, and then tensed at a movement behind me.

A shadow spread across my knee and on across the scooter's seat. I twisted round and looked up at the silhouette standing over me. Long-coated and top-hatted, it wasn't a shape I recognised, not at first, not until it leaned closer, craning forward on the balls of its feet, an ancient cackle rising in its throat.

'Gotcha!' the silhouette said. 'But this is no time for practical jokes. This is urgent, top priority. Ben Harvester, get up off that vehicle and come with me!'

✦19✦
THE BUTCHER AND THE
SHUFFLEHEADS

t was a new persona, not one I'd seen before. In this form he could pass for a distant relative of the pirate's, shorter and skinnier, thinner-faced and pointy-chinned with wild straggles of silver-streaked black hair jutting from under his lopsided top hat. The long dark coat flapped at his shins as he steered me back along deserted Camden High Street. The soles of his bright red, oversized clown boots crackled on the pavement.

'Not meaning to rush you,' he said. 'You're in no fit state, but that's why we should hurry. This won't wait until we return to headquarters. There's no time. We'll have to improvise.'

'What's happening, Mr October?' I said. 'Where are we going?'

'Not far. There's a little place around the corner, an office we keep for times like this. The poison running through your veins has to be tackled soon, not later.'

'How serious is it?' I was scared to ask.

He shook his head and somewhere in the recesses of his clothing he discovered a black leather doctor's bag, which he slid out to carry at his side. It bumped against his leg as we went.

'Potentially lethal,' he said, 'but its effects are reversible. How long since you were first exposed?'

'Dunno. Maybe a week. I suppose it was when—'

He hushed me, glancing away. 'Wait. We'll continue this in a moment. See there. . .'

Two figures on the far side of the high street were keeping pace but not looking towards us. Their outlines were familiar but their faces fell into shade. If these weren't the same two spies I'd been seeing all week they looked pretty close.

'See how bold they're becoming,' he said. 'They've kept to the dark ever since their defeat, but now they're gaining confidence. They're starting to come out. This way, quickly.'

He led me off the high street along a short alleyway and on through a tangle of residential rows with pink and blue painted walls, up one street and down the next. Faint and breathless, I had to strain to keep up, and he kept slowing to encourage me on, the anxiety clear on his face. Whoever those followers were, we needed to lose them.

'Along here, not much further,' he said, turning onto a mews of cottages with doors that opened straight onto the cobbled street. This place had the same out-of-time feel as the alley outside Pandemonium House, and I wondered if, like Eventide Street, it was far off the map.

'So far so good,' he said, rattling a large bunch of keys and unlocking a door on the right. 'They're still behind us, but they know we're on to them so they've gone into hiding. Follow me.'

We stepped inside a low-lit entrance hall, which brightened as he adjusted the hissing flame of a gas lamp whose light bloomed up the bare plaster walls. The floor was cluttered with office materials, file boxes and dusty manuals and tall piles of books. A rusty bicycle with a missing wheel leaned against the wall below an uncarpeted wooden staircase.

'Excuse the state of the place,' he said, keeping the front door open a crack to peek outside, then locking and bolting it after him. 'The work just keeps piling up. This way.'

At the end of the hall he ushered me through a door on the left. The room we entered was as fusty and old as the receipts office, but it clearly had a different purpose. The ceiling-high shelves were stuffed with medical texts and journals, books on anatomy, toxins and surgical procedures. At the far side, near the curtained window, was a handbasin with a paper towel dispenser and a trolley bed with a pillow but no sheets. A mahogany desk and two chairs stood by the near-side wall under a medicine cabinet and a variety of medical posters which showed diagrams of male and female bodies with vital organs colour-coded in soft pastel greens, purples and pinks.

'Take a seat, boy,' he said, planting his bag on the desk. He removed his long coat, under which he wore waist-high trousers and a checkered waistcoat buttoned to the throat. Finding nowhere to hang the coat, he draped it over his chair.

'Who were those two following us?' I asked.

'Who do you think? But never mind them – we have to get started.'

He began rooting through the cabinet, scattering bottles and blister packs of pills to the floor. Finding what he wanted, he returned to the desk and poured a dense deep green liquid from a narrow bottle into a thimble-sized measuring cup and pushed it towards me.

'Drink this. It will stall the effects while we find a way to reverse what the toxin is doing.'

Lifting the tiny cup between my thumb and forefinger, I sniffed at it, then downed it in one. It didn't have the bitter medicinal aftertaste I'd expected, but a sharp minty flavour with a slight burn and long aftertaste.

'Not so terrible, is it?' he said. 'Something like crème de menthe, but I don't expect you'll have tasted that at your age.' He seated himself, less flustered now. 'So tell me about the poison. You were saying, before we were rudely interrupted. . .?'

'It started about a week ago, but I didn't know it was poison then. I thought I had the flu.'

'Yes, of course. An insidious thing, a slow, systematic, airborne dosage.' Finding a small notepad and pen in his desk, he scribbled something in an illegible hand. 'And you said this came by way of a cactus plant?'

'I didn't say. Did Kate tell you that?'

'Her report was very thorough.'

'So where is she now? I thought she'd be with you.'

'She did what she had to and went home,' he said. 'Like you, she isn't allowed to work all hours.' He frowned at his notes, scribbled something else. 'I've heard of these cacti. They don't exist in this world.

The enemy bring them in from the dark territories they call Abhorra. This particular genera, toxi-poloxi, is native there.'

I moved restlessly on my chair. 'Well, I wouldn't know about that.'

'You wouldn't, and no matter. I'm certain it's the source, though, so at least we know what we're up against. But think hard now, boy . . . could the poison have been delivered in any other way?'

I shook my head. 'Not that I know of.'

He scribbled on. 'So you weren't fed anything, given anything to eat or drink against your will. You didn't eat at Vileheart's house, did you?'

'No, but. . .' I stopped, feeling the trace of a memory fluttering just out of range.

'No unusual foodstuffs, concoctions or medicines?' he went on.

'Wait a minute.' Suddenly it came to me, even though I'd been semi-comatose in a darkened room at the time. 'Vileheart's friend, Dr Rosewood.'

'What about him?'

'He saw me at the house this afternoon, gave me an injection, he said to take my temperature down.'

A light snapped on behind his beady eyes. This was significant. Dropping the pen, he rounded the desk and was on me in a flash, feeding me a thermometer, shining a pen-torch into my eyes while his thumb pinned my lids open.

'Confound it,' he sighed.

'Why? What's wrong?'

'Well, obviously that was no ordinary doctor but Vileheart's accomplice, and the injection he gave you was more of the same – a more concentrated dosage of mescahydrocarciomyathalate.'

'Mesca what?'

'No matter. There's less time than I thought.' He rounded the desk to take up the pen again. 'How do you feel? I don't mean just generally. How do you feel this very minute?'

In truth I couldn't tell. The wasted, heady feeling had never been far away all day. At the edge of my sights the small room was gently warping like a reflection in a hall of mirrors.

'Funny,' I said. 'Just funny. Like everything's distorted.'

'And the headache and the sickness?'

'Not so bad, but still there.'

He jotted this down, then looked at me again. Under his clenched brow the small dark eyes shone like a rat's, and his skinny chin twitched.

'What else?'

'Not sure.' The room was turning more violently. 'Look, can't you fix me up for a few hours? While we're sitting here we could be looking for Mum. That's why I wanted you.'

'First we have to fix you, then we'll fix the mere . . . the woman . . . your mother,' he said, and I blinked at him uncertainly. 'As you are now, boy, you're no help to her at all, and no use to the Ministry against such a great and dangerous enemy.'

'Then who. . .' The words rolled slow and thick off my tongue. A line of communication had been severed somewhere between my vocal chords and my brain, and I couldn't be sure what I'd say next. 'But how . . . but when . . . but can't you send someone to find her?' I managed to ask.

'It's all in hand,' he said.

Another thought, or part of a thought, was trying to reach me. There was something here – either in the room itself or in something he'd just said – that didn't add up.

'Where's Lu?' I asked.

'Pardon?' The small eyes were still and unblinking.

'If this is so urgent, where's Lu? Where's your

transport? How will we get from here to wherever Mum is without transport, and what about the other stops on your list?'

'That's not your problem. Our priority is to deal with what's happening to you before it gets out of hand.'

'But we should help Mum first. I'll take my chances.'

'You're delirious,' he said. 'Here, come with me. We need to get you settled before I begin.'

He was right. I was close to fainting, too weak to help anyone. When he took my arm I obediently followed to where he was leading me. The room and everything in it drifted in and out with his voice. A stomach cramp doubled me up.

'What was it you gave me to drink?' I asked sleepily.

'Don't question what I'm doing,' he said. 'This is for your own good.' The next few words after that were lost.

The soft mattress on the trolley was as welcoming as a real bed. As he helped me onto it I realised how badly I needed sleep, how long it had been since I'd slept properly. But an alarm was sounding in my brain. As I tried to sit up I realised I couldn't because of the first strap he'd secured across my chest. Now he was tying a second strap around my legs.

'For your own protection,' he said. 'A precaution to keep you from hurting yourself.'

'Mr October, please. . .' I began, and it was only then that everything began to make sense. 'You're not – you're not Mr October, are you?'

'Don't be silly.' He worked at the straps until three of them held me fast, then looked at me inquiringly, head cocked to one side. 'Who else would I be?'

'Dunno, but you're not him, that's all I know.'

'Delirious, as I said. Why would you think that?'

'Because of what you said, nearly said about Mum. What did you nearly call her?'

'I don't recollect. Probably nothing. In your present state you must have misheard.'

I lunged at him. The straps held me down. 'You said, "mere".'

'I said what?'

'You said, "mere" and then stopped yourself. You were about to call her a mere mortal.'

He sniffed and stroked his chin. 'See how the toxin does its devious work, first attacking the body, then the mind. If you'll be quiet for a minute we may still be able to do something about it.'

Now he brought the black leather bag and set it on the trolley by my feet and started fishing around inside it. A clink of metal objects did nothing to calm my nerves.

'Prove it,' I cried, rocking under the constraints. 'Prove to me you're Mr October.'

'And how am I supposed to do that?' he said, rifling through the bag. 'You know who I am.'

'No, I don't.'

'This is preposterous.'

'Show me something else,' I said, nearly choking. My mouth had become arid, bone dry. 'Show me *someone* else, another of your faces, and I might believe you.'

'If you insist.'

He did change then, only a little, not enough to convince me, only enough to plunge a needling terror into my heart. The thin jaw-line hardly wavered, the gaunt cheeks sucked inwards, and across his face came a slowly spreading grin, big-toothed and stretching from ear to ear.

'Seems you're as sharp as they say,' said Professor Adolphus Rictus, number one on the Ministry's Most Wanted list. 'It's true, there's no denying it. But now the time for talk is done.'

He swept from the bag the tools he'd been searching for – surgical instruments of some kind, one in each hand. In his left he held what looked like a chrome-clawed eagle's foot with gleaming needle-sharp talons, and in his right a long, silver, two-pronged fork. The instruments were alive in his grasp, quivering and stabbing the air, twinkling in the light.

'See how excitable they are,' Professor Rictus said. 'They know a good strong soul when they scent it.'

'Let me up,' I cried. 'Let me out!'

That was the furthest thing from his mind. The chilling grin broadened, dominating his entire face as he bent over me.

'You've been a long way today, boy,' he said, 'but you have no idea how far you still have to go. Shall I take you the rest of the way now?'

Gasping and snorting under the straps, I couldn't take my eyes off those hideous surgical tools as he swiped one against the other like a butcher honing his knives. The fork's prongs flickered. The claw-handed instrument flexed its talons, which squirmed like serpents on a gorgon's head. Professor Rictus eyed them with a gleeful grin.

'Lucky I found you first,' he said. 'Then again,

I suppose you're past believing in luck. It's hard to believe in anything at all when your own kind turn against you.'

Again he swished the tools together, and they twitched with pleasure, eager to begin the work.

'What?' I said. 'Who turned against me?'

'The Ministry of Pandemonium, of course. You've heard their silence. I heard it too, many generations ago. The Ministry's silence is the most dreadful sound imaginable.'

'You murdered Miss Webster's brother. You murdered loads of good people.'

The instruments collided again, and I heard a low tremble of thunder somewhere.

'Murder?' Professor Rictus said. 'I'd say that's a bit harsh.'

'You stole Mr Webster's soul.'

'Among others, yes.'

'Then you killed him. It amounts to the same.'

'I acquired his life force, but after that he gave up of his own accord. You'd be surprised by how many mere mortals continue on without their souls, dead in life. Not much of an existence, it must be said, but he didn't even try.'

The thunder again. Or maybe not thunder,

something more like a pounding knock. So far Professor Rictus seemed unaware of it.

'Sad for you that it should come to this,' he went on. 'At least you may think that now. But you'll see a glorious day before long, and then you'll wish you'd joined us sooner.'

If I'd had any spittle I would've launched it into his face. 'Wherever you take me, I'll keep on fighting you. You'll be sorry you ever thought of this.'

'Tough talk for someone in your position,' he leered, the corners of his grin now meeting the crow's feet beside his eyes. 'In time you'll see reason and wonder why you let yourself in for this. You'll be glad you were betrayed and thank the one who betrayed you.'

A feverish sweat ran into my eyes. 'Who betrayed me? How? You're lying!'

Professor Rictus steadied the eagle-clawed surgical tool. Its slender stem gleamed in the dingy room, and I braced myself for the first cut. The chromium talons flexed and tensed at my throat, then closed around my jacket zipper, easing the jacket open to my waist. Professor Rictus widened his eyes at the logo on my T-shirt.

'So which Bad Saturday would that be?' he said.

'Last week's or this one?'

'Go to hell.'

'Silence, please. I'm contemplating the first incision. And keep still, too. For your own sake it's best if we make this as brief and painless as possible.' His eyes were an insane match for his grin as he added, 'But it won't be painless, I promise you that.'

With the forked instrument he made a delicate movement in a straight line from the neck of my T-shirt to my solar plexus, slicing the material as if easing a knife through soft butter. The material separated with a faint ripping sound, but he hadn't touched my flesh, not yet.

'Well, it's goodbye and hello,' he said. 'See you in our homeland when we're done.'

He held both hungry twisting tools of torture aloft and ready.

Another growl of thunder resounded through the room. This time it was nearer and this time he heard it too. He froze, and the grin slipped a little. His gaze grew cautious and flashed from the door to me, then back to the door as it exploded inwards, bringing hinges and splintered chunks of door frame with it.

They were storming the surgery.

If the sight of the foursome at the doorway filled

me with joy and wonder, it must have struck cold fear into Rictus's heart. As his face fogged over, the deadly tools stopped moving, becoming worthless scrap metal objects in his hands.

'Oh. . .' he murmured. 'Oh, rats.'

For a split second he looked torn two ways – stand his ground against what was coming or rip me to shreds anyway, just for the sake of it – but Lu was on him before he could blink. Tearing through the room like a lightning bolt, her face as seriously set as a mask, she delivered a forceful high kick that wiped the grin off Rictus's face once and for all.

It did much more than that, too. The professor's head spun a full ninety degrees on his shoulders until it faced backwards. His top hat went flying and he dropped the surgical tools. This happened so quickly I hadn't even registered the others who'd come, but I saw the first of them now.

Tweaking his hat back on his head, Mr October flashed a silver tooth at me. Behind him were two indistinct figures standing in the shade in the hall. As Mr October started inside, Professor Rictus made his move, lurching at Lu with both arms outstretched while his turned-around face glowered back at me. Unable to see where he was going, he blundered past Lu, who stepped neatly aside, and thundered into a bookcase, bringing an avalanche of weighty reading matter down on himself.

The thickest and heaviest of the books, *Discorporation: A Surgical Reference*, landed squarely at Lu's feet. She looked at it a moment before picking it up, straining under its great weight, and batted Professor Rictus around the head with all her might – and Lu had considerable might.

The massive blow swivelled his head back the right-way around, face forward. His eyes twirled in their sockets and he faced Lu with a sabre-toothed snarl.

'Backwards . . . forwards . . . make your bloody mind up, will you?'

And he came at her again, catching her around the midriff with a tackle that brought the two of them careering over me and over the trolley bed to the floor with a crash that shook the room.

Mr October was meanwhile unfastening the straps, his fingers working speedily, his eyes searching my face with some concern.

'The poison,' I said.

'We know. Don't worry – our medical staff are ready and waiting.'

'Is it bad?'

'Bad enough, but we know what to do. We've seen this before.'

'He said it was lethal.'

'And why believe anything *they* tell you?' Mr October said. 'He's nothing but a butcher with a liar's tongue.'

The trolley rocked and skewed aside as Lu and the soul thief Professor Rictus slammed into it. Sitting upright, I leaned over to see Rictus holding Lu in a headlock, the strain of keeping her in place written across his vein-bulging temples. Lu was slippery, though, and in an instant she'd reversed the move, screaming from the effort as she locked her left hand to her right forearm and dug a knee into the small of his back.

'Aren't we going to help her?' I said, eyeing Mr October's companions as they came forward. 'Aren't *they*? And who *are* they, anyway?'

'I'll explain about them soon enough,' Mr October said, 'but honestly, does she look like she needs help? Let her have her moment. There's a little family history here.' He checked my eyes with a light as the professor had before him, then signalled me to open my mouth. 'Wider. Say Ah.'

'Ah.'

'That's good.'

'What family history?'

The struggle continued. Seizing Professor Rictus by his straggling hair, Lu began smashing his face against the washbasin, time and again. There was a crunch of bone on porcelain, and one yellow tooth pinged off a water pipe.

'Can you stay upright by yourself? Try swinging your legs round,' Mr October said. 'We've long suspected Rictus had some connection with the deaths of Lu's family. To this day her parents and siblings remain off our radar and not on any record. We believe the mah-jong cheat who drove her father to such desperate ends – bankruptcy and suicide – was one of Rictus's associates.' As Lu hurled the battered surgeon across the room and another bookshelf exploded around him, Mr October added, 'Lu believes this too, and has long sworn revenge, so it's best to let her work it out of her system.'

Lu came around the trolley, snarling and trembling. I'd rarely seen her so focused or furious. Professor Rictus scrambled blindly about the floor as she advanced, her wrists making slight but rapid movements at her sides, movements I'd seen her make in combat before. Whatever the invisible weapons she was able to summon up were, I knew they were lethal.

'Now I'll destroy you,' she told Rictus, but the bark of Mr October's voice stopped her.

'Lu! A reminder that destroying him isn't possible, since strictly speaking he's isn't alive. All we can do is banish or bind his kind where they can do no more harm. Besides. . .' He signalled the other two, who came forward to hoist Rictus to his feet. 'We need to find out what he knows of the enemy's plan. Take him to headquarters and punish . . . I mean interrogate him there.' Then he said to me in an apologetic tone, 'Not that I approve of Lu's methods, young man. We should lead by example, although sometimes drastic times do call for drastic measures.'

Lu looked thwarted. She turned to Mr October with the pleading eyes of a little girl whose toys had been confiscated.

'Just one more?' she asked politely.

He waved her on. 'Oh, go on, if you must. Just don't give me that look.'

It was all the encouragement she needed. Without any physical warning, she lashed the heel of a hand into Rictus's face, mashing his nose.

Professor Rictus sagged in the arms of the other two. He hissed and spat as they cuffed his hands, his features twisting and contorting to reshape themselves, but he hadn't the strength to change.

I looked at the two stern shapes who held him. Apart from their smart dark overcoats and highly-polished shoes I could tell very little about them. Even at close range their faces were oddly blurred and unclear and when I squinted I hardly saw them at all.

'Who are they?' I asked Mr October. 'I've been seeing these two everywhere, outside my home, on the high street just now. . .'

Mr October said, 'They're the Shuffleheads. No one knows their real names and no one knows what they look like. Their faces are ever changing to conceal their true identities – which makes them well suited to undercover work. It's a hard skill to master, too. I tried it once and it made me queasy. Had to lie down for a while. They were assigned to watch you and your mother because we knew the enemy had singled you out. If not for these two we wouldn't have found you tonight. It's them you should thank, not us.'

The Shuffleheads nodded at me, courteous and efficient, their faces unreadable.

'I'm Dan,' said one.

'I'm Don,' said the other.

'But not for long,' they both said together.

'Take him away, fellas,' Mr October said, and Lu had to restrain herself from delivering a further crushing blow to the professor before they dragged him out. She sighed and turned back, giving me a little bow.

'Sorry, got a bit carried away there,' she said. 'Are you OK, Ben?'

'I am now. I will be.'

'He will be as soon as the toxins are out of his system,' Mr October said. 'Better call ahead, Lu. Tell the medics we're on our way.'

CONVALESCENCE

The clinic was on an upper floor at Pandemonium House. While the staff settled me into a warm bed in a white-walled room, Lu joined the Shuffleheads and their prisoner below ground in a place Mr October called the truth cellar.

I'd heard of these other levels at headquarters but hadn't been allowed on either before. Apparently the building, like its records room, had no limit. There was more to it than I could possibly imagine, and its mysteries deepened every day.

In the private room, Mr October sat a while at my bedside before his next shift. I'd arrived in the clinic shaky and dehydrated, and my reaction to the journey between the walls from Camden Passage, Mr October said, was a classic sign of my condition.

'The mescahydrocarciomyathalate in all its forms does one thing and one thing only,' he said. 'Unfortunately for us it does it very well. You've inhaled it and been injected with it, and at the butcher's surgery you drank it undiluted. Most mortals wouldn't be affected – in fact they'd find the smell and taste quite pleasant. But to the gifted, that kind of dosage can be lethal. The toxi-poloxi cactus is cultivated by the Lords of Sundown for this very reason, to neutralise the weapons we use against them, which it does by attacking our higher senses – the skills that make us what we are.'

'Not sure I understand,' I said, watching a blue-uniformed nurse wheeling a drip stand inside the room. She was in her mid thirties, fair-haired, and wore glasses with loud red frames. 'You mean it takes away our powers, like kryptonite does to Superman?'

'Something like that,' Mr October said. 'Your gift isn't destroyed but dormant. The sickness shows you're missing it, the way you'd miss your own soul if it were taken.'

'So that's why it all went away, why I couldn't see the messages on the wall or even draw a simple picture at school?'

'Correct. It's why you couldn't find the entrance to headquarters today.'

'But I'll start to see again?'

'Most definitely,' the nurse said, setting up the apparatus by the bed. 'We need to run some tests and drain those nasty toxins away, and we'll give you something to help you sleep. Excuse me, Mr October.'

He stood back while she adjusted the drip bag on its stand and slipped an IV needle under the skin on the back of my hand, sealing it in place with tape and feeding the drip tube along the bed frame where it wouldn't be tripped over or trodden on.

'I'm scared of sleeping,' I said. 'I shouldn't sleep. I have to find Mum. . . I just have to.'

'We're on it,' Mr October said, very briefly becoming the elderly and kind-eyed empathiser. 'As we speak, there are very capable field operatives in all parts of the city working flat-out to bring her back.'

'So it's not too late? There's still a chance?'

'Of course, and there's little you can do until the good people here have treated you. We want you back full and strong. Rest assured, as soon as we hear anything you'll be the first to know.'

I wished I could feel more reassured. 'Tell me she's still alive,' I said. 'If I only knew that, it would give me something . . . some hope.'

'Can't tell you what I don't know,' Mr October said. 'Did Vileheart give any indication of his plans when you spoke?'

'Only to say they were leaving. And another thing that struck me as odd. He said they didn't often get to take mere mortals whole.'

'Hmm. I see.' Mr October mulled this over. 'Presumably he meant intact, body and soul, in other words very much alive.'

The relief I felt, hearing that, didn't last long.

'Which doesn't mean she's out of danger,' he continued. 'She isn't the first they've stolen this way. There are scores of recorded cases, including friends and family of some of us here . . . many of them taken alive but never seen again.' My distress must have been obvious because he hurried on. 'However, some – a few – were rescued and eventually returned to normal lives, as normal as their lives could be after such a trauma. All you can do, young man, is prepare yourself for the worst while hoping for the best. That should be your outlook all the time.'

'But where do they go?' I said. 'The ones who were saved, where were they found?'

'In this very city, but hidden. In holding.'

'Holding?'

'Held captive as the fire children were. But in cases like these, the living are held for briefing and debriefing before the descent . . . the journey to the place where the less fortunate ones were taken, the ones who never came back.'

'Abhorra,' I murmured.

'That's one name for it.'

'Like in the comic. The Lords of Sundown story.'

'That old propaganda,' Mr October said. 'They really should check their facts before they rush to print, you know. But we'd better leave this here. Soon the medics will give you something to help you rest and in the morning you'll see more clearly. We'll speak again on my return.'

Soon after he left me the nurse came again. She hummed an ancientspeak song as she checked my vital signs and gave me a knock out shot.

'Mr October says we're to take extra special care of you,' she said, scribbling on a chart which she hung on the foot of the bed. 'Which is a bit of a cheek, if you ask me. We take extra special care of all our patients. The bathroom's there, by the way, and the buzzer's above your head if you need anything. Now you should rest.'

I woke only once in the night, half-remembering an urgent question I'd meant to ask Mr October. The clinic was quiet and my room had none of the suffocating air of most hospital wards. While I listened to the soft-shoed comings and goings of staff on the corridor the question slipped away, forgotten, and sleep carried me off again.

In the morning I woke to find Becky napping in the armchair by the bed, making soft whimpering sounds as though running from something in her dreams. Suddenly she woke with a start, blinked and rubbed sleep from her eyes, pulling me into focus.

'Morning,' I said.

'Ben? I've been so worried,' she said. 'But it's going to be fine, we'll get her back, I swear. This is top priority. They're suspending all leave and recalling some agents who took early retirements. Mr October's had a long meeting with the Overseers, and he's got them onside. There's a rumour he threatened to resign if he didn't get the manpower he wanted.'

Too much information too soon. I couldn't take it all in. 'How long have you been here?'

'Oh, a while. Probably hours. So anyway, everyone's on call, something big is about to happen, I just know it. And Mr October needs your help. He said to give you these.'

She lifted a carrier bag from the floor and took out an A4 sketch pad and a pencil, placing them on the bed.

'What are these for?' I said.

'He wants you to draw something. The face of Luther Vileheart, last time you saw him. They have shed-loads of pictures of him on file, but Mr October believes he's using another face now, or was until yesterday. Anything you can remember will aid the search.'

'Not sure I can,' I said, thinking of last week's still life lesson. 'Suppose I can't do it anymore?'

'It'll come to you. The least you can do is try.'

She settled down to watch. I opened the pad but hesitated, the pencil wavering over the page. At first I couldn't see what I needed to. The picture of Mr Redfern's art class was much clearer, the basket of fruit and the invisible something gripping my hand. I nearly leapt out of my skin when Becky's fingers brushed mine.

'I know you can do it,' she said, 'and if you can – if you do this one small thing – you'll know you can do everything else. Don't give up.'

So I set to work, trying to summon up Vileheart's human face as it appeared in the photo taken by the harbour. This face wouldn't keep still for long, and the first marks I made on the page were messy and confused because all I could see in Vileheart's eyes was the monster hiding behind them.

Becky coaxed me on. 'Take your time. It's OK. Clear your mind and see what you have to.'

Turning to a clean page, I tried to use my imagination instead, picturing Luther Vileheart as Mum might have seen him the first time he entered the café where she worked.

I saw him in his business suit, at odds with the usual clientele of hoodies and pensioners, taking his seat and studying the menu, deciding on the six quid roast dinner. I saw steam rising from the kitchen area behind the counter where an old cash register pinged like a typewriter when its drawer opened. I felt the smooth laminated menu in Vileheart's hands as he smiled up at Mum, who smiled back and scribbled his order on her little pad.

She didn't know it, but her life had just changed. He hadn't come to dine but to plant a seed. She had no way of knowing that this charming man had her husband's blood on his hands. She would remember his kindness, paying for the meal with a twenty-pound note and insisting she keep the change, a gesture that would give the rest of the staff something to gossip about for days.

The next time he came he would do the same

again, and it sickened me to think that on those nights we'd eaten takeaways from Hai Ha's paid for by Vileheart's tips. Mum wouldn't see him again for a while but she wouldn't forget him, and when he came to her rescue in the HiperDino supermarket she almost felt she knew him.

'There,' I said, pushing the pad away and falling exhausted back on the pillows.

'See?' Becky said. 'If you lost it, it came back to you just like magic. You can still do it.'

So I could, even if the effort had worn me out. It was a start, a sign of something reconnecting, a cog turning one notch and clicking solidly into place. The portrait was complete, a good likeness too, so good that a part of me wanted to take up the pencil again and gouge out the subject's eyes.

'Wonder Boy.'

For a second I thought Becky had thrown her voice, but the voice came from the doorway where Kate Stone stood looking in.

'Sorry, am I intruding?' she said. 'They told me I'd find you here, and I wondered how you were doing, Ben. You were in a real state last night.'

'Was that only last night?' I said. 'Seems like weeks ago.'

'Mind if I join you? Only a quick hello 'cause I can't stay long. There's a big meeting downstairs soon.'

Becky was quickly on her feet, straightening her clothes, refastening her hair with a scrunchie. 'Sure. That's fine. I was leaving, anyway.'

'You don't have to go,' I said. 'They have enough chairs.'

'No, there's too much to do. Busy busy busy. You know how it is.'

'Well, thanks for coming, and for helping.' I offered the sketch pad. 'Will you take this to Mr October?'

'He'll be up to see you in a while. Give it to him then. And I didn't really help, Ben. You did it all by yourself.'

On her way out she passed Kate without a word or a glance. Kate waited while Becky's footsteps faded down the corridor, then came to the bedside, not sitting but leaning over to see the portrait.

'That's terrific, Ben. You're so good at this. Who's he?'

'A demon called Luther Vileheart.'

'Right. The one the Ministry's looking for. Is that how he looks now? The pictures I've seen of him aren't anything like this. You can't always tell from a face, though, can you, what's really behind it.'

For some reason that reminded me of the question I'd meant to ask Mr October. Did Becky know something, and was that why she'd been so cool towards Kate just now?

'Kate?'

'Yes, Ben?'

'About last night. . .'

'You don't have to thank me,' she said.

'I wanted to. But tell me . . . what happened after you left?'

The question caught her off-guard. She took her time before answering. 'I did like I said. I called it in.'

'Where? To dispatch?'

'No, to my team. They were still in the field. Why?'

'No reason.'

'There must be a reason to ask something like that. Did I do something wrong?'

'Dunno,' I said. 'You tell me.'

This time she didn't answer at all. Her eyes became timid and mouse-like and her smile drained away.

'You see,' I said. 'I've been putting two and two together and it keeps coming up five. If you called in, how come Professor Rictus found me first? He came straight to me. And how come Mr October didn't hear of it? It was the Shuffleheads who traced me in the end.'

Kate looked shell-shocked. 'But I did. I did what I said.' She started edging back from the bed. 'Why are you doing this, Ben?'

'You were here the day we had the lockdown, weren't you? The day Sukie was screened.'

'Yeah, I was here some of the time. So were a lot of others. Half the staff were called in, remember? That doesn't mean anything.'

'Well, it means something to me. Yes, there were others here. But you were the only one I saw in Camden last night.'

She was looking at me in open-mouthed shock.

'What's your special gift, Kate?' I said.

'How do you mean?'

'Everyone they recruit has something that makes them special. Becky senses things no one else can and Sukie hears every thought in the house when she's not being blocked. So what's your talent? Why are you here?'

She looked at the floor, shaking her head. 'I don't know, Ben. I see strange lights sometimes, and sometimes I get flashes of things before they happen, but that's it. I don't even know why they want me here. They say I have potential, developing skills that aren't quite there yet, but I'm out of my depth, really. It's just, I feel more at home here than I do out there.'

'I think there's more to you than you're telling,' I said.

'There isn't. There really isn't.'

'And you know what else? I think Sukie didn't know what she was dealing with when she recommended you to Joe. If you were able to screen her thoughts, she'd never know you were working for the other side.'

'That's not true. I don't even know what screening is. I'm no traitor,' she said, her eyes shining.

'The Ministry will decide about that,' I said.

She'd heard enough. She made for the door in tears, only turning back at the last moment.

'Why are you being so mean, Ben?' she said. 'It's not right to say things like that about people you don't really know. And I only came to say hello. I thought we were going to be friends.'

She ran out, sobbing, nearly colliding with Mr October in the doorway as she went.

'What was that about?' Mr October said, staring

after her. 'Why the waterworks?'

I stared at the wall, not wanting to discuss it, smarting from the betrayal.

'That was one of Joe Mort's team, wasn't it?' Mr October said.

'Yeah, her name's Kate.'

'Ah, of course. Miss Stone. The girl whose call was intercepted last night.'

'The . . . what?'

'Yes. That quack Rictus spilled it all in the truth cellar just before dawn. Lu's been over him like a rash all night between shifts – he's in a heck of a state. Can't see how we'll ever put the pieces together again. It's not the only thing he confessed. He eventually gave us much more, but he also gave us this vital lead.'

'What are you saying?' I asked.

'Everything's under control,' Mr October said. 'I'd been wondering why the girl's distress call never reached us. Turns out another member of Joe's team, Curtis Noonan, took it, and then relayed the message – not to us but straight to the enemy. We have a confession to that effect signed in Rictus's blood, and Noonan was captured on the M1 this morning, making his getaway. The Vigilant he'd been working with is in for questioning too.'

·21·
THE BRIEFING

After the medical team had examined and discharged me, Mr October waited at the bedside, poring over my Luther Vileheart sketch while I washed and dressed in the bathroom.

'Very good. Perfect for our needs. Are you ready?' he called. 'The meeting's in five minutes and all teams will be there.'

'I feel terrible,' I said, studying the mirror. The scar on my cheek was pink and clearly visible again. I turned off the light and went through to the room.

'You shouldn't feel so bad,' Mr October said. 'The staff gave you a great report. You'll still experience headaches and dizzy spells, but not for long, and they'll be nothing compared to what they were.'

'I don't mean that. I feel fine in myself.' And I did – revitalised, steady-legged, stronger than I'd been for days. 'I mean, I feel terrible about what I did to Kate Stone. I really ripped into her.'

Mr October tucked the sketch pad inside his coat.

'Fear,' he said vaguely, leading me out and along the corridor.

'Fear?'

'Yes, fear. Although it keeps us alert and focused, it also leads us to make mistakes. The enemy push fear into our lives, and we rush to judgement and make poor choices, wrong decisions. We look for someone to blame for our woes and we falsely accuse. You miscalculated, but that's no surprise after all you've been through. Apologise to the girl in your own time.'

'I will.'

'But first there are other, more urgent matters – your mother's capture, and the capture of five others who were taken whole on Bad Saturday.'

At the end of the corridor Mr October tapped a keypad beside the security door and the door buzzed to let us downstairs. On the first flight down he rummaged around inside his coat, bringing out a bulky package which he pressed into my hands.

'You're officially reinstated as of now,' he said, 'and here's your journal. The Ministry have given it careful consideration and don't believe it poses a security risk. You were right – even if it fell into the wrong hands no one would believe it. To outsiders it would seem too far-fetched.'

'Blimey,' I said. 'I mean, thank you!'

'However, if I may,' Mr October continued, 'your grammar does leave something to be desired. There are several split infinitives, a slew of unnecessary modifiers and far too many mixed metaphors. Don't they teach you anything at that school of yours?'

'They try, but it's not really my subject.'

'Aside from that, the Overseers find no reason to object. They're keen to see you progress here and feel you should be free to keep a record as long as it remains private and doesn't interfere with your duties.'

'I won't let it,' I said.

'Very well.'

Turning onto the operations floor through another security door, the first thing I saw was the Vigilant named McManaman blundering up the hall. His hands were cuffed and two other security staff were escorting him. He'd been going without a struggle until he clapped eyes on me. Then his face reddened and he fought to break away, bucking and straining while the other guards held him fast.

'Three of my colleagues died because of you,' he spat. 'Three of my mates! If I ever get my hands on you, kid, you'll wish you'd never been born.'

'You're finished, McManaman,' Mr October said, his features darkening to match the prisoner's. 'Take him away,' he told the guards with a wave of his hand, and then he turned to me. 'Noonan found a willing accomplice in McManaman, who badly wanted to avenge his friends. The evidence he planted during the raid was useless – the Bad Saturday list was days old by then – but what he did was unforgivable, costing us valuable time and manpower on an investigation which should never have taken place. You're aware of the resentment the Vigilants still feel towards you?'

'Yeah. They don't do much to hide it.'

'Most are loyal, but there may be other rebels who've yet to show themselves. Tread carefully, Ben.'

'I will.'

'Now take these pages to a safe place and join us in the briefing room without delay. And Ben?'

'Yes?'

'Good to have you back.'

The floor was buzzing, a steady stream of operatives heading down the hallway towards the briefing room. Receipts was unmanned, the telegraph inactive. As I fitted the typescript behind the ancientspeak volumes and started outside, it began to fizzle and groan again. Closing the door on it, I hurried away, hoping the meeting wouldn't take long.

The briefing room was a small theatre with low ceilings, soft lighting and a slightly raised stage on which Joe Mort and elderly white-suited Mr October were sitting. Most of the twelve rows of seats facing the stage were occupied, but Becky had kept me a place near the front. The room became hushed as Joe Mort and Mr October stood to bring the meeting to order. Joe looked tired, presumably rattled by the discovery of a traitor on his team.

On the wall behind them was a roll-down map of the city, marked here and there with bold red crosses. On a bulletin board beside it was my sketch of Luther Vileheart and six other artists' portraits including – I had to look twice to be sure – one of my mother.

A side door creaked and Lu entered, all eyes upon her, and made for a seat behind ours. Her hands were bandaged like a boxer's and her clothing was spattered with Professor Rictus's blood.

'Great work,' I whispered. 'I heard all about it.'

Lu looked down modestly. 'That's all right. It had to be done.'

A movement further back drew my eye to Kate Stone, still tearful and making a point of not looking at me. A cough from Becky turned me around to face the front as Joe Mort clapped his hands.

'Attention! Listen up for Mr October.'

'We've made good progress in the last few hours,' Mr October began, sweeping his brass-handled walking stick out of thin air and lowering his weight onto it. 'Thanks to the efforts of the Shuffleheads and Luna San Lao, better known to most of you as Lu, we now have a sense of the enemy's plan. Tomorrow, Monday night, that nefarious plan will reach its end. We must work to prevent it at all costs.'

Joe stepped forward to aid Mr October, who turned on weak legs to point the walking stick at the artists' sketches.

'Memorise these faces, burn them into your minds,' he said. 'Here you see Luther Vileheart, the entity charged with carrying out this plan under the direct command of Lord Randall Cadaverus. This is his latest known guise, and here are the six unfortunate souls in holding. One, Donna Harvester, was stolen by Vileheart himself, the others by junior demons at the scene of the atrocity now known as the Bad Saturday bombing. Their whereabouts are unknown. Reconnaissance? It's your job to trace them. They could be anywhere in the city, in any abandoned and boarded-up house, in any loft or cellar. We believe they're being held captive until the time of departure.'

Mr October broke off, wheezing, straining for breath, and Joe again steadied him as he turned to the street map.

'The enemy have many points of entry into this world and just as many points of exit,' Mr October said. 'This city is a honeycomb with countless routes in and out, but only a few of these can be used for transporting the living. They can't be moved safely through cracks and vents and pipelines. Their flesh and bone makes this impossible. However, under questioning in the truth cellar Professor Adolphus Rictus told us of three gateways through which mortals may be moved to the enemy's territory. The gateways are here, here and here.'

Mr October's walking stick prodded three places on the map marked by red crosses.

'They'll be carried by train, like cattle,' he said, 'an extraordinary train which runs between here and Abhorra. This train has no schedule, no timetable. It may run twice in a week or once in a generation, whenever there are mortals to transport. Well, the enemy have had a successful week – it's rare to see so many taken alive at once – and we believe the train will run again tomorrow night. If we're unable to find the prisoners before then, we'll have to intercept the train as it leaves the city . . . a daunting task, and for this we'll need all the forces we can muster.

'The first location,' he said, tapping a point at the map's north-western tip. 'As you're aware, there are sealed-up stations and mothballed lines all across London, such as the old Post Office Mail Rail tunnels between Paddington and Whitechapel. But there's another line, not on the underground map and almost impossible to find because it isn't meant to be found.

'This hidden route crosses the country to here in Harrow, the first subterranean stop in the city. The place of access lies below a storm drain close to Saint George's shopping centre. There's no indication of it, no marks on the street or walls nearby. Any prisoners entering here are likely being held in the immediate vicinity as we speak. Teams will be assigned to search the area.'

Mr October now pointed to the map's centre, continuing without Joe's support. The room remained silent as he explained.

'This second stop seems a more likely departure point. It's close to where Donna Harvester was last sighted and is situated on the property occupied by Luther Vileheart before their disappearance. Professor Rictus was most helpful with this. To the rear of the property there's a great maze, purpose-built to Vileheart's own specification, and the gateway lies at its centre. But the maze is guarded, watched over by zealous enemy forces. When we enter we should expect furious opposition, but it's a risk we must take.'

The tip of the walking stick flipped east to De Beauvoir Town.

'The third and final gateway is here, in a place well known to two of you in this room. It's beneath a school on Mercy Road, close to where two corridors meet at the building's centre. The platform isn't accessible from the school, but can be reached through an underground walkway leading from the chapel crypt across the street. Additional teams will be assigned here, with armed Vigilants providing support. If we fail to intercept the train by this point, there'll be little hope for the prisoners on board. Are we clear?' Assorted murmurs and nods circulated the room. 'Good, then let's get cracking. You all know what's required. And folks – let's be careful out there.'

'That's all,' Joe Mort said, helping frail Mr October onto a chair. 'Everyone to their posts.'

The briefing room began clearing. Kate again avoided my look as she joined the queue filing out. Through the crowd I saw Mr October waving us over. Sukie had already joined him on the stage but, becoming the gunslinger-pirate again, he didn't need assistance to stand.

'I knew there was something about the school,' Becky said as we went over. 'In fact, I could've sworn I heard a train the other day, but then I thought, no way, you're imagining it. Shows how wrong you can be.'

'Lu!' Mr October called. Lu looked back from the exit. 'Go to the clinic and have your hands checked. We don't need you for transport until later today.'

'OK.'

'What about our shift?' I said. 'There'll be a new list in receipts by now.'

'Other teams will cover for us,' Mr October said. 'Public transport will take us where we need to go.'

'So we're looking for Mrs Harvester?' Becky said.

'Later we will, but first we have a social call to make.'

Sukie gasped, alarmed by something she'd read in his thoughts. 'You're not,' she said. 'You're not really going to see *him*, are you?'

'Who?' I asked.

'Kirk,' Sukie said. 'He's mad-dog crazy. Completely out of his tree.'

'An old colleague,' Mr October elaborated. 'It's true that he has a few anger management issues. He's a former employee, now gone to ground, but at one time he was a warrior who struck terror into the enemy's heart.'

'Loop the loop,' Sukie said, twirling a fingertip at her temple. 'And if you don't mind me saying, Mr October, you might be a bit mad yourself if you're thinking of doing what I think you're thinking of doing.'

'There's a little madness in us all,' Mr October said. 'Yes, he's unstable, so unstable the Ministry encouraged him to take an early retirement, but if we're to stop the train reaching its destination, he's the man for the job. A one-man army, in fact.'

'Kirk. . .' I said. The name meant nothing. I'd never heard it mentioned until now.

'The reason he's never mentioned,' Sukie said, 'is that everyone's afraid of him, afraid even to speak his name.'

Mr October agreed. 'True, but he's as loyal as they come, a Ministry man through and through. So this is our task,' he said. 'We'll travel to the forest where he lives and persuade him to join our mission. I believe, Ben, that your mother and the others in enemy hands stand a greater chance if we can bring him onside. And when we explain our situation it'll be easier to convince him if he sees your face.'

'I still think it's nuts,' Sukie said. 'But that's just me. Just my opinion.'

'My decision is final,' Mr October said. 'Oh, and Sukie? There's another matter to clear up before tomorrow night. We'll need your help on this.'

'I know what's coming,' Sukie said, her eyes lighting up. Whatever it was she already knew, it must be good.

Mr October continued. 'It's a small assignment but a vital one. It concerns the school on Mercy Road.'

On the way to receipts he described the plan he had in mind, detail by detail, and Becky squealed with pleasure. Most of what he said washed over me, though. I was too concerned with other things – Mum's ordeal, my returning gift, and the fearsome one-man army we were soon to meet – to make any sense of it at all.

❧ 22 ❧
THE LAST BERSERKER

On the train from Liverpool Street to Chingford, Mr October briefed us on what to expect from the man named Kirk.

'Above all else, he's a proud man,' he said. 'Violent and volatile, yes, without question, but loyal to a T and proud of his achievements with the Ministry, most of all proud of his lineage. He's a descendent of ancient warriors, the last of his kind, the last berserker. He still wears his heritage as a badge of honour, so much so that he changed his own surname from Engelstad to Berserker.'

I looked askance at Mr October. 'So he calls himself . . . what, Kirk Berserker?'

Becky stifled a laugh.

'That's his name,' Mr October said, watching the silver-frosted open spaces of Hackney Downs passing our window. 'I know, I never thought the name change was a wise move myself, but don't show your amusement in front of him. In fact, take care not to say anything to upset him. He flies off the handle easily, but that's why he's so vital to us. That's why we must see him.'

'Now you're scaring me,' Becky said. 'Will we be safe? I'm starting to not like the sound of him.'

Mr October fussed around inside his coat, seeming surprised to find two chocolate bars and two coffee cups with drink-through lids, which he offered to us for the journey.

'Afraid I'm out of sugar,' he said. 'There's no reason to be scared, Becky, if you stay on the right side of him.'

'And how do we do that?' she said.

'Just be respectful. Compliment him. Don't hurt his feelings in any way. Be nice to him.'

Becky wasn't the only one with reservations. The more I thought about Kirk Berserker, the less I imagined I'd have anything to say when we met. I'd be too afraid to speak, let alone compliment him.

As the train trundled towards Epping Forest, I wondered if Mr October's furious warrior face, which I'd seen for an instant during the lockdown, owed anything to Kirk and his kind. He'd once told me that everyone we meet in life becomes a part of us, for better or worse. Apparently a little part of Mr October was pure berserker.

From Chingford station we went the rest of the way on foot, crossing a deserted golf course and following a wide path over frozen ground towards the dense forestry of Bury Wood and on into a darkness of trees.

The towering oaks and hornbeams grew thickly together, closing out the sky except for a few chinks of daylight above their bare branches. After a time I scented a sweet pine smokiness on the air and heard a regular hammer-like thump and thud in the middle distance. We came to a clearing, the sky brightening where the tall trees had been cropped or burnt back. At the centre of the clearing was a tumbledown shack that looked thrown together without design, its walls made from mismatched lengths of timber and sealed with clay and strips of animal hide. The front door sagged open on leather hinges nailed crudely to its frame, a small window beside it was frosted and dark, and white smoke curled from a lopsided chimney at one end of the flat roof. A black pollarded beech tree stood by the shack, its ten remaining branches reaching for the sky like a witch's fingers. A sudden movement off to our left caught my eye, and I turned to see the man called Kirk.

The berserker bent his powerful frame over

a broad flat tree stump, lifting and positioning a hefty log with one hand, then straightening up, raising a short-handled axe above his head. His limbs were as thick as the log, and he had a lion's mane of stringy golden hair and a darker, black-streaked tangle of beard. He wore a stitched-together coat of bear or wolf skin, knee-high leather boots and a broad belt with a buckle shaped like a runic symbol that glimmered as Kirk swung the axe.

The stout log became two logs, then three before he looked up. When he saw us, his whole body shivered with mistrust. We'd caught him unawares. He'd been somewhere else in his mind, not chopping wood here in the forest but off in some far away world, and he was still coming back. Then his penetrating gaze found Mr October, and he let loose a cry that rattled the ground.

'Well, my old sparring partner!'

'Hardly a sparring partner,' Mr October said. 'I would never have been so bold.'

Kirk swished the axe one last time, burying its head in the stump, and came forward, offering a huge hand to crush Mr October's.

'So how are you, sir?' Kirk said. 'Have to admit I didn't recognise you straight away. It must be the hat.

Makes you look like Jack Palance in *Shane*.'

The handshake made Mr October wilt and he introduced us in a feeble voice. 'Pleasure to see you again. This is Ben Harvester and Becky Sanborne, our latest recruits.'

Kirk bared his teeth at us in what I supposed was a smile. 'Any friend of Mr October's,' he said, and I was relieved that he didn't offer to shake our hands too. 'Come inside, folks, warm yourselves up. Not much to look at but it's the place I call home.'

He steered us to the front of the shack. The doorway was quite a bit lower than Kirk's full height and as he started inside he cracked his head against the frame with a force that would've flattened a bull. A murderous look crossed his face. For a moment I thought something terrible was about to happen. But, taking a deep breath to control himself, Kirk stooped to clear the frame and led the way in.

It really wasn't much to look at, everything crammed into one dingy living space, an unmade bed at one end, a sturdy oak dining table under the front window, and in between a spitting wood-burning stove which didn't give out enough heat to combat the draught blowing in at the door. Tacked to one wall was a photograph of a brunette woman and two blonde children, boy and girl, all with the same blue eyes as Kirk.

'Who're they?' Becky whispered.

'Please be seated,' Kirk said, either ignoring or not hearing her. He crossed to the stove, lowering a tin kettle over a burner while we settled, shivering, at the table.

Through the window we had a partial view of the clearing, everything white and still. The kettle whistled, and Kirk delivered tin mugs of steaming tea, which he banged down in front of us before pulling up a chair for himself.

'I see you still wear the belt,' Mr October said.

'I still wear it with pride,' Kirk said, turning to offer Becky and me a clear sight of it. 'The buckle is Uruz, a symbol of tenacity and courage. I've worn it every day since my first encounter with the enemy, and I wear it now in retirement because the blood of a warrior still runs through these veins. I never chose to leave the Ministry, but I know when I'm not wanted. I had good times there, though, once.'

A distant look came into his eye. Somewhere behind the fearsome mask there was a longing for what he'd lost, a sadness that for some reason made me less wary of him.

'Not everyone at the Ministry wished you to go,' Mr October reassured him. 'In fact, that's why we're here. You've probably guessed this is more than a social call. We didn't come just to say hello.'

'Oh?' Kirk said as if the possibility hadn't occurred to him. 'Then what can I do for you, sir?'

'We have a situation,' Mr October said, and then he went on to explain the nature of it, from Luther Vileheart's first contact with Mum at the Mare Street café to the leaking of the Bad Saturday list and the living soul train due tomorrow night. Kirk listened in silence, bristling at the mention of Luther Vileheart, Nathan Synister and Professor Adolphus Rictus.

We sipped our teas while Mr October outlined his plan. The tea tasted stewed and soapy, but it seemed wise not to mention that or the freezing draught we were sitting in.

'So you see, timing is everything,' Mr October concluded, 'and we'll need to meet force with force. As you know, we prefer not to resort to mindless violence except as a last resort. But sometimes it's necessary, and I know of no one more mindlessly violent than you.'

To Kirk Berserker this was a major compliment. 'Much appreciated, Mr October. You weren't so bad in your day either.' To us he said, 'He was always my greatest champion and we won many memorable battles together years ago. In one of his other guises he fought like a whirlwind, with superhuman strength and the speedy reactions of a fly. You should've seen him.'

'Those days are long gone,' Mr October said. 'That warrior is all but retired. I must admit he always frightened me a little. I'm afraid to let him out again now.'

'You may have to, come tomorrow night,' Kirk said. 'I wish him well if you do, and I'm sorry I won't be able to join him.'

'But you're invited, and very welcome.'

'I appreciate that, but there's no honour in a forced retirement. I've nothing but respect for you, sir, but as far as your superiors are concerned. . .' The anger was surfacing again, reddening his face, coursing through him like the first stirrings of a quake. 'Where they're concerned, I've nothing but contempt. I gave them my best – my all – and see how they repaid me.'

'I know you and the elders always had your differences,' Mr October said. 'But you should know they approved our visit here today. Personal feelings aside, consider this boy's mother and the other victims. Imagine the consequences if we should lose them.'

Kirk stopped at that. The quake seemed to be passing, no damage done. Now he looked at Becky and me with sudden new interest, head cocked to one side, something stirring behind his eyes.

'They both have it, don't they?' he said to Mr October. 'The boy most of all, but the girl too. It's everywhere around them like golden light, more light than I've seen on anyone besides your good self. I knew they had to have it or you wouldn't have enlisted them in the first place. I just didn't see until now that they had so much of it.'

He slurped his tea, making a face at the soapy taste. He looked tempted to hurl his mug across the shack in disgust, but instead he placed it carefully on the table and gave me a quizzical look that reached deep inside me.

'It's because of this gift that they came for your mother,' he said. 'I see that now. I know the enemy well, and a gift like yours would terrify them. You're a warrior too, in your own way. I see your strength and I see your anger . . . a great deal of anger.'

'They murdered his father,' Becky said without prompting, then quickly fell silent.

'The boy saw him off safely after four lost years,' Mr October said. 'More recently they crippled his gift by means of toxi-poloxi poisoning, and yet here he is sitting before you, ready to play his part.'

Now the prickly mood had left Kirk Berserker, all I saw on his face was respect. 'You've been through so much, kid,' he said.

'Yeah,' I said. It was the first time I'd spoken to him directly.

'But what you've faced already is nothing compared to what you'll face next,' he said. 'What would you give to bring your mother back?'

'Anything. Everything.'

'Would you go to the dark side?'

'Yes. Wherever it is. Whatever it is.'

'I speak not of a place but a state of mind. The day may come when you'll have no choice.' He glanced at Becky, who was cowering down on her chair. 'You're young – much too young for that yet – but you should still be prepared, as my own family should have been prepared. . .'

He broke off, and with a pained expression looked over at the woman and children in the photograph. His family, then. Something had happened to his family. And I remembered what Mr October had said in the personnel room. *With grief comes anger.*

'I wouldn't wish that journey to the dark side on anyone,' Kirk continued. 'It's to be hoped Mr October's rescue plan succeeds, otherwise you may just have to go there.'

I wasn't clear about his meaning, but he didn't say more. Having spoken his piece, he sat back from the table to study me, fascinated by whatever he saw in the air around me.

'So what do you say?' Mr October asked. 'The offer stands, regardless of how you feel about the elders.'

'Let me sleep on it. You'll have my decision in time.'

'That's fair. I can't ask for more.'

We left soon afterwards, our tea unfinished and cooling on the table, and crossed the clearing while Kirk watched us off from the door.

Returning through the shade of tall trees, I wondered about the golden light he'd described. I'd never seen anything like it around my reflection in mirrors. Becky must have been thinking the same thing, because as we followed the path out of the woods she said excitedly, 'Did you notice how he looked at us, Ben? I mean, how he looked at you in particular?'

'Yeah. Something he saw seemed to interest him.'

'It was more than interest. Not even respect. It was something else. Maybe it didn't show on his face but I definitely felt it. It was there all right, no mistaking it.'

'No mistaking what?'

'Fear,' she said. 'You could knock me down with a feather. That man – that beast – was afraid of you.'

SUKIE

'd been starting to think I'd never see home again, but I was back on Middleton Road before nightfall. The first thing I did was take out the trash, stuffing the harbour-side photograph of Mum and Vileheart into a waste bag with the flowers he had brought to dinner. Later I'd find Dad's photo and put it back where it belonged, but there were more unwanted gifts to throw out first.

As I added the comic, the Moleskine sketchbook and the pencil case to the bag, my trainer bumped something solid on the bedroom carpet – the tin box containing my four-leaf clover chain.

The last time I'd seen it, the clover chain had been rotten and shrivelled. Now it nestled lush and green inside the box, good as new. I stared at it in wonder, turning it around between my fingers. How could it still be alive? Returning it to its box, I closed the lid and set the box back on the shelf.

After dumping the bag down the waste chute outside, I went to the bathroom and scrubbed the feel of Vileheart's gifts off my hands until my fingers were raw. Later, I lay awake on the bed, feeling Mum's absence in the empty maisonette. I should've been out there helping with the search, but there were many highly-skilled agents on the case and Mr October had insisted I'd need all my strength for tomorrow.

Sleep wouldn't come. There was too much to think about, too many questions. Kirk Berserker, the mighty warrior who made the enemy quake in their boots . . . afraid of me? He'd seen my gift, but what else had he seen? Would Sukie's assignment succeed as planned? In the darkness I saw grinning Professor Rictus jump at me, the living surgical instruments twisting in his grasp.

In the end I drifted off at around two in the morning and woke just before seven, about the same time our PSHE teacher Miss Whittaker was waking with a sneeze in her small flat across town on Wellington Row.

Today Miss Whittaker bathed, dressed and breakfasted with a tingle in her throat. Typically, the head cold hadn't come over her until Saturday, three days after her winter flu jab. But she would see off this bug like all the others. She hadn't missed a day's teaching in her life and she wasn't about to miss today for something as trivial as this.

After breakfast she washed and put away the dishes, leaving herself no after-work jobs. Everything in Miss Whittaker's studio flat, like Miss Whittaker, was orderly, organised and slightly old-fashioned. On her dining table was the thick novel she'd started reading last night and a vase of freesias and lilies she'd bought at yesterday's flower market around the corner on Columbia Road. She was refilling the vase with fresh water at the sink when her doorbell sounded the first four notes of 'Frère Jacques'.

Miss Whittaker left the vase and went to peer through the spyhole. Framed in her fish-eye view, a young dark-haired woman in a black and white houndstooth coat stood outside holding a clipboard. She looked harmless enough and smiled politely when Miss Whittaker unchained and opened the door.

The visitor introduced herself as Tabitha and apologised for calling so early. She was here on behalf of the residents association, she said, to conduct a Q & A about the building and its services. Her emerald eyes were unblinking and her voice was soft and mesmeric. Miss Whittaker never felt herself being hypnotised while she explained she was due at work and asked Tabitha to call again later, after four.

Tabitha said that would be fine, and turned away as Miss Whittaker closed the door. It had taken just fifty seconds to instil the thought. The girl's name wasn't Tabitha and she wasn't from the residents association, but Miss Whittaker had no way of knowing this or of knowing what had just happened.

Closing the door, re-attaching the chain, she looked across her lonely flat at the bookmarked novel on the table. The first three chapters had hooked her last night. She wished she'd started it sooner. Miss Whittaker finished refreshing the flowers and returned them to the table and picked up the book.

It was still dark out. More ice and freezing mists to come, the forecasts said. Not a day to be out and about, she thought, and it wouldn't be wise to carry this cold – she sneezed again as she thought it – all around school, and risk spreading it to the children and other members of staff.

She checked her watch. Ten past eight. The office wouldn't be open yet, so she'd call in half an hour and then unplug the phone. If she had to miss her first day ever, so what? She'd feel much better tomorrow.

Besides, the best books of your life were those you read when you were sick and at home in bed on school days. Kicking off her shoes, Miss Whittaker snuggled fully clothed under the duvet and opened her novel to the start of chapter four.

Thirty-five minutes later, the principal of Mercy Road school had a visitor. A woman in a houndstooth coat arrived at reception, introduced herself as Polly from the *Hackney Gazette* and asked to see Mr Hatcher. As it happened, Mr Hatcher was free.

As she entered his office the phone rang on the desk and the receptionist lifted the receiver to take Miss Whittaker's call. The meeting between Polly and Mr Hatcher lasted exactly three minutes.

We were passing the cold spot, Becky and Sukie and me, when Polly came marching down the corridor towards us. I hadn't known what her particular talent was until now. She had a confident, purposeful walk and her eyes were fixed straight ahead. She flicked a stray strand of hair from her forehead and winked as we passed.

'Job done. It's up to you now. Good luck.'

She was turning off the corridor when Mr Hatcher stepped out in front of us from the reception area, staring after her with a bleary-eyed and distracted face.

'Mornin', sir. What's up?' Becky said.

Mr Hatcher gradually brought the three of us into focus. 'Pardon? Oh, nothing. We find ourselves short-staffed today, that's all. Three teachers have called in sick and our usual supply staff have commitments at other schools.'

'Our mate's a supply teacher,' Becky said, introducing Sukie. 'A really good one, too.'

'Lucky she has a free day,' I said. 'She only came along with us to pass the time.'

Mr Hatcher gave Sukie the once-over. She hadn't given school dress codes much thought and wore a black motorcycle jacket over a Motorhead T-shirt, frayed blue jeans and brown cowboy boots. She couldn't have passed for a teacher in a million years, but the meeting with the woman whose name was not Polly had made Mr Hatcher docile, easily manipulated.

'A supply teacher,' Mr Hatcher said. 'Someone must have been reading my mind. And you are?'

The three of us looked at each other. We hadn't

thought a lot of other things through, including Sukie's supply teacher name.

'Hurd,' Sukie said at random.

'Miss Hurd?' Mr Hatcher said.

'That's right. That's me.'

'And what's your area of specialisation, Miss Hurd?'

'My what?'

'What do you teach?'

'Oh, this and that, anything, everything, really. What have you got?'

'It's mainly PSHE today,' Mr Hatcher said.

Sukie sniffed as if that presented no problem at all. 'Sure. I could do that easy,' she said.

'Fantastic,' Mr Hatcher said, and then he became more businesslike. 'I don't suppose you have references with you? Commendations from other schools, certificates of qualification and so forth.'

'Not really, not on me,' Sukie said. 'I was just keeping my mates company, that's all. Didn't really expect this.'

'Neither did we, and I realise it's all a bit short notice. I suppose . . . yes, I suppose we could sort out the paperwork later. Is there any chance you might take Miss Whittaker's classes before and after lunch, say eleven and one-thirty?'

'Dunno. I'll have to think about that.' Sukie thought about it for all of five seconds before saying, 'All right. I'll do it. Do you pay cash?'

Mr Hatcher didn't bat an eye.

'I'm sure that can be arranged,' he said, 'even if I have to break into the school piggy bank. If you'd like to join me in my office, Miss Hurd, we'll get something on paper to make this official.'

'Why not?' Sukie said. 'I wouldn't say no to coffee and biscuits either. See you later, you two.'

Leaving her there with Mr Hatcher, we hurried off to registration with Miss Neal.

Nothing had changed. The tension still gripped Miss Neal's class, and 8C were again quietly obedient while Miss Neal remained terse and snappy. As registration ended I looked outside, following the flight of a raven which sailed across the yard to perch on the climbing frame and fluttered its wings as Miss Neal clapped her hands.

'Harvester! I see that three days of suspension have taught you nothing. Keep this up and I'll be having words with your mother.'

'His mother ain't around anymore,' Raymond Blight gloated, and I shot him a warning look before it struck me. There was no way he could possibly know. That wasn't Raymond speaking but the Whisperer speaking through him. At the back of the room, Simon Decker wiped his mouth and looked away.

The lockdown was still in place, so at break we sat by the window in the school canteen, under observation, not daring to speak. The strain tugged at Becky's lips as she stirred her tea and the table vibrated under my fingers. I was wondering if the soul train had set out early when Becky trapped my hands on the tabletop.

'Keep your cool. That's not the train making things shake, Ben, it's you.' With a quick look around the canteen she added, 'Let's hope Sukie can pull this off. Otherwise there'll be a lynching.'

It seemed fitting for Sukie to take Miss Whittaker's class in the room where Dad and the fire children Mitch and Molly Willow had first shown themselves. If I hadn't known about the cold spot and what lay underneath it I might have thought this room was the heart of everything, the place where the departed made their way in and out.

For the first five minutes there was no sign of Sukie. 8C were subdued, the Whisperer keeping them in check. All eyes were on the unoccupied desk at the front and the pile of magazines and newspapers Miss Whittaker always kept on it. Becky frowned at me as if to say, 'Where is she?'

We didn't have long to wait, though. When the door crashed open and Sukie marched in, the whole class caught its breath. She clattered across the floor in her cowboy boots and creaking leather jacket, seized a marker pen and squiggled her supply teacher name in big capitals across the board. There were confused looks and shrugs as Sukie grabbed a broadsheet newspaper off the pile, fell onto the chair and plonked her feet up on the desk.

'Your teacher's feeling a bit blah today,' Sukie announced, 'a bit under the weather. So she's staying home to read a book, and I'm her replacement. That's my name right there on the board.' She scanned the room, her kinked gaze landing on Decker, causing the two pupils either side of him to shrink down on their seats. 'Now I've not been here long,' Sukie said, 'not even a full minute, but already I can tell there's a bad influence in this class, a very mal . . . mal. . . What's the word I'm looking for?'

'Malign, Miss?' I offered, raising a hand.

'Thank you,' she said. 'A very malign influence, and it isn't who most of you think it is, either. Look, I'm only here for one day and you'll probably never see me again, but I'm not putting up with any nonsense in this lesson. I just won't stand for it, all right?'

'Yes, Miss Hurd,' the class mumbled.

'So anyway, I don't have much of a lesson plan,' Sukie went on. 'This was all sort of sprung on me, unexpectedly. So instead of an actual lesson you're having an hour of silence. You can read, catch up with your homework, do what you like, I don't really mind, and I'm going to sit here and read my paper without interruption. Are we clear?'

'Yes, Miss.'

Sukie opened her newspaper and the quiet hour began. Every so often she would look up from reading, narrowing her eyes at the rustle of a book page, the clearing of a throat, the rasp of a pencil sharpener. At the back of the class Simon Decker stared sullenly at the street, and for once his lips were sealed and unmoving.

'Don't you dare,' Sukie said, not looking up. 'You can't fool me. I know what you're doing. Any more thoughts like that and you're out on your ear.'

The pupils looked at each other, bewildered. The silence grew, the tension stretching towards snapping point. It was a different tension, though, not the same thing we'd felt in Miss Neal's or any other class. For once, the hostility wasn't directed at us. Instead it was passing between Sukie and the hidden enemy.

The next half hour went the same way. As long as Sukie was in charge the Whisperer was gagged. It needed to make itself heard but couldn't. At times I could almost hear it trying to send out its thoughts, and whenever it did Sukie would rattle the newspaper and glare.

'Quiet,' she said, although no one had spoken. 'Don't think I can't hear you. You're coming through loud and clear.'

I'd never seen Sukie at work in the field, but now I saw what made her such an asset to the Ministry. It wasn't only her ability to hear what no one else could but the way she used her gift to draw the enemy out.

'You!' she said suddenly, speaking directly to Decker, and what she said next left Becky and me reeling. 'Yes, I'm talking to you, Simon Decker. Don't sit there looking sorry for yourself. It won't be like this forever. I know you're miserable and scared, you've been miserable and scared since you came here, all because of the bad seed in this place. But it's nearly over. It can't hurt you now.'

Decker's eyes widened in surprise. His face cleared, and for the first time I saw him for what he was – just a vulnerable kid who knew something was wrong here, something was bad, a kid who felt the malign influence too and muttered to himself in fear. He stared at Sukie, a tear draining from the corner of his eye. Someone understood. At last someone understood.

'It's all right,' Sukie said gently. 'There are others in this room –' she sent an accusing glance our way '– who think you're the cause of everything, all the bad feeling here. And who put *that* idea in their heads, I wonder? Who convinced them it was you?' She took in the class with a long sweeping look. 'You may as well come out and show yourself. There's nowhere for you to hide anymore.'

So I'd mashed Decker's nose and split his lip in two places for nothing. If he wasn't the Whisperer, then who? Not Raymond Blight, who was too dumb to manipulate anyone. Not the Ferguson twins, who shared so many unspoken secrets. They'd been at Mercy Road long before I started in September, and nothing like this had happened until recently.

It hadn't begun until the week Simon Decker and Fay De Gray joined the class.

Sukie slapped down the newspaper and took to her feet in the same instant two chairs crashed aside and two girls, Mel Kimble and Francine Hart, squealed and leapt clear of the desk they'd been sharing with Fay De Gray. A stunned silence held the room, and then the panic spread like wildfire as the enemy inside Fay began to come out.

Fay gripped the sides of her chair, quaking and jerking as if an electric current were running through her. There was a crunching sound like splintering bones and another chair screeched behind mine. I couldn't take my eyes off Fay, whose whole body was cracking apart like a pupal case while the creature – the thing hiding inside her – came scuttling out.

It was almost the size of Fay herself, fuzzy brown-bodied and spindly-limbed, and it scurried to the desktop to orientate itself, pumping blood through its papery wings until they expanded like sails with intricate skull and crossbones emblems at their centres. Its face was unmistakable – a Deathhead face, eyeless dark sockets and shorn-off lips. It stared dazedly around the room, a rattlesnake vibrato in its throat.

The entire class was screaming, huddling in corners, diving for cover under desks amongst a shriek and crash of furniture. The hypnotised look had left their eyes, which were now filled with fear and wonder.

'So there you are,' Sukie said. 'So that's what you look like. Even uglier than you sound. Ben?' she called, but she didn't have time to finish before the moth-thing took flight.

With a stiff beat of its wings the Deathhead went airborne, slamming into fluorescent ceiling lights, spraying hot slivers of metal and glass. Then it dove straight at Sukie, careering into her with such force she collapsed to the floor, a grey-brown cloud of wing dust rising around her.

'Ben,' Sukie cried. 'It's up to you now. . .'

'Stay down,' I said, and to Becky, 'You too!'

Becky peered out from under our desk in alarm.

Sukie had driven the demon out, but the next part wasn't her strong suit. It was mine. But I had no time to fit it together in my mind before the Deathhead was on me, its gaping mouth missing my face by a fraction.

The shrieks and sobs were deafening. Everyone had gone to ground except Fay De Grey, whose outer shell sagged on her chair like a reptile's cast-off skin. Drawn by the daylight, the moth-thing thudded the window before flexing its wings and turning, letting loose a full-blooded scream as it came again.

Above us the shattered ceiling lights puffed smoke and sparks. As the demon swept down, I pushed a clear, bright thought out towards it – a picture of how this would end – and the Deathhead moth rocked in mid flight, jolted off course and straight upwards.

It struck the exposed guts of the broken light fitting. Another dust cloud showered down, and a cascade of sparks belched from somewhere inside the ceiling. There was a rushing noise and a crackle of electricity rolled through the air as the creature burst into flames.

Its cries were the worst thing, drowning out even the howls of the kids. The wing-beating ball of fire tapped and thumped its way across the ceiling, scorching the white paint black before dropping like a heavy sack to the floor in front of Miss Whittaker's desk.

Sukie rolled clear as it landed, then scrambled to her feet and stood back to watch as the creature blackened, twitched and stopped moving, and the fire steadily burnt itself out.

Before long there was nothing left but ashes. The classroom filled with dense black smoke. Becky wriggled out from cover to open a window, and gradually, one by one, the rest of 8C reappeared too. Their faces were rigid with shock and their eyes skipped nervously between the Deathhead's remains and me.

Oh no, I thought. Now they know.

'So what do we do?' Becky said. 'They've seen everything. They've seen that thing, they saw what you just did. What do we do about *that*?'

Sukie glanced at the door a second before it opened. The woman in the houndstooth coat peered in through the smoke at the cremated heap on the floor. It could have been anything by now, a torched bundle of rags or newspapers, offering no clue to what it had been before. The woman looked at it dispassionately, not a trace of emotion on her face, and turned her striking emerald eyes on the class.

'Hello 8C,' she said, crossing to the teacher's desk. 'A quick word, if I may. . . This won't take more than a minute of your time.'

The rest of 8C returned obediently to their seats and sat to attention, all ears. As the woman cleared her throat and began, Sukie signalled us to follow her out.

Soon they'd forget everything they'd seen. The next time they saw us they'd know us, and the Whisperer wouldn't be telling them what to think. The last thing I saw, leaving Miss Whittaker's room, was Simon Decker listening, enthralled, no longer muttering to himself, a normal kid with nothing more to fear.

◆◆24◆◆
LUTHER VILEHEART'S MAZE

With roaring engines and blazing headlights the convoy crossed the cobbles of Eventide Street and sped through the narrow passageway into the night.

From Upper Street the procession split three ways, one deployment heading the short distance south-east to Mercy Road, another north to Harrow, while ours set out for the Vileheart residence in Belsize Park.

'I'm not sure Becky should come,' I told Mr October as Lu wove the rickshaw through the high street traffic. 'If the maze is guarded like you said, she'll be at risk.'

'I'm inclined to agree,' Mr October said. 'She may be talented but she isn't made for combat. Perhaps we should drop her here. Lu?'

Lu slowed, steering us closer to the curb.

'Don't talk about me like I'm not here,' Becky said. 'Don't I have a say? So I can't fight, I can't do what you lot can, but I'll find what we're looking for faster than anyone else.'

'Possibly,' Mr October said, 'but if and when the fireworks begin we'll be too stretched in battle to carry you. Which makes you a liability.'

Becky stood her ground. 'Then give me a weapon, one of those DEW things the Vigilants use. Give me something like that and I'll do my bit. Just because I'm a girl doesn't make me a risk.'

'Whether or not you're a girl is neither here nor there,' he said. 'You're a healer – or will be when your skills are fully developed – that's your nature. You're not a destroyer of agents of darkness.'

'Well, I'm coming, anyway,' Becky said, as if that settled the argument.

'Your friend is so prickly,' Mr October said to me. 'She tests my infinite patience.'

'She'd test anyone's patience,' I agreed, flinching when Becky's elbow found my ribs.

We parked in front of the yellow stone wall on Lawn Road. The Vigilants had broken through the security gate there, and beyond the gate a night frost glittered across the forecourt under a cloudy moon.

The house lights were out, the windows boarded,

the front door smashed in. The bronze sculpture was missing from the forecourt. I'd been here only two days before, but the place looked long abandoned. It was as if Luther Vileheart had never been here at all.

'Flashlights,' Mr October said, starting up the steps and indoors.

A tangle of beams – ours, and those of another team in front – searched the walls as we crossed the entrance hall, picking out shadow-spaces where pictures had hung. There wasn't much left here – no priceless paintings, sculptures or statues. The few remaining tables and chairs were draped with white cotton sheets and skulked in the great rooms like crouching ghosts. One sheet covered the sofa where Vileheart's accomplice Dr Rosewood had treated me. A pale rectangular shape marked the wall above the fireplace where the mirror had hung. At the back of the building the swimming pool was drained and dry, and around its tiled floor insects foraged through dead leaves blown in through the open doors.

Moving out to the garden, we were met by a sickly sweet-sour scent. I recognised it, and recoiled, holding my breath. An orange-yellow fire flickered on the far side of the stream. The hulking figures of

Vigilants were filing from the maze, carrying armfuls of vegetation, which they dumped into the flames before returning inside again.

'It's all right, they're making it safe,' Mr October said. 'The maze has been lined with cacti from Abhorra, which would put us at a great disadvantage. The Vigilants have been here for hours clearing a path.'

'Won't it make them sick?' Becky said.

'They don't possess gifts like yours, so the toxin has no affect on them,' Mr October said. Crossing the stream, he called to a Vigilant offloading another handful into the fire. 'What's the status?'

The guard dusted his hands and saluted. He was one of the pair who'd arrested me at Halloween, the traitor's partner. He recognised me too, but there was no resentment in his eyes. Unlike McManaman, he didn't hold a grudge.

'We're giving it one last sweep, sir,' he reported. 'But as we expected, Shifters are watching the maze, and there's something else in there we don't understand, something that messes with your eyes. It's like a hall of mirrors. Some of our men have made it to the square but others are still lost along the way.'

Mr October nodded. 'Thank you, Heller.'

The last group of guards were leaving the maze empty-handed. One of them spoke briefly to Heller, who signalled Mr October with an all clear.

'Very well,' said Mr October. 'Stay close together, you three. We can't be sure how they'll come at us once we're inside, but come at us they will.'

We started through the entrance, pausing to check the map on the noticeboard. The plan looked subtly different from the last time I'd seen it and seemed to be changing even as we looked, its network of pathways squirming and spreading in new directions. We could easily lose our bearings in here.

'It's like snakes and ladders,' Becky remarked. 'One wrong move and you're back to square one.'

The sound of Vigilant-enemy combat near and far rocked the night air as we set off, the rifle shots visible in the darkness as sparks of light. Lu and Mr October strode ahead, following a path that ran straight for twenty metres before curving sharply right. A little way short of the bend, Lu stopped dead to flag us down.

'Something's coming,' she called, and she and Mr October backtracked until the four of us were bunched together, watching and waiting.

At first I only felt what was heading our way

– a malign presence like the cloud in Abney Park Cemetery. Becky whimpered, sensing its hostile mood an instant before the shape came into view. The dark mass spreading across the ground, rounding the curve on the path, looked like an enormous shadow. I glanced up at the sky, wondering what could be casting it – but this wasn't a shadow. It wasn't even a single large mass but thousands of smaller ones, parts of the whole, black eyes glinting and pink tails twirling in our flashlight beams.

'Oh God, anything but this,' Becky groaned.

'Shifters,' said Lu.

'*Rattus norvegicus shiftus*,' said Mr October, who had time, just, to flash out a hand and unload a fireball before they were on us.

The wave nearly carried us off our feet. Becky fell sideways and would have plunged headlong into the quivering swarm if Lu hadn't held her up. In no time the pathway was heaving with slick-bodied creatures – not rats, I had to remind myself, but Shifters in rat form. They came in all sizes, some as large as terriers, others small enough to burrow up inside trouser legs. They scrambled about us, biting and clawing and flowing up our limbs, clinging to coat-tails and cuffs as we fought them off. I howled as one closed its incisors on the back of my thigh just before someone – Lu or Mr October, I couldn't be sure which – tore it away.

Becky screamed, dragging one from her hair and tossing it back to the crowd. At the same time Lu waded forward, stamping her feet and swishing the invisible blade she gripped with both hands.

The shrill shrieks of the *rattus norvegicus shiftus* were as unbearable as their bites. The sound needled into my head, and when I went to cover my ears I found one dangling from my sleeve by its teeth. Its legs beat the air as I took it by the tail and slung it aside, and Lu flicked a hand at it – swish-swish – lopping it in two in mid-air.

But even lethal weapons like hers couldn't cope with this many, and now they were overrunning the path behind us, cutting us off both ways. I tried to hold on to Becky, who was yelling and shaking and covered to the waist, but the numbers under and around our feet were pulling us further apart. Even Lu was screaming, finding three of them writhing inside her jacket, slippery and plump, and another smaller one poking from her sleeve.

Because Lu was screaming, because Mr October unleashed a second fireball at that moment, and because of the piercing shrieks of the attackers as they thrashed and burned and cooked, I could only just make out the quiet voice that spoke to me then.

'Ben. . .'

I turned to see who'd spoken. The fireball's light had imprinted itself behind my eyes, but through the afterglow I saw Mr October's silhouette drawing something from his coat, something flat and rectangular and far too large to cart around in a pocket.

'Ben,' he repeated. 'Ben, do you see this, the frame I'm holding?'

You couldn't really miss it. The empty picture frame was at least half a metre tall and twice as wide. I winced at a stabbing sensation behind my knee, and for a moment the pain was all I could think of. I could only nod but I couldn't reply.

'I need you to fill this empty space,' Mr October said. 'Forget the pain, work your way through it, and think of Abhorra.'

'I don't . . . I don't know what you want.'

'The comic,' Mr October reminded me. 'The story of the Great and Dangerous. See it again now, piece it together in your mind and project it right here.'

I couldn't imagine why he'd want that, but when

Mr October asked you to do something you had to do it in trust. Closing my eyes, trying to recall, I couldn't see anything but a blank canvas. It was hard to focus at the best of times but with an army of rats scrabbling around you it was almost impossible. Nothing there. Nothing at all.

'Don't think,' Mr October called. 'Just do it.'

Yes, I thought. See it, don't think it. Easier said than done.

But something was stirring, fading in out of the grainy dark. Inside the empty space of the picture frame a scene was taking shape: a red sky and red landscape, two demons sitting on the beach of bones and the beach bathed red under twin crimson moons.

Abhorra, home to Luther Vileheart and the Lords of Sundown. Home to the enemy. Home to the Shifters.

The rectangular frame burned such a bright hole in the dark I had to squint to see anything. It might have been the open door of a furnace, aglow with orange and scarlet and black. A wave broke on the beach like a tide of blood, washing up a deposit of bones. As the bones stirred and turned in the ebb and flow, the frantic squeals and bites of the attackers tailed off and stopped.

The ones clinging to the girls sprang away to the floor, as did one which had found its way to the small of my back. Lu and Becky were as mystified as I was, clueless as to what they were seeing. Only Mr October knew.

The fiery vision held the attackers in its spell. Losing their taste for flesh, the *rattus norvegicus shiftus* now saw nothing else. They ran to the shoreline as they'd come at us, in a squabbling, squirming mass. There must be something irresistible about the scene, I thought, as the first of them leapt into the red beyond. Another Shifter-rat followed, then another, tails twirling, and Mr October held the frame low to the ground as they scrambled towards it. The exodus to their homeland had begun.

'Step right up,' Mr October said, cracking his voice like a ringmaster's whip, adding a few words of ancientspeak, unworldly sounds in Ministry dialect. 'Back where you belong.'

The ground was clearing at both ends of the pathway. All but a few of the Shifters raced for the frame, and those that didn't had other ideas, fleeing the way they'd come, changing shape as they went.

One moment they were rat formed, the next

they were more like rat shadows, then shapeless, low-flying clouds of black vapour. At the bend in the path they left the ground, flocking high above the maze walls, then swooping down to burrow inside the hedgerows.

'Shifters in their natural state,' Mr October said, watching the last rat-shaped entity leap into the hellscape. 'Shifters as living shadows – shadows cast many centuries ago by the most hideous of Abhorra's inhabitants. They're darkness incarnate, darkness itself. And now the survivors have gone to regroup. They'll be back in another form, no doubt. It seems some are more resourceful than others. They weren't all taken in by this old Pied Piper party trick.'

With a wiggle of his magician's fingers, Mr October folded the bright landscape picture in half as if snapping an open briefcase shut. The light vanished at once. The rest of us watched in amazement as he folded the frame again and again until all that remained was a small cubic shape about the size of a dice between his thumb and forefinger.

The dice was shiny and jet black with silver-grey runic symbols on all six sides. With a spring-loaded thumb Mr October flicked it high in the air – a long moment passed when it seemed it would never come down – and then caught it in one outstretched hand and tucked it inside his coat.

'How's everyone holding up?' he said. He looked around at us: ripped and torn and bloody, numb with shock, but we'd survive. 'I've seen worse, but we'll get you patched up as soon as this is over. Let's continue.'

He started out again, striding on along the pathway and around the bend, turning a sharp left onto another path and left again, then right. We fell into line behind him, wincing from our injuries. The maze wound deeper. The crackle of firearms sounded nearer. We took another right, then another, and at the next turn Mr October came to a standstill.

'Oh bother,' he said. 'Who would've thunk it?'

We were back at the start of the maze again, in front of the noticeboard map.

Snakes and ladders. One wrong move. I could've screamed. We'd come all this way, we'd gone absolutely nowhere and now all we could do was start over again.

'Double back and double quick,' Lu said.

'One moment,' Mr October said. Training his flashlight on the map, he pushed back his hat and scratched his brow.

Becky shrugged her shoulders and looked at me as if to say, 'What is he doing?' It wasn't like Mr October to waste time, but I could feel the seconds draining. We had to turn back now, and I'd go alone if I had to. What I couldn't do was wait.

'Wait,' said Mr October, inspecting the map. 'This is what the Vigilant – Heller – was talking about. I believe I see what Vileheart did with this plan. Quite ingenious, but I should've spotted it sooner.'

'I don't care how ingenious it is,' I said. 'We need to move.'

'And move we will. But you see, the map is deceptively simple. It's ninety-nine per cent misdirection. There are so many criss-crossing routes and dead ends and loops it's nearly impossible to see, especially with this op art design boggling your eyes.'

'What's there to see?' I asked. 'What *do* you see?'

'We're still on course. It's a straight line all the way to the centre,' Mr October said. 'The whole maze, like the map, is a series of optical illusions. Its strange perspectives make walls seem to appear where there are no walls, paths where are there are no paths. And I have to say this is a good one. It even fooled me.'

I was puzzling over what Mr October meant when

he suddenly stepped towards the noticeboard and marched straight through it, vanishing from sight. The map rippled in the air like a reflection on water.

The three of us looked at each other, slack-jawed. In front of us the map was still settling, its pathways warping, and Mr October was still invisible when we heard his voice somewhere on the far side of it.

'Step this way. It's a visual trick. See?' Now his face reappeared, growing out of space, out of the map as he peered back from wherever he was standing. 'It's only one of many such tricks. Follow me, and don't let yourselves be sidetracked as you go. If you see hedgerows blocking the way, close your eyes and keep going. They're not what they seem.'

Becky ran her light up and down the map and over Mr October's disembodied face. 'You're telling us there's nothing there, no noticeboard or map or anything?'

'Absolutely,' Mr October said. 'Your eyes are telling you one thing, I'm telling you another. Now hurry.'

He turned away, again disappearing, leaving behind the wavering map that wasn't there.

'Well,' Lu said. 'If we can go through a brick wall to Eventide Street we can go through this.'

She took a couple of tentative steps forward, then broke into a run, dissolving into space as Mr October had done. With a nervous flutter I started after Lu. The map parted around me like a cinema projection, and I felt a brief rush of cold as I felt my way forward. An instant later I was back on the path, falling in behind Lu and Mr October while Becky stumbled along after me. Behind Becky there was no sign of the noticeboard at all.

The pathway we were taking continued uninterrupted for a while but gradually narrowed, the leafy walls closing in from both sides until they were brushing our shoulders. They seemed to converge ten metres or so further on.

'But they don't converge,' Mr October said. 'They run parallel all the way. It's the maze playing games with your eyes. Do as you did before, disregard what your eyes tell you and feel your way through.'

Passing through this next illusion, I shut my eyes and shielded my face, expecting the hedges to scratch and claw, but I didn't feel a thing. When I looked again we were still on the unbroken path, wider than before, and the hedgerows were rustling as if something quick and agile were moving through them. Another sequence of shots rang out, sparking like fireflies, but I couldn't gauge how far off they were.

'Twenty or thirty seconds away by my calculation,' keen-eared Mr October said. 'Less if we pick up our pace.'

He'd only just spoken when something whirled past me in the dark, throwing cool air across my cheek. I flipped a light towards where I thought it had gone but saw nothing except darkness. Probably only a breeze, I supposed, with a stronger wind getting up behind it – that had to be why the maze walls were shaking.

Then Becky cried out behind me, and I swung the flashlight around.

'What the heck's that?' she said, swatting the air in front of her face.

'They're here again,' Mr October said. 'Look sharp, you three, don't even blink.'

All I could make out was the same inky dark, the same leaping and darting shadows that covered everything else. But that was exactly what Mr October meant. He meant the shadows themselves. The Shifters had entered the hedgerows at one point in the maze, and now they were emerging in another. They hadn't changed shape in between.

They could have taken any form, rat or rattlesnake, pterodactyl or wolf, but as shadows they somehow seemed at their worst. As shadows they were faceless, hiding worse things inside them than anything we could see. They soared up from the maze, swirling and hovering about our heads, merging for a second into one larger mass, then splitting apart and separating into four, then eight, then sixteen – and then they attacked.

'Down!' Mr October called.

Becky hit the deck first, dropping as if she'd been shot. Lu, meanwhile, held her ground as if to prove she had nothing to fear. Her hand fluttered at her side and I heard the swish of the blade. In another moment she would have used it, but suddenly her head and shoulders vanished as the darkness covered her like a cape.

It flowed over and down her until only her legs were visible. She looked to have been sliced in two at the waist. Suddenly other Shifters were on her too, flapping and rushing about her in a terrible feeding frenzy. They seemed to have forgotten the rest of us. Maybe one catch, one prize, was enough.

'Take her legs,' Mr October said as Lu's feet left the ground.

She kicked out frantically as I grabbed her left ankle, Becky her right. If Lu was yelling and screaming up there I didn't hear a thing. The darkness muffled every sound. I felt its great force drawing her in as I strained to pull her back, and for a second I thought we might be lifted up too. Then Mr October drew another few choice phrases from *Ancientspeak Unexpurgated* and spat them into the heart of the shadows.

At least I supposed it came from the unexpurgated version. There was much more to it than the odd phrase or two. It was more like a rant. The words poured out of him in a babbling stream, and their effect was immediate and violent.

A mighty electric charge ran through me, wiping my mind and sending me back in time. As a three-year-old, left unattended for a minute while Mum answered the phone, I'd found a screwdriver inside a drawer which should have been locked and poked it inside the nearest electrical socket, just out of curiosity. I'd blanked out then too, coming round seconds later on my backside halfway across the kitchen where the electric current had thrown me. The stunned surprise I'd felt as a toddler came flooding back to me now as the powerful wave punched me clear and across the hard ground.

The first thing I saw was Becky reeling on the grass close by, shaking the cobwebs from her head, and then Mr October reaching once more inside his coat of wonders.

With one last verbal assault on the Shifters – if there were swear words in ancientspeak he must have used them all – he took the black dice from his pocket and tossed it high at the sky.

This time it didn't come back.

The dice rose and rose against the foggy moon, twirling and turning, untouched by gravity, and it kept rising until it blew apart, lighting up the sky and bathing the path with dazzling blue light. The earth juddered from the aftershock and the Shifters lost their hold on Lu, dropping her like a hot potato and fleeing inside the hedge walls they'd come from. Lu landed hard with a winded 'Oof!' There was a slap and squelch of juices that coated her from head to waist, a colourless, watery goo.

'Ugghh, that is *disgusting*,' she said, sitting up and wiping her face with the back of a hand and wiping her hand on the grass. 'I'll need a shower when this is all over. Otherwise, don't ask – I'm OK.'

You had to admire her focus. Another few seconds

and they would have digested her, but to Lu this was a distraction, an inconvenience. I wondered what she'd seen, how the shadow forms looked from the inside, and I hoped there'd be a time when she'd tell me about it, but that time wasn't now.

We were quickly on our feet and moving again, heading to where the latest volley of shots was coming from. Something was burning that way too. I could see the leaping flames in the middle distance. Suddenly and without a word between us we were running.

The ground rumbled underfoot. Whatever waited at the maze's heart drew closer with every step, and now I knew the earth tremors didn't come from the explosion, the underground heating or anything else.

The night train bound for Abhorra was here.

❋ 25 ❋
PANDEMONIUM EXPRESS

The path ended suddenly, blocked by a towering bramble wall, no optical illusion this time. But the Vigilants had blown a huge yawning hole through the thorny barrier and the scorched opening fizzed and spat orange sparks. A keen smell of smoke came from whatever was burning beyond it, and the shots were only occasional now, the last exchanges of a dying battle.

Following Mr October through the smouldering entrance, we came to the central square, a walled-off expanse of pock-marked earth around which the remains of enemy defenders were scattered.

Their torn torsos lay on the silvery grass like heaps of refuse, and the air hung heavy with stinging petroleum fumes. Vigilants were dousing the remains with flamethrowers, and small fires lit up the square from all corners. In the middle distance was a larger fire, a blazing moat surrounding a small black island.

The last few survivors were crawling towards

the hedgerows for cover but not many made it that far. One wyvern-like being with slow-beating wings and long snapping jaws sent a feeble trail of smoke from its snout as a cluster of rifle shots toppled it. A many-armed, squid-like demon jetted a stream of darkness from its bulging ink sac but hadn't time to flee inside the shadow it made before another round of shots stopped it short.

Mr October called to one of the Vigilants, requesting a progress report.

'Been securing the area since mid-afternoon, sir,' the guard said, reloading his rifle. 'Nearly done with this lot but more took off below, so good luck down there. You'll need *lots* of luck where you're going,' he added, indicating the moat of fire.

Now I noticed a shape on the island, a small domed building half obscured by the flames. That must be the gateway entrance, but I couldn't see a way to reach it past the fire.

Typically, though, Mr October could.

'Well . . . in for a penny,' he said, and without explanation he set off to the moat, quickening his step along the way and spreading his arms for balance before scrambling down its steep near side and vanishing into the furnace.

I stared after him, dumbstruck, following the movements of his outline as it passed between the flames and the flames warped and reshaped themselves around him.

'Now us,' Becky said.

I looked at her. 'Are you serious?'

'It's OK, Ben. Don't you see? It's like the other illusions, like the map and the hedgerows. It looks like fire but it's not. It's another trick.'

She had to be right. Mr October had just this second reappeared, his wide-hatted silhouette standing tall on the island. We were looking at the maze's last illusion, the only thing between us and the journey below. Giving each other the nod, the three of us broke into a run and tumbled down into it.

The flames billowed around us, dazzling orange and yellow and white, but they gave out no sound or heat because – unlike the fires back on the square – they weren't there. Moving through the blinding haze I soon lost track of the others, but I had a feeling they were somewhere ahead of me all the way. The hardest part to navigate was the nearly vertical slope on the far side. Straining for purchase up the hard ground, I twice reached the top before sliding back, but then Lu was above me, hauling me up.

The dome resembled a squat mausoleum with pillars either side of a blistered black door. Mr October gave the door a push and it opened with a haunted house creak. It was pitch black inside, and a rumble reached us from deep underground – the soul train at its platform.

How long did we have? How far from here to the train? Lu found her flashlight and swept it through the dark, over a filthy wet floor and across a graffiti-covered wall. A sequence of runic symbols carved into the wall caused Mr October to cluck his tongue and shake his head but the message meant nothing to us.

'What's it say, then?' Becky asked.

'It loses a lot in translation, but in any case I won't pollute your ears with such talk. Ah, here we are. . .'

The light settled on a grimy lift door and the control panel on the wall beside it. Lu hit the call button and the lift juddered far below in the shaft, beginning its climb.

It was a long climb, too, because something like two minutes passed before the doors rattled open. There wasn't much room inside, and the lift cage wobbled under our weight. I wouldn't have trusted it to carry more.

The descent began. The cage dropped at speed, making my ears pop, and with the sudden rise in pressure Becky sighed and held the bridge of her nose. We seemed to be in freefall, plunging through space with nothing to hold us. Then the lift stopped with a bone-crunching shudder and settled, taking its time before opening its doors.

Exiting into a grimy low-ceilinged walkway, we were met by a wall of sound from somewhere away to the left: engine noise, booted footfalls, voices shouting orders in the same reverse-sounding language we'd often heard on the rounds.

Mr October listened carefully, then said, 'My grasp of their Abhorrentongue is patchy, but without question they're preparing to board.' Other voices, banshee cries and rattles, joined the call and response. 'They're bringing the prisoners – the mere mortals, they call them – from holding. There's no time to intervene, so we'll have to take our chances on the train.'

An almighty siren rose and fell, and a voice crackled from a tannoy, repeating the same short phrase over and over in Abhorrentongue.

'Just a warning to mind the gap,' Mr October interpreted, ushering us towards our first sight of the platform.

The train stood along it, its corrugated steel sides covered with graffiti slogans written in runes. The doors were open, and from the little I could see from the walkway the insides looked like bare drab cattle cars, but this train hadn't been built for comfort. Above the engine noise the siren wailed on.

'Move to the end but stay out of sight,' Mr October said. 'If we're spotted this will end before it begins. Wait till I give the word.'

We crept to where the walkway met the platform and huddled against the wall, not making a sound. With a rushing heart, I chanced a peek around the corner.

The platform was as busy as a marketplace, patrolled by guards in uniforms and helmets of bony armadillo armour. Their deathly grey faces were blessed, or cursed, with many spider-like eyes which glanced all ways at once. In their hands were scaly hooked and clawed weapons, which writhed like Professor Rictus's terrible tools. Their jackboots smacked the concrete as they moved along, checking compartments. There were scores of them, at least as many demons in other forms, Shifters and Deathheads and feral dog-like beings which the guards held on leashes, and now another wave of guards turned onto the platform from a tunnel at the train's midway point.

Their arrival sent a charge through the air. All those present stopped and turned to look, and some bowed their heads respectfully.

'What's happening?' I said. 'What are they seeing?'

Mr October's eyes never left the crowd. 'It's the distraction we've been waiting for. Everyone to the train while they're occupied.'

The open carriage faced us, perhaps ten paces away. Mr October waved us on. The girls ran ahead and slipped neatly inside, but I'd only half crossed the platform when I saw what was causing the disturbance further down.

When the guards stood back to make way for the new arrivals, I had a clear view of her through the crowd. It was only a glimpse, and the great relief I felt at first was quickly replaced by horror. What had they done to make her look like that?

Swathed in a tatty grey blanket, eyes downcast and head hung low, Mum looked broken – a hollow woman with her soul ripped out. She glanced neither left nor right as they steered her along and she didn't react when the tannoy squealed with feedback. She was in a trance, unaware of where she was or what was unfolding. While she and three other captives were being ferried to the train another face appeared in the crush, and the sight of that face turned my stomach.

It was Luther Vileheart as I'd first seen him in the personnel office, an almost human figure whose hateful eyes with their vertically slitted pupils were anything but human. A poisonous aura surrounded him like a storm cloud, and the guards jumped to attention at the snap of his voice. He gestured up and down the train, barking instructions, but that was all I saw before Mr October dragged me to the doors.

'She's there. . .' I said. 'She's alive.'

'I know, but you can't help her if you're seen, can you?'

But maybe I'd been seen already. As Mr October bundled me inside, the guard nearest our end of the train turned and looked our way.

If he'd spotted us, he'd alert the others, it would all end here. We huddled in the train, Becky gnawing her knuckles, Lu watching the door space ready to fly at whatever came through it, me still reeling from what I'd just seen of Mum. I looked down the empty, wooden-boarded compartment as the doors slid shut. A tremor ran through the train, and we were moving.

But the guard had entered the carriage in front. His spider-eyes were peering straight at us through the door, and he wasn't alone. The door opened and a second guard followed him through.

Their sixteen sharp eyes held us. The weapons morphed restlessly in their hands. Lu spun round to face them, and I moved in front of Becky to shield her from what was about to happen. At the same time, Mr October set off up the carriage, meeting the guards halfway and raising a hand as if preparing to launch another fireball.

The guards tensed, their eyes blinking nervously. Those weapons, whatever they were, looked a match for anything he might throw at them. But Mr October had only reached to tweak the brim of his hat, and the two guards clicked their heels and saluted.

'Status, please,' Mr October said.

The one on the left answered first, his watchful spider face flickering, switching rapidly between several sets of features.

'The four are being held at the centre of the train,' he said. 'They're heavily guarded and there are other hostiles in the carriages either side of theirs.'

'And what of our teams?' Mr October said. 'How many made it aboard?'

The second guard answered, his features scrambling too.

'Only a handful besides us,' he said. 'Others are waiting at Mercy Road, where the last two prisoners are due for collection. If we haven't recaptured these four by then, they'll storm the train there – subject to your order, sir.'

It wasn't until then that I knew I'd met these two before. I hadn't recognised them with their spider masks, but these blurry ever-changing faces were still fresh in my memory.

Becky tugged at my sleeve. 'What's this about, Ben, and who . . . I mean what *are* those things?'

'The Shuffleheads,' I said. 'Undercover specialists, masters of disguise. Nobody knows their real names.'

Lu sighed and relaxed. They'd fooled her too, though she knew them well enough from the field and the hours she'd spent with them in the truth cellar interrogating Rictus.

'So far, so good,' Mr October said. 'Now take us to the prisoners. We'll go as prisoners with you as our captors.'

'Yes, sir,' they said together.

'Pardon?' I said. 'Are we giving ourselves up?'

'On the contrary,' Mr October said. 'Rather than fight our way through, we'll join them in peace, but we should do so before the next stop.'

The Shuffleheads nodded, their faces reverting to those of spider-eyed guards. The way those eyes blinked at different times and stared in different directions unsettled me, so I tried not to look too closely.

'After you,' they said. 'Stay in single file.'

We worked our way along the bucking carriage and on through the next, steadying ourselves against the train's motion with the stirrups that dangled from the ceiling. Black tunnel walls rushed past the windows. The lights stuttered on and off. Behind us, the Shuffleheads' boots clomped the wooden floor.

'Mercy Road in two minutes,' one said.

'Enemy in the next car,' said the other. 'Put your hands on your heads to show you've surrendered.'

We did as he said. The occupants of the carriage, seeing us coming, opened the door before we reached it. Twenty or more demons waited inside. Some were armoured guards, suspicious and alert, levelling their weapons. Others were horned and reptilian. Still others, the dog-like beings, had salivating mouths all over their muscly bodies, as many mouths as the guards had eyes.

A weird clicking and rattling came from the guards' throats. It could have been a cautionary sound, an alert, or joyful noise at the sight of new mere mortal prisoners. Their inexpressive faces made it hard to tell which.

One of the Shuffleheads spoke in a calm, authoritative voice, addressing them in their own language. The guards listened carefully and two replied with what sounded like questions. The Shuffleheads answered curtly, wasting no words.

The guards fell back to let us through but couldn't resist prodding us with their weapons and suckered hands as we passed. We were curiosities, they hadn't seen many like us, and they treated us with the same reverence they'd shown towards Mum and the others on the platform. Although they seemed in awe of us, I was worried the demon dogs might bite.

A guard at the end averted all its eyes and obligingly opened the door. In the next two carriages the Shuffleheads again took charge, demanding the armed guards make way, and again we were allowed to continue.

'The prisoners are here,' one Shufflehead whispered as we neared the fifth compartment. The train jerked and the lights went out, turning everything black for an instant, then flickered on again as we trooped inside. Every face in the carriage turned towards us except one.

She sat on the floor with the others, the blanket around her drooping shoulders. Her hair was drab and unwashed and she was shivering and staring vacantly ahead. It would have been better to see fear or confusion – or anything – in her eyes, but there was nothing there at all.

If she heard my voice would she recognise it? If she saw my face would she know me? Tears prickled my eyes as I started towards her. Becky held me back, touching a finger to her lips.

Wait, her look said. Just wait.

The other prisoners had the same docile, beaten-down appearance as Mum. One, a woman in her forties, chattered to herself between gasps and sobs. The other two were children no older than Mitch and Molly Willow. Blue-eyed and red-haired, they held each other and trembled.

If they were defeated and afraid, Mum was an empty shell. She never looked up, never knew I was there, and she didn't react when Luther Vileheart's voice cut across the bustling carriage.

'What have we here?'

Wiping my eyes, I turned towards the voice. At the same time I felt the restraining pressure of Mr October's hand on my shoulder.

'A prize catch, unless my eyes deceive me,' Luther Vileheart said. 'Imagine the welcome in our homeland tonight when they see the ten living souls we've brought for the price of six.' His piercing eyes found mine. 'Such prizes too, but did you really have to capitulate so easily, Ben Harvester? Frankly, I expected more of a challenge. Have you lost your nerve, or have you simply lost your will to live, like your mother?'

'Don't listen,' Lu cautioned me. 'He's baiting.'

'I'll tear him to pieces,' I said through my teeth.

My voice carried well enough to send a shocked murmur through the carriage. The guards drew breath and one prodded my ear with his rifle. In their world it must be unthinkable to make threats against demons of Vileheart's high standing.

Ignoring me, Luther Vileheart addressed the Shuffleheads in that reverse-sounding tongue. They pushed us towards the prisoners.

'Take your place with the others,' one Shufflehead said. 'Steady now. One false move and they'll . . . we'll hit you with all we've got.'

The train rocked and a shrill squeal of brakes needled into my skull. Outside the window, ghostly tunnel lights gave way to a first sight of the platform under Mercy Road school and a splash of white wall running alongside it.

'It won't be long, Mum,' I said, kneeling over her. 'It'll soon be over.'

She stared into space, frail-faced as she'd been on the day of her first hospital clinic.

Now Becky settled down with her, gathering Mum's good hand in both of hers. If Becky was afraid, she was putting on a bold face. 'I swear I won't let anything happen, Ben. Don't worry about us, think about what *you've* got to do.' She paused. 'You know what I mean.'

The brakes shrieked again. The train was slowing. Luther Vileheart's eyes fixed on something outside the window.

The platform was as busy as the one before, but there was no order here, only chaos and confusion. Vigilants who'd come to seize the train had been met by heavy resistance and were running pitched battles with enemy guardsmen. Bodies from both sides littered the red-spattered platform under a shroud of smoke. Some defenders were attack-dog-shaped, iron-jawed and sharp-fanged, like those on the train. Three were playing tug-of-war with a Vigilant who lay tattered and struggling on the ground. His eyes met mine through the glass for an instant, then rolled up to white. A demon staggered past the window in flames, thrashing its many limbs until a hail of rifle shots felled it. The thing lay still, radiating black smoke and ashes.

There were shots and cries and jets of flame everywhere. Shadow-like entities swirled above the mayhem, others swept down to join in. One closed itself over a Vigilant, smothering him from head to foot in darkness until there was nothing of him to see. The Shifter soared away, carrying him screaming with it.

Meanwhile, further down the platform and barely visible through the smoke, four figures were making an exit. A blast of fire at their heels – a Vigilant torching a many-mouthed attack dog as two others sprang at him from behind – made one of them, Kate Stone, stop and turn.

Even from here I could see the nerves tugging at her face. She and Joe Mort had the last two Bad Saturday prisoners, a hobbling elderly couple, and were guiding them towards a walkway tunnel. The conflict had given Joe's team a perfect opportunity to steal in, and it was still escalating along the platform when they quietly slipped away.

Luther Vileheart gave a furious shout, and the train jerked ahead without stopping. Without the two elderly souls the Ministry had recaptured, it had no reason to stop. While I hadn't understood a word he'd said, I knew he'd given the order to keep going.

Moments before we re-entered the tunnel, an almighty roar went up on the platform and a figure flashed through the warring crowds towards the train, moving so fast I saw only a black and bronze blur. Its power must have been enormous. Enemy guardsmen scattered around it like wind-blown leaves, collapsing to the ground in a blood-red mist. The train lurched, struck by an incredible force. A shock wave rolled through the carriage, throwing a number of demons to the floor while others flapped for balance.

'True to his word, as ever,' Mr October said to Luther Vileheart. 'Unless I'm mistaken, a certain one-man army has just crashed your party.'

Vileheart's eyes faltered. His expression turned rapidly from bewildered to terrified to murderous, and if looks could kill, I thought, Mr October's name would be arriving on the telegraph anytime now.

'The berserker,' said Vileheart.

The enemy guardsmen shuddered.

The train rolled on into the dark.

'The very same,' said Mr October. 'So why don't you and your pestilent minions cut your losses while you can and give back what you've taken?'

'Over my festering body,' said Vileheart.

'As you wish,' Mr October replied – but it was Luther Vileheart who struck first.

With blinding speed he lashed out a hand, and a streak of white lightning leapt from the tip of his long curving index finger to thump Mr October full in the chest, rocking him back on his heels. A smell of singed clothing filled the cramped space. The guards held their straining attack dogs, ready to unleash them on Vileheart's command. The train thundered on, dipping and swerving from dark to deeper dark.

'You shouldn't have done that,' said Mr October, his features contorting. 'You won't like me when I'm angry.'

'I never liked you in the first place,' said Vileheart. 'Or did I not make that clear?'

We'd entered a kind of stand-off, us and them, everyone silent and twitchy and waiting for the next move. And all the while a confusion of roars and screams further back in the train were coming nearer.

'Becky?' I said.

Becky nodded. She knew what I wanted and had already draped herself over Mum to protect her. She knew it was about to start, and Mum sensed it too, letting out an anguished cry.

'There now,' Becky said. 'It's all right, it's all right. . .'

Becky shouldn't have come, I hadn't wanted her to, but now I was glad she had. I couldn't trust anyone else to do what she was doing. If anyone could take care of Mum, it was her.

'Forget about us, Ben,' she said. 'Get your mind right!'

'Quit jabbering,' Vileheart said, training his lightning finger on Becky.

I stepped in front of her as he let rip, and a bolt of pain jarred my hip, spinning me full circle. It felt like something had bitten a chunk out of me.

A metallic scent of blood mingled in my nose with the smell of scorched clothing, and I only kept my footing because Lu put out an arm to steady me.

'You go to hell,' I told Vileheart, and without effort, hardly aware of what I was doing, I rolled a thought out towards him – a little parcel of anger.

Vileheart looked at me in total astonishment and touched his upper lip, feeling the first trickle of the nosebleed. He frowned at his slick red fingers, then glowered at me, baring a mouthful of pointy off-white teeth.

'Well, now,' he said. 'What else have you got?'

'There's more where that came from,' I said. 'I'll show you.'

And then it began.

All at once the attack dogs were free. Another lightning bolt lanced across the carriage, missed Lu by a fraction and punched out a window behind her. In response, Lu turned her invisible blade on the first snarling dog that came her way, stopping it dead in mid-leap, while Mr October flicked a fireball which took out two guards at once. One moment they were shouldering arms, the next they were tottering figures of flame.

But I'd turned my sights on Luther Vileheart. Our

eyes locked across the carriage. I knew what should follow – that nosebleed was only the start – but a hooked weapon sliced my midriff, and a stunning blow caught me under the jaw, knocking me off my feet.

For the next few seconds I was gone. Like the train, I was hurtling through a tunnel with no light at the end, but a thunderous roar brought me back, a terrifying sound from the carriage behind.

The adjoining door disintegrated, and the Shuffleheads jumped aside as a procession of enemy guards poured through. We were already outnumbered, we didn't stand a chance against this many – but they hadn't come for us. They were fleeing in terror from the full-blooded battle cry behind them. A tidal wave was crashing through the train, an unstoppable force of nature, and its name was Kirk Berserker.

He came like a man possessed, twirling an axe in one hand and a sword in the other, slicing and flattening everything in his path. On his head he wore a helmet with a red Uruz symbol, across his chest a breastplate of burnished bronze. His face was a bare-toothed picture of fury as he tore through the carriage, spraying the walls with enemy blood, and all the while his shout rose and soared. He paused only to tip me a wink as he went.

'Hi kid, how's it going?'

He then set his sights on a charging attack dog, plucking it from the floor with one huge hand, making a face in disgust at the snapping mouths that covered its body and hurling it with great force at the doors.

Meanwhile another fearsome warrior had materialised in the carriage, a shield and gleaming sword in his hands. He fought in a frenzy, tearing into the guardsmen as they threw themselves at him, and when some reverted to shadow shapes he sliced with precise strokes of the blade, carving apart their darkness until there was nothing left but empty space.

The two warriors exchanged a glance and a respectful nod. I'd been wondering who this new one was and where Mr October had gone, but now I knew that they were one – this was the personality Mr October preferred to keep hidden, the one Kirk called the whirlwind.

The train raced on, sucking hot air through its fractured windows. The demons were still multiplying, their shadows drifting in from the tunnel through air vents and cracks in the glass. The darkness they brought threatened to overtake us, and now the lights were failing again.

'Ben!' Lu said.

She was sprawled on the floor nursing a scalp wound, the blood matting her forehead and darkening her fingers, but she wasn't the least bit concerned about the injury. She was gesturing at the far end of the carriage, where Luther Vileheart was backing away, feeling for the door-handle behind him, beating a coward's retreat.

If he thought he could slip away unnoticed, he'd better think again. Setting off after him, I ducked to avoid a flying head severed by a swing of Kirk's axe. The head rebounded from a window to land at his feet, its lips spitting curses and its eight eyes staring hatefully up at him until Kirk kicked the thing away like a football.

I looked again for Vileheart. Vileheart wasn't there. The door he'd taken flapped open and shut in time with the train. A pathway had opened all the way to it between piles of hacked-off limbs and twitching tails, but the injured hadn't given up the fight yet. One severed hand lashed at my ankles as I ran, and a suckered arm looped itself around my knee, tightening like a vice. Lu, on her feet again, sliced it away.

I didn't look back. Leaping clear of a snake demon slithering across my path, I flung myself through to the next compartment.

Luther Vileheart had reached the far door when he sensed me there and spun round. A forked tongue flicked around his lips and his vertical pupils sent a wave of icy bad air my way.

I started towards him. He stood his ground. A fireball detonated in the prisoners' carriage behind me and I felt its heat on my back but refused to look. It was just me and Vileheart now.

Fear, Mr October had said, makes us make mistakes but also gives us focus. I was gripped by fear, frozen by it, but I had something else – and all my pain was directed at the entity in front of me. All of this carnage and hurt and misery were because of him.

He knew what I was thinking. The doubt crossed his face and he again touched his lip, expecting the nosebleed. His dark aura crackled, and I felt a pressure in my skull as if the bad vibes he was sending out carried a physical force. I didn't dare turn away, but it sounded like the hostilities were tailing off. Kirk Berserker's roar was becoming a triumphant cry.

'It's ending,' I said. 'Vileheart, you're finished.'

Vileheart scoffed. 'Didn't they tell you? There is no end. There's no beginning. This is how it always was and will be. You're marked for life, Harvester, because of the choices you've made – and not just for life. In a moment I'll break you to pieces and then you'll see for yourself.'

'Why should I listen to you? You're a murderer, a liar, a coward—'

'And you're even less than that.' The black cloud snapped with white lightning. 'You're a statistic, a number on our hit list.'

'You know what you can do with your list,' I said, but I didn't get to finish what I'd started.

I'd been watching his hands for sudden movements, but the lightning bolt leapt from the aura itself, flashed across the carriage and caught me full in the chest. Its force was astonishing, like nothing I'd ever known. It slammed me back against the wall, stopping my heart for several beats. My mind whited out and I started to sag, but the next thing I knew I was being lifted off my feet, not by Vileheart's hands but by the strength of his mind.

His face was rigid with concentration and his hands were uplifted like an orchestral conductor's.

When he flipped at the ceiling I must've hit it hard enough to leave a permanent imprint across it. The impact was still rattling my bones long after I'd hit the floor.

'Imagine an eternity of this,' Luther Vileheart said in a voice that sounded miles away, trapped in an echo chamber. 'An eternity of suffering. That's what you signed up for when you took sides.'

I was straining for consciousness, willing myself not to slip away. As my head slowly cleared I looked down my body, aware of a throbbing pain coming from somewhere. I must have broken something, at least cracked a couple of ribs, but the sight of my left hand's little finger doubled back on itself nearly made me pass out.

The commotion in the prisoners' compartment sounded more muted. A series of shots, a gargling high-pitched cry, the ferocious swish of a blade . . . all of these sounds floated past me. But then another sound, the faintest of voices, came into my head.

'Ben . . . where's Ben?'

My mother. She was still here, still with us, and she knew my name. That was all I needed to know. Thank you, Becky, I thought. Thank you for being there.

And somewhere inside the whirling space in my head I found what I needed, I saw what I wanted to see. With every rattle and roll of the train the picture came clearer.

The train I was hearing wasn't this one. It was the train Dad had taken from Edinburgh to London four years ago. I saw him now, seated by the window, looking out at the green and brown land, not knowing that this journey home would take so long to end. And I heard him years before that, reading me bedtime stories in a mellow voice that made me feel safe. I saw the mischievous look in his eye one night when Mum went to bed early and he let me stay up with him to watch my first horror film, *Brides of Dracula*. I remembered how he'd covered my eyes with his hand during the scary parts and said, 'Don't look now!' Mum would've gone spare if she'd known, but she never found out. It was our secret, something we shared, and next morning at breakfast Dad had smiled and winked at me over his newspaper when Mum asked why I looked tired.

Don't look now, Dad, I thought. This one's for you.

As I hauled myself to my knees, Vileheart made a whimpering sound and stumbled back three, four paces. By the time I was on my feet he was visibly shaking. The nosebleed hadn't started again, but instead his bloodshot eyes were streaming crimson tears down his cheeks. He clamped both hands to his head as if to stop it exploding, but that wouldn't help him – nothing would help him now.

Vileheart staggered back, his mouth locked open in a silent scream. The pain poured out of me and all the way through him. This was for what he'd done to my family, for everything he'd taken, for Mum and Dad and all the hope and faith and love he'd tried to smash.

And when hope and faith and love run out, I thought, remembering the comic adventures of the Lords of Sundown, you're left with one thing only.

'You're out of luck,' I said, and that was when Luther Vileheart's face began to cave in.

A few more seconds and it would be over. I'd teach him a thing or two about suffering. I had my focus, the picture was bright and sharp, and I was only vaguely aware of the raised voices and heavy footsteps in the carriage behind me.

Two guardsmen passed me left and right, skirted around Luther Vileheart without looking at him and ran to the carriage in front. I didn't give them a glance or a thought. I couldn't be distracted now. The picture was nearly complete, and it was time to finish what I'd started.

Vileheart slumped to his knees, clawing with both bony hands at his rupturing face. 'Please. . .' he said, although it was hard to understand because he no longer had much of a throat. 'Please, I was only following orders. . .'

'Orders to kill and steal,' I said.

'Ben?'

A voice at my shoulder. I shrugged it off.

'The train, Ben,' the voice came again. Becky's voice. 'The Shuffleheads went to stop it. We have to leave. We have to get off now.'

My concentration snapped. My body went slack. That must have been the moment Luther Vileheart slipped away.

A firm hand steadied me and I looked up into the placid eyes of Kirk Berserker. Behind him were a range of other familiar faces – Lu and Becky, still holding on to Mum, and Mr October with the three Bad Saturday survivors.

'Sometimes, kid,' Kirk said, scratching his beard, 'you have to know when the battle's won and there's nothing more to do.'

But I was shaking, still seeing red.

'Ben, that's enough,' Becky said, looking at me as if she didn't recognise me. 'You have to stop now. Let it go.'

'But I had him,' I said, looking at the bloody patch on the floor where he'd been. It had taken him only a fraction of a second. He must had fled in shadow form through a vent or a door-space, perhaps changing shape again after that. He could be anywhere now. 'I could have finished. . . I should have. . .'

'You're forgetting,' Mr October said, beginning his sentence as the warrior and ending it as the gunslinger-pirate. 'We have what we came for. Your mother is safe, their forces are in tatters and our business here is done. I've told you about personal feelings, Ben. There's no place for revenge in our work.'

'I see you have a few anger issues,' Kirk Berserker said. 'Believe me, no one knows more about that than me. We'll have a little talk sometime, just the two of us.'

'Anyway, you need to get that looked at,' Lu said, frowning at my buckled finger. 'Soon as we're out of here, we'll run you to the clinic.'

An empty platform came into view through the window, a station stop without a name.

'We're under the river,' Mr October said. 'It's an unscheduled stop, but it'll do for us. We have a bit of a walk to the Embankment, though. Do you think you can manage that, Mrs Harvester?'

Mum hadn't much of a voice yet, but she nodded, and at last her eyes found me.

'Darlin'?' she said.

She still knew me. Nothing else mattered.

Looking at Becky with her arm around Mum, I began to see what she'd been all along – as much an empathiser as Mr October's old man persona, the caring soul I'd first seen in Highgate. The one who took the pain away.

The journey was ending. The doors hissed open, and we spilled together onto a cold and gloomy platform. The Shuffleheads were waiting there. They'd dispensed with the guards' heads and uniforms and their fuzzy, rapidly changing masks were restored.

'Don't stand too close to the doors,' Mr October said, but Becky hung back anyway to let Mum through to me.

Mum didn't say anything as she clung to me, but I felt her love and the warmth of her tears on my neck. I must have been crying too, because when I looked up Becky seemed to sparkle and glow. She had a kind of aura, too, one filled with shimmering lights.

'Love you, son,' Mum whispered.

'Me too,' I said awkwardly.

We stood trembling on the chilly platform, and the anger – an anger that frightened me as much as it frightened Kirk Berserker – slowly lifted, and all I felt then was relief and gratitude.

Finally Mum relaxed and let me go, and Mr October passed her a handkerchief while I looked over at Becky. 'Thank you,' I mouthed, and she smiled as if to say, 'Oh, that's OK.'

She was still smiling when the fuzzy dark shape flitted past the open doors behind her. She was standing too close, altogether too close to the train. There was no time to warn her, to call her away.

It was on her before anyone could react. In the blink of an eye the shadow took physical form, snaking one of its hands around Becky's mouth and hauling her back inside the train.

The doors slid shut at once. The engine boomed and revved. Becky's hands pressed the glass as she stared out with stunned, confused eyes, and behind her was another face – a different, altered face from the last one I'd seen, but I knew without a thought whose it was.

The suddenness of what had happened threw everyone into shock. Before Mr October could call the order – 'Stop this thing! It mustn't leave!' – the train was moving, gathering speed along the platform.

I sprinted alongside it, screaming, hammering the windows and doors where Becky was trapped. Her breath misted the glass between us. Luther Vileheart's leer at her shoulder, a victorious grin, wasn't even the worst thing about what I saw then. The worst thing was the look on Becky's face in the instant before the train carried her into the tunnel, a look I'd never forget. It wasn't even a look of terror, but one of resignation that seemed to say, 'Sorry. Ben, I'm so sorry. My fault.'

Then the darkness took her. The train hurtled on. There was a tremendous crash further back on the platform when Kirk Berserker ripped away a pair of sliding doors with his bare hands. But the train was travelling too fast and furiously even for him. Thrown off balance, he keeled over and fell back on the concrete with the two severed doors skidding away either side of him.

The train's lights shrank into the tunnel, and all that remained was its throbbing sound. Seconds later that faded too, leaving only a memory of the train and its echo, and after that only silence.

I looked frantically up the platform. Every face was pale with shock. I started back towards the others, numb to the bone and empty inside, as if a large part of me had been torn out and taken with the train.

'Please,' I said to Mr October. 'Tell me . . . what do we do now?'

And for once Mr October, who knew everything, had no answer. Instead, he threw back his head and emptied his lungs with a grief-stricken cry.

More than a few times I'd heard the enemy mourning its losses, sending out heartbroken wails like cats in the night, but I'd never heard a sound as chilling or terrible as the one Mr October was making now.

26
A DISPATCH FROM THE MINISTRY

Days later I can still hear Mr October's cry inside the wind at Pandemonium House. I'm back at the desk in receipts, bringing my account up to date on the old Olivetti typewriter, and the candlelight shivers and the wind fills with mournful voices.

The place is in a state of shock. The Ministry is missing one of its own and I'm missing my friend. The apologetic look on Becky's face just before the train took her – I can't get it out of my head. I see it all the time, whether I'm wide awake or dreaming, and I see it again now as I sit typing.

That night, as we were leaving the platform under the river to begin the long walk to the Embankment, Kirk Berserker took me aside, resting a heavy hand on my shoulder.

'Never give up, kid,' he said. 'Never stop hoping. Hope's one thing that can bring her back, and believe you me the Ministry will not rest until she's safe. Others have been where she's going, some have even returned. I was there once, and look at me – I made it back.'

If that was supposed to make me feel better it didn't really help, partly because of the haunted look that came into his eyes when he spoke of it. He'd been to the dark territories and seen things I couldn't even imagine.

Later at HQ, while I was in the clinic, Mr October spent an hour with Mum in a private room on the same floor. They were joined by Tabitha, also known as Polly, the woman in the houndstooth coat whose real name wasn't Polly or Tabitha.

Mum didn't look any different after their meeting, but she'd forgotten all she'd seen. I quizzed her about it on the way home – we took a taxi while Lu ran Mr October to a 3618 in Waterloo – and she recalled very little after her last days in the Canaries. She'd never heard again from Tom Sutherland, she said. A typical holiday romance, she said.

And the first thing she said when we got home was, 'Darlin', where's Dad's picture?' Surprised to find it hidden in a drawer full of bills and receipts, she kissed the photo and returned it to its rightful place on the shelf.

At the weekend we wrapped up in warm clothing

and took a flask of coffee to Dad's bench in London Fields. I opened my sketch pad and drew Mum in profile while we spoke of better days, the memories we had of Dad when we were all together as a family. After half an hour a spiky rain began falling and as we left Mum smiled sadly and said, 'You know, I'll never love anyone else like I loved him.'

Her health could be better. She's back to square one – snakes and ladders – where she'd been before her holiday. The clinics continue, the nurses give her encouraging reports, but I still worry, not just because of her illness but because the enemy haven't finished with us yet.

The Ministry's twenty-four-hour watch on Middleton Road continues. The Shuffleheads are never far away.

At school the lockdown has been lifted, the notices torn down. Simon Decker is finally settling in, and while we never have much to say he doesn't blame me for anything, probably because like the rest of 8C he remembers nothing. Raymond Blight will never change – one more smart remark and I swear I'll swing for him – but Becky's old gang keep asking after her, genuinely concerned. They don't hold our friendship against me now, they just want to know, but all I can do is shrug and say I haven't heard from her lately.

Meanwhile the Sanbornes' house is under reconstruction. The insurers came through after all and Parkholme Road was crawling with hard hats the last time I saw it. But the place will feel so empty if Becky's folks move back there without her. I've tried to work up the courage to meet them, to explain what happened, but I wouldn't know where to start. It seems unfair not to tell them anything, but I wonder if it's better to know nothing than to know a truth like this one.

The other night, after attending an 8847 on Tottenham Court Road, I stopped outside a TV showroom window. Every TV in the bright display was tuned to the same news channel with the same scrolling red ticker tape. The newsreader looked solemn and heavy-eyed, and the image cut suddenly to a black-and-white still of Becky – Becky looking aloof, lips pursed, the soft lights in her eyes shaped like four-leaf clovers.

Not the most flattering picture of her but probably the most recent, I'm seeing it everywhere lately, on news-stands and 'Missing' posters all over town. On the poster are the words *Have you seen me?* and when I took a closer look at one outside the park I realised the head and shoulders image – the one her folks must have given the police and the media – was the portrait I'd done of Becky in Mr Redfern's class before we were friends.

Break times at the crypt tea rooms aren't the same without her. I sit at our table in an alcove near the steps leading up to the exit, stirring my coffee and watching the money bubbles, then I look up quickly in the hope she'll be there. But she never is.

In school I sometimes hang about on the corridor near the cold spot. There's no sign of the ghost Becky saw there that time, and no matter how hard I listen I never hear anything of the soul train. It may run again a week from now or it may not run for another generation. There's no intel at headquarters to suggest when the next one will be. All I know is that one day or night, sooner or later, it will run again.

'Don't even think of it,' Sukie said yesterday, simultaneously reading my mind and typing another batch of cards. 'Even if you could, people don't come back from there. OK, maybe one or two have been known to, but in general they just don't.'

'Kirk Berserker did.'

'Yeah, but he's Kirk Berserker. You're not. He's crazy and you're not. And you'd have to be crazy to even try.'

Still, the idea is never far from my mind.

The small tin box containing the four-leaf clover chain sits on the desk by the typewriter. It's a kind of talisman. I'm keeping it close this week. The lid is open and inside the box the clover chain remains healthy, which Mr October says is a sign of my own health too. As long as it lives there's still hope and faith and love and luck, all the things Luther Vileheart came to steal away.

Earlier, Kate Stone stopped in at receipts to say how bad she felt after hearing about Becky. If there was anything she could do, she said, I only had to ask, and I thanked her and apologised for the way I'd behaved that time in the clinic. It was the first chance I'd had to say sorry.

She smiled and said no problem. We'd all been under so much pressure it was no surprise mistakes had been made. Then she spotted the clover chain, her eyes widening when she saw it for what it was, and I explained what it meant as Becky had once explained it to me.

'Wherever she is now, she's fine,' Kate said. 'No

idea how I know, I just do. And anyway, she isn't on the list.'

But that's the thing. There are always more lists. Soon there'll be another, and another after that. If we knew what they were about to bring it wouldn't be so bad, but no one ever knows what's incoming.

Tonight there's a strange calm about Pandemonium House. The wind warbles on, and on the floor outside receipts there's barely a murmur, just a faint motorised hum: Mr October in old man form getting the hang of the mobility scooter he detests. It thumps lightly against a wall, then moves along, its drone fading down the hallway.

Meanwhile the telegraph machine is silent. It's never silent for long, and it's never possible to sit here with an easy mind – there's never any real peace even when it's quiet – but this is the job.

The job is waiting and watching. It's knowing that somewhere out there new names and numbers are floating through space and eventually they'll find their way to this room. When they do, the telegraph will creak and groan into action again, and then all you can do is hope the names it gives out won't belong to anyone you know.

The war goes on, and I'm still waiting.

Chris Westwood was born in Wakefield,
West Yorkshire, the son of a coal miner and
a school teacher. His first published writing was for
the London music paper *Record Mirror*, where he
worked as a staff reporter for three years.
His first children's book, *A Light In The Black*,
was a runner-up for the Guardian Children's
Fiction Prize. His second, *Calling All Monsters*, was
optioned for film three times by Steven Spielberg.
After a break from writing, spending seven years
caring full-time for his father, Chris returned with
Ministry of Pandemonium, the first in a series
of novels set in a secret, alternative London.
He now lives part of the time in East London,
and the rest of the time in a world of his own.

✤ ACKNOWLEDGEMENTS ✤

Well, I may have written it, but there's no way this book could have happened without the great help and support of the folks behind the scenes who rarely get the credit they deserve. I'm therefore hugely indebted to the following:

The whole team at Frances Lincoln Children's Books, in particular Maurice Lyon and Emily Sharratt for the editorial insights, solutions and suggestions which helped transform the raw early drafts of *The Great and Dangerous* into something very much like the book you now hold in your hands.

My agent Mandy Little – not just an agent but a friend for many years, and a darn good diplomat too!

And speaking of friends, a big shout to:

Amy, Anne, Alex, David, Liz, Pete, Anuree, Tina, Helene, Matt, Lloyd, Heather, Jan, Craig, Rosana, Julian, Nick, Mary, Fola and Seun. . . We're all on first-name terms now so I think you know who you are.

And of course the amazing Gill, my first reader, for constant encouragement and infinite patience through all the months of work and well beyond. Thank you!

Last but by no means least, a special mention for Alex Stanley and Della "Devil Dog" Webber, who inspired the 77772 which takes place in Chapter Six. Just for the record: Alex and Della are real, not figments of my imagination. As for the rest of this story, some of it's real, some of it isn't – which is which is for you, dear reader, to decide.